TONY PIGNAT

RAZORBILL

UNSPEAKABLE

CAROLINE PIGNAT is the award-winning author of four critically acclaimed YA novels, including *Egghead*, a Red Maple Honour book, and *Greener Grass*, the 2009 Governor General's Award winner. A high-school teacher, she lives in Ottawa.

ALSO BY CAROLINE PIGNAT

Egghead

Greener Grass
(Book 1 of the Greener Grass series)

Wild Geese
(Book 2 of the Greener Grass series)

Timber Wolf
(Book 3 of the Greener Grass series)

CAROLINE PIGNAT

razor
bill

RAZORBILL
an imprint of Penguin Canada Books Inc., a Penguin Random House Company

Published by the Penguin Group
Penguin Canada Books Inc.
90 Eglinton Avenue East, Suite 700, Toronto, Ontario, Canada M4P 2Y3

Penguin Group (USA) LLC, 375 Hudson Street, New York, New York 10014, U.S.A.
Penguin Books Ltd, 80 Strand, London WC2R 0RL, England
Penguin Ireland, 25 St Stephen's Green, Dublin 2, Ireland (a division of Penguin Books Ltd)
Penguin Group (Australia), 707 Collins Street, Melbourne, Victoria 3008, Australia
(a division of Pearson Australia Group Pty Ltd)
Penguin Books India Pvt Ltd, 11 Community Centre, Panchsheel Park, New Delhi – 110 017, India
Penguin Group (NZ), 67 Apollo Drive, Rosedale, Auckland 0632, New Zealand
(a division of Pearson New Zealand Ltd)
Penguin Books (South Africa) (Pty) Ltd, 24 Sturdee Avenue, Rosebank,
Johannesburg 2196, South Africa

Penguin Books Ltd, Registered Offices: 80 Strand, London WC2R 0RL, England

First published 2014

2 3 4 5 6 7 8 9 10 (WEB)

Manufactured in Canada.

LIBRARY AND ARCHIVES CANADA CATALOGUING IN PUBLICATION

Pignat, Caroline, author
Unspeakable / Caroline Pignat.

ISBN 978-0-14-318755-4 (pbk.)

I. Title.

PS8631.I4777U57 2014   jC813'.6   C2013-908063-5

eBook ISBN 978-0-14-319201-4

Visit the Penguin Canada website at **www.penguin.ca**

Special and corporate bulk purchase rates available; please see
www.penguin.ca/corporatesales or call 1-800-810-3104, ext. 2477.

FOR GRANNY

MY GUILT HAS OVERWHELMED ME
LIKE A BURDEN TOO HEAVY TO BEAR.

Psalm 38:4

∽ THE MORNING AFTER ∾

May 29, 1914
Rimouski, Quebec

☙ *Chapter One* ☙

"THIS WAY," THE SAILOR COAXED US from where we huddled against the cold, hundreds of us on the deck of the small steamer. Dazed, we stumbled down the gangway into the early morning light.

This isn't real. It's a nightmare. It has to be.

But try as I might, I couldn't wake. I couldn't forget. And I couldn't stop shaking.

I thought that long night would never end. That I'd never see the sun again, never feel it on my face or the solid ground beneath my bare feet. I staggered forward on my trembling legs and stopped for a moment to reassure myself. But nothing felt steady. And neither the sun on my head nor the stranger's shirt that reached my bare thighs did anything to keep away the chill.

The other ship had docked behind us, and I walked partway down the quay as hundreds of disoriented victims left her gangway and trudged past. Most were injured. Many nearly naked. But all looked numb. From the cold, yes, from the freezing waters and biting winds, but mainly from the shock. It was all too much. Their vacant eyes didn't see me even as I stood before them. Survivors, still lost at sea. Though their bodies had survived that long, horrific night, for many, their minds and hearts had not, as they watched their loved ones lose blood and heat, lose their very lives, seeping away in the cold depths.

Meg.

I closed my eyes. Tried not to see her in those last moments, then opened them to search for him.

He's here. Somewhere. He has to be.

I scanned every bruised and battered brow, but no face was his. They moved past me, drawn by the kindness of strangers offering woollen blankets and mugs of tea. Even at this early hour, the townspeople of Rimouski had rallied quayside, their farmers' carts piled with whatever clothing and food they could spare.

"Thomas! Thomas!" shrieked a young woman in a ragged nightdress as she shoved past. A man coming off the other ship lifted his face, his eyes, his hopes. His soul sparking back to life as he heard his name, as he saw her come. She pushed through the crowd and flung herself into his arms, and they fell to their knees where they stood.

"I thought I'd lost you ..." He gripped her face, as though convincing himself she was real. "Dear God—" He kissed her roughly as he pulled her to him. "I thought I'd lost you."

The crowd thinned to a few stragglers, and some towns-people rushed down to shoulder the injured and carry those too weak to walk. Face after face, yet none were his. By the time I reached the empty gangway, my legs, my hands, my very heart trembled as I gripped the rope railing.

He had to be here. I'd already searched in vain for him while aboard the *Lady Evelyn*, and the only thing that had kept me going was the belief that he was right behind us. That I'd find him. That I would run to him. That he would take me in his arms again and, this time, never let me go.

I glanced back at the crowd dispersing into Rimouski homes or the temporary hospital at the train station. The reunited couple walked away, arms tight around each other's waists, each holding the other up. Their prayers had been answered. Why not mine?

A bald-headed man called up to the sailor on deck. "The shed is ready for the others."

The others. I shuddered.

"Claude!" a local woman scolded the man, gesturing at me. She put a blanket around my shoulders. "*Viens-t'en Monique*," she urged, firmly pulling me from the ship's gangway as Claude and the men of the town climbed up. "*Ça va être correct.*" She patted my arm and gently muttered sympathies, but there was no way she was letting me on that ship or leaving me here.

I let her steer me back quayside. Let her slip a dress over my head and help me shrug off the dirty old shirt. I couldn't stop thinking of him.

Hundreds survived. He had. He had to.

Monique poured a steaming cup from her flask and put it in my hands. It burned my fingers but I gripped it tightly, wanting to feel something—for I feared I would never feel anything again.

I STARTED AT THE HOSPITAL and then moved to the nearby homes. All that afternoon, I ran from house to house, calling their names until I was hoarse. Monique came with me, speaking fast French to neighbours who looked at me with sad eyes and shook their heads. And when my search had led us road after road, house after house down to the thick-planked quayside shed, I knew I'd looked everywhere. Everywhere but there.

And I just couldn't go in. I couldn't.

The door opened and two men exited. The tall man with slick hair glanced briefly at Monique before resting his dark eyes on me. He wasn't from around here. Even before he spoke, before I heard his American accent, I knew. His clothes were too smooth and tailored. But more than that, his gaze held no pity. He was no farmer. No victim. He wasn't here to offer or seek help. He smiled at me. Any other time and place, I might have thought this twenty-something young man handsome, might have longed for his attention, but here and now, his intensity unnerved me.

"Were you a passenger, mademoiselle?" the shorter of the two asked.

"Stewardess," I mumbled, wondering if they might be Canadian Pacific Railway officials.

"Mind if I take your picture," he said, raising the camera to his eye, "for the *Montreal Gazette?*"

"Actually," I said, lifting my hand to cover the lens, "I do mind."

"Wyatt Steele, *New York Times.*" The taller man held out his hand. I didn't take it. "The world wants to hear your story, Miss ..." He fished for my name and once again came up empty. But he wouldn't be deterred. He flipped open his notebook. "Can I ask you a few questions?"

I eyed the door, considered what was behind it. "Let me ask *you* something. What business do you men have in there?"

"Memorial postcard," the short man said.

"What?" I looked at him in disbelief. "You actually took a picture of the dead ... for a *postcard?*" The rage surged from a place deep inside me. "Did you ask them if they minded?"

"Just doing my job." He shrugged. "The public have a right to know."

"And what about the deceased?" I snapped, pointing at the shed. "Do they not have any rights? To dignity? To privacy? To respect?"

"They deserve to have their story told," Steele answered. "By someone who was there, by someone who survived." He rested his hand on my shoulder. "Don't you think you owe them that?"

"Get away from me," I yelled, shrinking away, "you—you vultures!"

Monique stepped in and, in no uncertain terms, put the men in their place. I don't know if Steele spoke French, but he got the message just the same. She took me to her home then, murmuring her words of comfort, tucking me under her wing. I let her fuss. Let her stoke up a roaring fire and wrap me in a thick quilt. Let her make a cup of tea I wouldn't drink and back-bacon sandwiches I wouldn't eat.

Maybe at least one of us would feel like she was doing *something.*

They thought I was sleeping in the guest room—as if I would ever sleep soundly again. I heard Monique puttering about making Claude's tea, the spoon clinking on his cup, the knife scraping his sandwich in two. And the halting sound of his voice. This tough old farmer, reduced to tears as he told his wife what he'd done that day. What he'd help carry from the ship decks to the shed. I didn't understand a word of French, but I knew exactly what he said.

For now we all spoke grief.

∽ FOUR MONTHS BEFORE ∾

January 1914
Strandview Manor, Liverpool

$\backsim$ *Chapter Two* $\backsim$

GRIEF WAS NO STRANGER TO ME. I'd known more than my share of it in my short eighteen years. My mother. My father's love. My innocence. My hope. All of it had been stolen from me. In many ways, I was a victim long before the *Empress* tragedy. I'd arrived on the steps of my great-aunt's Liverpool house two months before with nothing but my losses. And I hadn't the will or the strength to do anything more than wallow. To bury myself under the covers and never come out.

But apparently, Aunt Geraldine had other plans.

"You can't make me," I yelled from my bed that damp December morning, gripping the quilts in my fists as I burrowed deeper. "I won't do it!"

Aunt Geraldine ripped the bedding back and dumped it on the floor. Her strength surprised me. So did her temper. Not just because she was ancient, like some wizened apple doll, in her eighties at least, but because my aunt rarely came out of her study. I'd ignored her these past long weeks. Why couldn't she do me the same courtesy? Hadn't she done that for most of my life?

She pointed her finger at me as I sat shivering in my nightie. "You will go on that ship, Ellen Hardy, and you will work hard, bloody hard. Mr. Gaade is doing you a favour taking you on at all."

"Some favour," I sulked.

"You will learn to be grateful for all you do have," she continued, as if I had anything to be thankful about. "Maybe, just maybe, you will learn how to make a life for yourself."

"As a stewardess?" I couldn't believe her. What kind of life was that? Outraged, I bolted from the bed and stood before her. Though we were the same size, my great-aunt's greatness seemed to loom over me, snuffing out whatever my words might have sparked.

Her young maid dropped to her knees to gather up my bedding, tending to my every need as she had since I'd arrived. Fetching tea. Bringing trays. Warming water bottles.

"Leave it, Meg," Aunt Geraldine said, and the quiet girl stood. "Ellen will do it."

Meg curtseyed and left.

"You can't write my life. You can't just order me about." I crossed my arms. "I'm not some halfwit maid you can—"

I never saw my aunt's slap coming, but I still remember its sting. How it made both of us watery-eyed. I raised my trembling hand to my burning cheek. No one had ever slapped me before. Not even my father, though he surely must have wanted to after what I'd done. I felt hot with the memories, the shame, the smouldering flush of a victim who is powerless to do anything but burn.

"Why didn't you just leave me where I was?" I said, defeated, as she turned to go. "You've only traded one jail for another."

She rested her wrinkled hand on the doorknob and, slumping, looked back over her shoulder. Her eyes were tired. Her face, sunken. For the first time, Aunt Geraldine seemed as old as she truly was. "I promised your mother I'd watch over you."

"Well," I said, gloating somewhat in the small power of my words, "I'd say she's sorely disappointed, isn't she?"

"Yes," Aunt Geraldine said softly, her eyes meeting mine. "I'd say she is."

She paused. "You know, Ellen, I always thought you had more of your mother in you. I guess I was wrong."

TRUE TO HER WORD, within the week Aunt Geraldine had me signed on, suited up, and shipped out as a stewardess on the ocean liner the *Empress of Ireland*. And her maid along with me. That's all Meg was to me then. My aunt's hired help. Her eyes on the ship. I'd no idea then that Meg would become so much more. That I would become a victim of a shipwreck because of my aunt's actions, or that I'd survive it because of Meg's.

Oh, Meg. She always had a wide-eyed wonder about her. So something as grand as the *Empress of Ireland* literally left her speechless. As soon as we boarded, bags in hand, the stiffly starched Matron Jones led us for what seemed like miles, through passageways and back stairs from one long hall to another. Meg followed, fascinated by the grand dining halls, the stocked library, the lush carpets and rich wood panelling—even the bloody doorknobs were worth a mention. Everywhere she turned she seemed even more amazed, but all I felt was trapped. Meg saw grandeur. I saw work. More places to clean. More places to get lost. I'd never be able to find my way around.

"Is this the front of the ship?" Meg asked, trying to get her bearings.

"The *bow*—yes," Matron Jones corrected. Her dark skirts swished as she marched. Her keys jangled on her belt like a jailer's. "Stewardesses' cabins are located on the Shelter Deck."

Meg's smile widened. Perhaps it was being referred to as a *stewardess* or the idea of having a *cabin* on the *Shelter Deck*. But I knew neither were going to be as glorious as Meg imagined. Not by a long shot. Not for me, anyway. Matron Jones finally stopped outside a door and knocked brusquely before entering. As soon as it opened, I knew there had to be some mistake. This wasn't a room, it was a cupboard. A closet of bunk beds.

"Them's the new girls?" A short stewardess stood at the small sink between the bunks patting her reddish-brown hair. She looked to be in her early thirties. Solid. Ruddy. She reminded me of a potato.

"Kate, this is Ellen Ryan and Meg Bates," Matron Jones replied in her clipped voice. She glanced at us. "Change and report to the galley in five minutes." She left as abruptly as she spoke.

I didn't like being ordered about by this old goat. And hated even more that this was my life now.

"Well, here's the grand tour." Kate flourished her arm, taking in the tiny room, the two sets of bunk beds, their green curtains swagged up either side. " Bed. Bed. Bed. Bed. Sink. Closet."

"It's lovely," Meg gushed. "And look, there're little drawers right by our bed. We can each have our own."

A tantrum roiled in my stomach. I didn't want my own drawer. I wanted, I needed, my own bloody room, not to be shelved away like one of my aunt's books. "This is our room … I mean, for all *three* of us?"

Kate snorted at the ridiculousness of it and I felt my shoulders relax. Clearly there was some mistake.

"Actually, we're four. Gwen is upstairs giving the toilets another swish. I dunno the fuss, really. But you know, some passengers can be so finicky—every bowl must sparkle, even the one for their shite."

The already cramped walls started to close in. This can't be happening. How could Aunt Geraldine do this to me?

"Don't worry," Kate said, no doubt reading my expression, "we hardly ever spend time in here other than sleeping or dressing. The passengers keep us hopping."

That didn't make me feel any better.

"You working second class?" Kate asked.

Meg looked at me, unsure.

"Probably," Kate concluded. "Funny, they don't normally sign them on so young. Or pretty. Most of us are working widows or spinsters." She tilted her head at us. "What are you, eighteen?"

Meg clutched her bag and nodded enthusiastically. "Lady Hardy knows Chief Steward Gaade so she put in a—"

I glared at her blathering our business. My business.

She blushed again and added lamely, "… good word for us."

Had the girl no sense? I'd told her not to speak of it.

"Either way," Kate concluded, "I doubt Gaade will let you wet-behind-the-ears serve first." She lifted a white apron from her bunk and slipped it over her dark uniform, efficiently knotting it in a looping bow in the back before adjusting her white cuffs and collar. I hated the sight of the drab uniform, the knowledge that I'd be forced to wear it every day, like some inmate. "The last thing the chief steward needs is for you to piss off some upper-class brat."

"What do you know about upper class?" I didn't like her tone. Or her suggestion that all upper class are brats or that I couldn't serve them. If anyone knew what an upper-class person wanted, surely it would be me. I *was* upper class, or had been, once.

She laughed and busied herself with her cap, securing it in place with four hairpins. "Nothing personal, Ellen, but you don't know your galley from your glory hole. And if there's one thing rich people expect, it's a servant who knows the place." She tilted her head. "A servant who knows *her* place."

"She has the right idea." Kate nodded at Meg. "Look at her, all eager to please. You must have served first class before, love. Am I right?"

Meg hesitated and glanced at me. "Um, I've only ever worked as a maid. For Lady Hardy."

"We both did," I added. "As maids. I'm a maid, too."

"Oh?" Kate seemed amused by my overinsistence. "Just the one mistress, then?"

"And her young grandniece," Meg added. Her eyes flickered from Kate's to mine, terrified she'd said too much.

"Let me guess," Kate continued, smoothing down her apron and brushing her hands together. "Rich, spoiled brat who speaks of nothing but her clothes and her hair and her debutante dress?"

Meg said nothing and stared at the floor, but her blush made Kate laugh.

"Do you know the Hardys?" I asked. It hadn't occurred to me that anyone but Chief Steward Gaade knew my family. And even he didn't know the whole story.

"No." Kate shook her head. "But they're all the same, aren't they?"

I thought of my old friends. Of our visits that summer before everything changed. And we did talk of clothes and hair and dresses. Until Declan Moore appeared. Then all I spoke of was him. And look where it got me.

"Hurry up and change into your uniforms or Jones will have our heads." Kate moved to the doorway. "I'll meet you at the stairwell down the hall. Can't have you lost already." She smiled and closed the door behind her.

"She seems nice," Meg said.

"She seems like a bossy know-it-all," I grumbled, folding my arms. "Just what I need."

"Exactly." She opened up her bag and put her meagre items in her newly acquired drawer. "I mean, who better to teach us than someone who knows everything?"

I slumped into my bunk. This was going to be a long trip.

❧ THE DAY AFTER ❧

May 30, 1914
Rimouski, Quebec

∽ *Chapter Three* ∽

THE WHISTLE SHRIEKED as the train pulled into the station, steam puffing in the afternoon chill. It felt cold for May. Maybe it was just me. I hadn't stopped shaking since I'd arrived in this small town yesterday, and no amount of hot tea or quilts or roaring fires helped. I doubted I'd ever feel warm again.

"*Tiens*," Monique said, taking off her shawl and draping it across my shoulders. Willing her warmth into me.

About three hundred of us stood on the platform, clad in the homespun generosity of those hard-working strangers who literally gave us the clothes off their backs. Even the richest men among us, who had worn nothing but ties and tails on the ship, now sported farmers' jeans and mackinaw jackets, their wives in calico and old bonnets. We were not first or third class. Passengers or crew. Not anymore. We were victims. Only victims.

I scanned their faces one more time—spending a bit more of my hope. But not too much. I'd always thought I had hope in endless supply. But I knew now I didn't. Hope was a fistful of pennies. Each prayer and every wish meant tossing one more penny into the depths. Every time, it cost me. I knew that soon enough I wouldn't have any hope left, and a part of me was afraid to waste it. But there was no sign of either of them.

The doors to the cars opened and, numbly, I followed the crowd onto the train. We didn't want to think. Just tell us what to do. Where to go. *Take this dress. Drink this tea. Take this train to Quebec. Take that ocean liner back to Liverpool.* It didn't matter that getting on another boat was the last thing any of us wanted to do. *And what then?* I pictured old Bates in his butler uniform, leaning against the car as he waited for us at the Liverpool docks, how he used to fuss over whatever small trinket Meg brought him back from across the sea. This time, all I'd be bringing him was the news that Meg, his only granddaughter, was never coming home.

Take this seat. Yes. That was enough for now.

I leaned my forehead on the cool window and closed my eyes.

Jim was there, as always. In that moment. His face before me. His arms around me. And his eyes, those eyes, seeing right inside me. Even now I could almost feel his warmth, almost smell his scent as he drew me inside his peacoat. His voice, strong and sure.

"*You* are my hope … and I won't lose you, Ellie. I won't."

That was the last time I saw him. For all I knew, he—

I opened my eyes.

No.

Don't go there.

All I had was a fistful of memories. Stolen moments at the

ship's rail. Wishes. Hopes that he felt the same way about me. I knew it was him I wanted above all else. I just never knew for sure if he felt the same.

I never told him my truths. I never asked for his.

The train lurched forward. Through the window, I saw Monique raise her hand to me as we pulled away.

I never said thank you. I never said goodbye. I suppose I never said a lot of things these past few days.

And now it was too late.

"Ellen!" The young girl clambered up on the seat beside me, her blue eyes wide in their dark pockets. She wore a sailor dress of white with blue trim, a gift, no doubt, from some family in Rimouski.

"Gracie." I managed a smile. The man with her wasn't her father. I recognized him as one of the Salvationists, but when I glanced behind him, there was no sign of Bandmaster Hanagan or his wife, Edith. He met my eyes and shook his head—a tiny movement that said it all.

"Ernie Pugmire," he said, offering me his hand. He sat across from Gracie.

"Well, well, " a man said, as he stepped between us and settled in the empty seat across from me, "you must be Gracie Hanagan." The reporter from the shed, Wyatt Steele. How the hell did he get in here? Instinctively, I rested my hand on Gracie's leg.

"Can you not leave us in peace?" I snapped. "She's a child, Mr. Steele. A *victim*."

"She's no victim." He smiled at Gracie. "She's a *survivor*."

Gracie sat a little taller, strengthened by his words. "How do you know my name?" she asked shyly.

"Why, you're famous. One of the four children who survived."

My stomach sank. *Only four?*

There were over one hundred and thirty-five children on board. I remembered the way the young boys cheered when the huge ship sounded one long blast from its tall stacks before pulling away from the Quebec docks; the bonneted babes mesmerized by their mothers' hankies fluttering as they waved to those ashore; the little ones skipping around the deck, dancing to the music as Gracie's father led the Salvation Army Band, trumpets and trombones winking in the sunlight.

Could they really be gone? All of them—but three and Gracie?

"The world wants to hear your story, Gracie," Steele continued with his familiar sales pitch. But I wasn't having any of it.

"I doubt her parents would've wanted her … " My voice trailed off as she turned to me. I'd just mentioned her parents. Spoken of them in the past tense. But it didn't seem to bother her.

"It's all right, Ellen. I want to tell Mr. Steele my story," Gracie explained. "We can ask permission when we get to Quebec. Mama and Papa aren't on this special train, but they'll be on the next one."

I met Ernie's sad eyes. He hadn't told her—or perhaps he had, and like the rest of us, Gracie didn't want to hear it.

I faced Steele. "How many people … survived?"

He pulled out a black leather notebook and flipped back through the pages, giving me the toll as if he were merely telling the time. "Four hundred and sixty-five."

We'd sailed from Quebec with 1477 souls aboard. I didn't let myself do the math that would surely tell me over a thousand were dead. Instead, I clung to the fact that four hundred and sixty-five were alive. Four hundred and sixty-five had made it.

Maybe he had, too.

Maybe even Meg. She could very well be coming on the next train with the Hanagans. Hope flickered in my heart and I cupped myself around it, protecting it against all reality that might snuff it out.

I didn't like the man or his mission, but Steele was right about one thing at least—Gracie's very presence gave hope to us all.

⌒ *Chapter Four* ⌒

I EXCUSED MYSELF TO USE THE LAVATORY as Gracie spoke. I never wanted to think about that night again, much less relive it through poor Gracie's eyes. Even as I came back down the aisle, I could see Steele scribbling furiously in his notebook, getting every detail. His readers would get their story—but they would never know what it was *really* like. And those of us who did know could never forget.

I sat back in my seat, and tired from her interview, Gracie put her head in my lap as Steele reviewed his notes.

"Can you keep an eye on her?" Ernie asked me. "I'd like to check the other cars."

I nodded and stroked her hair. Already, her breathing slowed, her eyes grew heavy. "You fall asleep faster than Emmy."

"Who?"

"Emmy—the ship's cat."

She drifted off for a moment then sat up in terror. "Ellen! Cats can't swim!" Her eyes flitted frantically. "What if ... what if she—"

"She's all right, Gracie." I held her face in both hands, forcing her to focus on me. "Emmy is fine. She's fine, pet. She wasn't even on the boat. She took off down the gangway right before we sailed."

I remembered seeing the bellboy going after her, running back at the last minute, his arms full of orange tabby. We'd never sailed without our shipmate Emmy. Some even thought of her as the captain's cat, even though she often slept in our cabin. Meg always kept her a saucer of milk. But as soon as the lad brought her on board that day, Emmy leapt out of his arms and scurried back down the gangway as though the devil himself were after her. At the time, we thought it was the strangest thing. Now I'm thinking it was the smartest.

Gracie relaxed. She could retell the facts of that night, but I wondered if she truly understood them. Hundreds dying. Hundreds already dead. Her parents drowning—that was too much for her. It was too much for most of us. And so she worried about a cat she'd never met.

"So she's waiting for us … at Quebec?" she asked, uncertain.

"Yes," I said, and ran my fingers through her curls. "She's waiting."

"Emmy knew." She settled back on my lap. "She knew what was going to happen."

I stroked her hair and watched her breathing deepen as the train rocked her to sleep.

Steele's pencil scratched across his notepad. The girl. The cat. This was good stuff. He flipped to a clean page and glanced at me. His eyes so dark they seemed all pupil. I felt exposed. Hunted.

"So," he asked, "how long have you known the Hanagans?"

I didn't want to talk to him. Didn't want to answer his questions. I had a story, but it was one I'd been hiding for nearly two years and I wasn't about to tell it to Steele. Good Lord, he'd be the last person I'd tell.

"I met them when they boarded." That truth seemed safe enough. "They were one of my twelve rooms this trip."

"Second class, is that right, Miss Ryan?"

I nodded. *How did he know my name? Did Gracie mention it?*

He flipped back through his notes. "Been a stewardess with the *Empress* since ... January this year?"

Gracie definitely didn't know that.

He raised his hands and added apologetically, "Ship's records, Miss Ryan. No big secret. Just doing my job."

I folded my arms and looked out the window. Let him get his damn story somewhere else.

We sat in silence as the train clickety-clacked along the river's edge, passing the lighthouse at the point. The shore looked so different now from this side, in the daylight, without him next to me at the rail—our rail.

Where would I find him now?

"Did you lose someone ... close?" Steele asked. He set aside his pencil and pad.

I nodded.

"Your roommate, Margaret Bates, was she—"

"Meg, her name was—her name *is* Meg," I whispered. She hated being called Margaret.

"What brought you to the *Empress*? You both worked for a Lady Hardy in Merseyside, or so the records said." He said it as if he knew it was not the truth. After months of secrecy, someone had unravelled me just like that. "But you're not from Liverpool. Yours is an Irish accent. Wicklow, if I'm not mistaken."

I met his eyes. Who was this man?

He shrugged, almost apologetic. "I make it my business to know things."

I clenched my jaw and turned back to the window. There was no way I'd be telling this man anything. He already knew more about me than most of my fellow stewardesses did.

"It must be so hard for you," Steele said after a few minutes. He leaned forward, voice low, eyes shining with sincerity. And for a moment, I felt as if he understood, really understood, how hard this all had been. He lightly rested his hand on mine, his fingers radiating warmth and strength.

"What happened that night—can you tell me?"

Images flashed across my mind—gushing water, people scrambling. Hundreds upon hundreds trapped in flooded cabins and hallways, unable to reach the deck. Bodies floating. And Meg's face. Always Meg's terrified eyes watching me as they disappeared beneath the black water for the last time.

No. I pulled my hand away.

"Yours is an incredible story of survival, Miss Ryan," he continued. "You must tell it. People need to know."

"I—I can't." I raised my hands to my ears, trying to block the thousand screams, the heavy silence of buoyed corpses drifting into the dark. A tremor ran through me. "I'm sorry … I just … I can't speak about it."

His eyes searched mine for a moment. I wasn't going to tell him anything. Ever. As though reading my thoughts, he settled back in his seat, picked up his notebook, and jotted in its margins.

Ernie returned and sat beside me. I didn't need to ask to know his search had been in vain.

My eyes flicked back to Steele from time to time as we rode along the track approaching Quebec, but he paid me no mind. Clearly, he'd done a lot of research about the ship and those aboard. He'd even managed to secure an exclusive train ride with the survivors. He was good at his job, I had to give him that. But I wasn't going to give him what he wanted. My eyes took in the measure of this mysterious man, cunning, relentless, resourceful—I wondered if he might know something that could help me.

Gracie woke and rubbed her eyes as the station came into view and the train hissed to a stop. After our goodbyes, Gracie and Ernie made their way to the front of the car. Steele flipped his notebook shut and slipped it into his pocket as he stood. He glanced out the window at the throng of reporters pressing closer. They waved their hands and elbowed for position as Gracie and the first few survivors stepped onto the platform, dazed and disoriented by the popping flashbulbs.

"We've already been through hell," I snapped. "Why can't they just leave us alone?"

Steele slicked back his hair and set his hat upon it. "Miss Ryan, the sinking of the *Empress* is Canada's worst maritime disaster. We are talking more dead passengers than the *Titanic*, which puts it as one of the worst tragedies in North American history. Do you know how big a story this is?" He paused. "And you lived to tell the tale."

Was that why I'd lived?

"Like it or not," he added, "you are somewhat of a celebrity now." He tipped his hat and turned to go, but desperate, I grabbed his sleeve. He might know something—I couldn't just let him go, I had to ask.

"What about the engine crew?" I bit my lip. "Do you know anything of them?"

He paused, brow arched, dark eyes searching. "Anyone in particular?"

I opened my mouth and shut it, unsure, but the name weighed on my heart.

"Miss Ryan, I can't find him if you don't tell me his name. I'm good but even I'm not that good."

"Jim," I whispered, and suddenly it all became real. The ship. That night. The last time I saw him at the rail. "His name is Jim Farrow. But they all called him Lucky."

⚭ FOUR MONTHS BEFORE ⚭

January 1914
The Empress of Ireland,
somewhere in the Atlantic

∽ *Chapter Five* ∽

IT WAS ON MY SECOND CROSSING that I first saw Jim. All blood and soot and cinder he was, lying on the cot in Dr. Grant's office with his right arm draped over his face as the doctor tweezed cloth from skin on the left. Jim had burned it raw from elbow to palm, like charred meat, in the flames of the boilers. The fire he was hired to stoke. An accident, they said. But Jim's knuckles said otherwise. Bruised and bloodied on the teeth of another, they told the truth of a fire within. One that never subsides.

I knew Jim was trouble, plain and simple. A scrapper. Sullen and surly. A right mess if I ever saw one—and, God help me, I could not take my eyes off him.

"That's all I can do for now," Dr. Grant said, washing his hands. "Clean around the wound, will you, Ellie?"

I'd been helping Dr. Grant since my first crossing. It was a welcome relief from scrubbing second-class toilets, making beds, and fetching spinsters cup after cup of tea. He'd called me in as I'd passed by one time, asked me to help hold a child's leg while he set and splinted it. Afterwards he'd praised my steady hand and nerve. It was no different to me than gentling a mare, and I'd done that enough times on the farm. Father always scolded me for mucking in. Said it wasn't fitting for a young lady of my station. But I liked the work. I liked feeling needed. I liked doing something that mattered. After that, Dr. Grant would ask for me by name—much to the annoyance of Matron Jones, the head stewardess.

Jim never made a sound. Still, I tried to be as gentle as I could as I wiped the wound, skirting the edges of his pain. I dipped the cloth in the bowl of water and, wringing it slightly, brushed down his thick biceps and around his callused fingers. The black of the soot wiped away easy enough, but not the cuts and bruises.

I'd heard the men talking. They'd said Lucky had gotten into another one of his rages, and in the fight, he fell into the open door of his furnace. The Black Gang were notorious for fighting as hard as they worked—and when docked, drinking as hard as they fought. Matron Jones had warned the dozen stewardesses to give them a wide berth. She made it clear those men were trouble and that any shenanigans would result in termination. Not that we saw much of the men. Our paths never crossed during duties, and Meg and I had no desire to enter the rowdy taverns they stumbled into and staggered from. Besides, Meg was smitten with Timothy Hughes, the ship's librarian—a bookish lad who scurried away at a sudden move. All they'd shared were a few magazines and even fewer words since our first voyage. And I had no interest in any man. Not after what I'd been through. No, Matron Jones had no fear of any so-called shenanigans, not from us.

At least, not until Jim.

Dr. Grant handed me a tube of ointment. "Apply this once it's clean." He turned to Jim. "Check back in a few days to see how you're healing."

Jim lowered his right arm and nodded, thanking the doctor as he left. I wrung the cloth once more and turned my attention to his face, discerning soot from bruise. After a few wipes, it was clean for the most part, but I kept dabbing at his bleeding brow, riveted by the blue fire in his red-rimmed eyes. It gave me an excuse to stare. Something, whatever it was, burned inside him with fierce intensity.

"What?" Jim met my eyes and held my gaze, though it seemed to cause him more discomfort than any wound.

I felt it too. Exposed. Seen. Known.

Could he read my shame as easily as I'd seen his? A heat spread across my cheeks and I looked away, busying myself with rinsing and wringing, pulling myself together before turning back to finish cleaning his brow. I cleared my throat. "Why do they call you Lucky?"

He said nothing.

"If you ask me, I'd say you're pretty lucky to be alive. Falling into a fire like—"

Jim grabbed my wrist and I stopped. My pulse increased in his grip and I glanced at our hands, unsure if he felt that, too.

"I am *not* lucky." His intensity radiated from his stare like an open furnace, but I didn't shy from it. If anything, it drew me in.

He released my arm and moved to get up. "And I didn't ask you."

"Oh no you don't." I put my hand on his chest and pushed him down. Gentle, but firm. It surprised both of us, but I'd handled enough large animals on the farm that I suppose those ways came to me instinctively. I let my hand linger a moment longer, aware of the solid strength of his chest, the warmth of it, and the quickening of his heartbeat under my touch. Had he a mind to leave, I couldn't stop him. The man was solid muscle. But he lay back once more and breathed deeply.

I didn't know this stranger, but I knew something the men didn't. Jim's anger, the fight in him, was only escaping steam. In him I saw a driven, haunted soul, one fuelled by some great secret.

I knew because I was too.

I took my hand away and opened the tube Dr. Grant left on the counter. I squeezed the thick salve onto my fingertips. "I have to put on the ointment yet. It will help with the healing. You won't scar as badly."

He snorted but let me do my duties. When I finished, he simply stood and left. He didn't want to be cleaned up, to be helped or healed. He just wanted to sit there and smoulder in all his unspoken pain.

It made me think he wished he'd burned more.

❦ *Chapter Six* ❦

"SHALL I OPEN THE WINDOW, MISS ELLEN?" Bates asked from the parlour doorway.

"No. I'm fine." I poked the fire and sat in the wing chair, one of the few pieces of furniture not draped in dust covers. Though he'd uncovered the chair and parted the blue drapes, opening the view onto the front garden, the room still seemed like a morgue. The dining table and chairs, the china cabinet, the settee, all of it lay hidden under great white sheets. Even the piano in the centre of the room stood deathly silent. Hidden. This front room was never used. Most of them weren't. Over the years, Aunt Geraldine had shut down Strandview Manor, closing it off room by room, storey by storey as she retreated eventually to her study in the turret. To the stories in her mind.

"Are you sure you don't want Lily to clear away these dust covers?"

"No." What was the point? For whom? It suited me to sit in dead rooms, shrouded in grief. I deserved no better.

"Mr. Cronin mentioned he'd need to discuss some legal matters … when you're ready," Bates added.

Poor Bates had been run off his feet answering the door, especially that first week after I'd returned, what with doctors and priests visiting Aunt Geraldine during the final days of her coma. Days when her body remained, but the woman inside was long gone. A shell of herself. I felt like that now, numbed, hollowed by grief and regrets. I'd no idea she'd been that ill. She'd been closed, withdrawn in our few conversations when I'd been back between crossings. I'd assumed it was me. That I'd disappointed her yet again. I'd been so caught up in my own story, I'd given no thought to hers.

The bell rang again. Bates's voice mumbled in the hallway. "Just another reporter looking for Ellen Ryan," he said as he returned. "I've told Lily to send them packing if they come around again."

I sighed. Somehow these men had made the connection between the young *Empress of Ireland* stewardesses and Strandview Manor. Perhaps they'd gotten a peek at the job files at the Canadian Pacific Railway head office. Who knew—they were resourceful, those reporters, and relentless.

Thankfully, Aunt Geraldine had had the foresight to register me under Ryan, my mother's maiden name. Only Meg, Aunt Geraldine, and Bates knew the truth—and two of them were dead now. Even Lily, the current young maid, believed Ellie Ryan was just a maid who used to work here. She didn't connect that name to me. My secret was safe.

"Right, then," Bates soldiered on. "Lily is here if you need anything."

I nodded. At fourteen, Lily wasn't much help. I was only four years older, but it felt like a lifetime. Bates had hired her to replace Meg when we set sail last year but the girl was hopeless. Still, it wasn't Lily's fault. She'd never fill Meg's shoes as a maid. And no one could as a friend. Not after all Meg and I had gone through.

God, I missed her.

Bates nodded as if reading my thoughts. Meg was his grand-daughter, his only family. How the old man must grieve. It was hard enough to say goodbye to Aunt Geraldine at her funeral yesterday, but she was elderly. And as I'd recently learned, she was ill. But the old should never have to bury the young—it isn't right. Bates cleared his throat and propped his driver's cap on his wispy white hair as he left. I wondered where he went, what he did with his free time now that Aunt Geraldine wasn't here to order him about. Without Aunt Geraldine here to tell us, none of us knew what to do, really. As much as we hated her controlling ways, she was both rudder and sail. Controlling my life, and now, even her death. She'd taken care of every detail, right down to her funeral reception's sandwiches. Who did she think was coming? I'd wondered when I saw the huge platters, for she'd outlived any friends and ignored acquaintances. She had no time for family—though she had only her nephew (my father) and me. Being the matriarch, living eighty long years, I suppose she could do what the hell she liked. And Great-Aunt Geraldine did exactly that.

The church had been full yesterday, true enough. Fans, I guessed. G.B. Hardy was a well-known novelist, though few, I suspect, knew the author was a spinster. Old women wrote household tips or fashion critiques, not adventure. But then again, Aunt Geraldine wasn't a typical woman.

It surprised me that my father hadn't come. They weren't close, each one with strong opinions about the other; still, I'd thought he'd pay his respects. I didn't know if I felt anger or relief at his absence. Maybe losing my mother years ago was grief enough to last him a lifetime. Maybe he just didn't care. *Did he know about the* Empress? *About me?* I wondered. Either way, he wouldn't have come to my funeral, that I knew. I was disowned. Dead to him already. He'd made that painfully clear when we last spoke nearly two years ago. My father had buried me with my shame.

I stared into the fire, unsure of what to do next. With the house. With my grief. With my life. I'd lost everyone that ever mattered to me, and I'd only realized how much after they'd gone.

The doorbell rang. Moments later, Lily appeared, followed by a tall, broad-shouldered man in a pinstriped suit. I assumed it was Mr. Cronin, but as the fire's glow lit his face and flickered in his dark eyes, I knew exactly who he was. And what he'd come for.

"Miss Ryan"—Wyatt Steele took off his hat and extended his hand—"good to see you again."

I stood, rigid, and glared at Lily. "You were specifically told to turn away reporters asking for Ellie Ryan."

"I'm sorry, miss." Her huge blue eyes darted between us. "Only he asked to speak to you, Miss Hardy. He didn't look nothing like them other reporters, neither." She blushed, clearly taken in by his handsome charm. His dark eyes and bright smile. Foolish girl.

"I mean—" she blustered on.

"Oh, go get me some tea." I waved her away.

"Make mine a whiskey," Steele added as she scurried out. He turned and smiled as though we were old friends. "I'm chilled to the bone. Does the sun never shine in Liverpool?" He sat on the wing chair on the other side of the fire and surveyed the room, his eyes observing every draped item, as if he knew in one glance what hid beneath. He stared at me with the same knowing appraisal. His confidence, his ease infuriated me. His very presence did. Who did he think he was, showing up here? Now?

"This is not a good time," I said. "I just buried my great-aunt yesterday and—"

"Yes, my sympathies, Miss Ryan." He paused. "Or do you prefer Miss Hardy?"

I stood there, wordless. Not only had he found me, he'd dug up my real name. What else did he know?

Lily appeared with our drinks. She handed Steele his whiskey and, hesitating at my clear annoyance, set my teacup on the end table. "Um … will there be anything else, Miss Ellen?"

I shook my head and she disappeared into the kitchen, seemingly grateful to get away. If only Steele picked up the hint.

Instead, he raised his glass. "To G.B. Hardy." He took a swig. "Huge fan of her work. Brilliant writer. Loved her Garrett Dean novels. Climbing Kilimanjaro, sailing the Nile, hunting lions on safari—each great adventure was as real to me as if I'd lived it myself." He stared into the fire, and for a moment he seemed like the boy he must have been.

A scallywag if I ever saw one. "He was every boy's hero. I wanted to be Garrett Dean."

"And yet here you are," I said, revelling in catching him off guard. "Hounding people in their grief. Heroic, indeed."

He blinked a few times and I could almost see the shift in his eyes. A tightening intensity, like the slight turning of a telescope lens as he refocused upon his purpose.

"The paper sent me to do a feature on the British army," he said. "War's brewing, you know."

I didn't, actually. My personal hell had overshadowed all else.

"I saw the obituary. Thought I'd pay my respects at the funeral. Turns out G.B.'s grandniece is the mysterious Ellie Ryan." He took another sip, eyeing me over the rim. "You're a hard woman to find, Miss … Ellen."

I swallowed, rattled by how easily he'd tracked me. "Well, now you've found me. Good for you. But you've wasted your time. I have nothing to say." The words gushed as though it was myself I was convincing. He unsettled me, so he did. With his swarthy looks and arrogant swagger, he may look like Garrett Dean, I'd give him that, but to me he felt more like the lion's roar in the black beyond. Circling. Closing in. As if he knew I was wounded and the fire was dwindling.

I grabbed the poker and rattled the embers. They flickered to life for a few seconds then throbbed orange.

"You are the only surviving stewardess of the sunken *Empress of Ireland*, Miss Ellen. As I said on the train, like it or not, you are famous. Readers want to know your story. And

I want to be the one to tell it." His eyes gleamed. "A profile piece like this, and I'd be a shoo-in for the editor's chair."

I shook my head as he spoke. Wasn't he listening?

"I don't want to talk to anyone about the *Empress*!" I just wanted to forget. To stop the flashbacks, the relentless nightmares. To never speak of it again. My heart thudded in my chest. "What makes you think I'd want to tell you anything?"

"Because I have something you want."

My laugh echoed in the stillness of the dead room. I sounded like a madwoman. Perhaps I was. Perhaps insane people don't even realize they truly are.

"You flatter yourself, Mr. Steele." I tried to give my voice more of the confidence I lacked. "I assure you, you have nothing—"

He reached into his pocket and pulled out a small black notebook. The edges were frayed now and the pages rippled with water damage, but I'd know it anywhere. Jim's journal. The leather spine creaked as he opened the book and thumbed through the yellowed pages to where the thin red ribbon lay.

January 23, 1914

What sort of a fool stoker falls into his fire? I was so riled from the lads taunting me, I barely noticed how badly my arm was burned. I wish they'd just leave me alone. I didn't even want them to bring me to Dr. Grant. But I'm glad they did. If they hadn't brought me, I never would have spoken to her.

I saw her. Up close, and not from the shadows along the ship's rail. I don't know why she stands there each night all alone. I don't know why I could never find the courage to talk to her. All I do know is that she's even more beautiful than I thought.

And her name. It's Ellie. Ellie Ryan.

I sank onto the edge of my seat, wordless, breathless, as Steele read from Jim's journal.

He glanced up at me and turned the page.

She rubbed the ointment into my arm and I swear it hurt like the dickens. I nearly fainted with the pain of it. Still, I'd endure a thousand burns to have her look at me like that, to feel her touch me again. She warned me (like Mam would) to be sure to use the ointment Dr. Grant left. Said otherwise the burns would leave me scarred.

If only she knew the scars I have. Ones that no ointment will remove. No, she'd want nothing to do with me then.

I'd often wondered what he wrote in that small black book as he stood jotting at the rail while he waited for me at the end of our shifts. I swallowed and looked at Steele through my puddled tears. Jim carried that book with him always. How could it be here in Steele's hands?

"Is he—" I couldn't say it. As though voicing it made it real. It had been three weeks since the sinking. Three weeks since I saw or heard from Jim, but something in me refused to believe he was gone. He couldn't be.

We sat in silence for a few moments as my mind raced.

"Miss Ellen, we each hold a story the other desperately

wants." Steele closed the book and held it like a winning ticket. "You tell me yours—and I will give you Jim's."

"How did you get the journal?" I blurted. "Did you see him? Do you know where he is?"

Steele smiled. "You have the mind of a journalist."

"And you have the heart of a devil."

"The choice is yours, Miss Ellen." He shrugged. "You may have your privacy or your answers, but you can't have it both ways."

How could he? How could he sit there holding my heart as ransom? What kind of man does that?

No, there was no way I'd trust him with any of my secrets. Clearly, he had every intention of exposing them on the front page of the *New York Times*. My life would be ruined.

Sensing my hesitation, Steele slipped the journal back into his jacket pocket and stood.

But this was Jim, my Jim. My life already was ruined. I needed answers, and though Steele was obviously a poor excuse for a man, he was a skilled journalist. If there was any information to be had, he'd find it, as surely as he'd found me.

"Fine," I exhaled in defeat. "I'll do it … on one condition. You can't use any of Jim's journal in your piece." It was bad enough Steele had read Jim's private thoughts and I would be reading them too. I owed it to Jim to protect his innermost self, even if that meant exposing mine.

Steele considered the request. "*All* of your story?"

"Yes." I held out my hand for the journal, willing to tell him anything, everything, just to have it. "Whatever you want."

He pulled it from his pocket and flipped it open to the ribbon. In one quick swipe he ripped out the yellowed page he'd just read. The sound tore my heart as though it were Jim himself we were dissecting. I suppose in some way we were.

He laid the ragged page in my palm, a drop of water to someone dying of thirst. "Surely you didn't think I'd give you the whole book up front?"

"Surely you can give me something I don't already know." I looked at him, desperate for more.

Turning to the front pages, he tore out the first entry and handed it to me before slipping the book back inside his jacket. "Consider it a down payment. But you owe me, Miss Ellen. Remember that."

He pulled a few newspaper clippings from his satchel and laid them on the table. "Some samples of my work for the *Times*. One on the *Empress* based on my Rimouski interviews and a few on the *Titanic* from a few years ago."

Then, donning his hat, he tipped it to me like the gentleman he was not. "I will be back tomorrow at ten for our interview."

I didn't see him leave. Didn't notice the fire die or even hear Lily until she put Aunt Geraldine's throw over my shoulders and eased me into the chair. I don't know how long I'd been standing alone in that room staring at Jim's cramped scrawl. Seeing, but not reading, his words as they slowly faded with the light.

∞ *Chapter Seven* ∞

COLD RAIN TAPPED AT THE WINDOWS as I sat in bed, the torn pages trembling in my fingers. Jim's journal. His private thoughts. It felt wrong to read them and, yet, impossible not to. Perhaps they'd have the answers I longed for. If nothing else, they were at least Jim's words. As Steele read them earlier, I could almost hear Jim's deep voice speaking them inside my heart. A flicker of him—just enough to dispel the dark thoughts that threatened to pull me under.

I brought the papers closer to the bedside candle's light. I'd been so struck by seeing Jim's journal, at hearing my name read from it, it was only now as I reread that first entry that I realized the weight of Jim's secret shame. What burdened him so? What had left him scarred long before the marks on his skin? Perhaps the journal had some answers. And even though I knew Jim wouldn't have wanted me to know what he'd long kept hidden, I turned to the next page.

May 28, 1913

The lads on this ship all call me Lucky. I wish they wouldn't. I'm not lucky—not by a long shot. It's cursed, I am. Bloody cursed. They want to hear all about it—all the gory details. So I just keep to myself most of the time.

Mam bought me this book on my last layover at home. Told me to write in it, though I don't see the point. She thought it might help with the nightmares, might give me something to do when I wake up in a cold sweat and can't sleep. You were the smart one, Da. Not me. You always had a way with words. She told me to write about how I am feeling—but all I ever feel is angry. And the more I try to stop, the hotter it burns.

The last place I want to be is at sea again. But I suppose I belong in the boiler room. I've shovelled my way cross the pond four times now. Liverpool to Quebec City and back again twice. The company men brag about the Empress taking only six days to cross from dock to dock, but it's the firemen—the trimmers and stokers—they should be bragging about. She might have two engines three decks high, but where do they think she gets that 18,500 horse-power to turn the twin screws? What do they think propels all of her 14,000 tons?

The sweat of the Black Gang, that's what. While the hobnobs sip their brandies and marvel at her speed, eight levels down, men blackened by soot drive the ship by their muscle and sweat. It's like some bloody Roman galley. The Black Gang shovel tons of coal into the white-hot furnaces. A hundred or so of us, taking turns, labouring non-stop

until we reach port. Gruelling work, and hotter than hell's
bowels. But I deserve no better. Mam wanted me to get
on as a bellboy, not a stoker. Work my way up to assistant
steward and, like you, maybe even smoke room steward
someday.

But I'm not you, Da. As badly as Mam needs me to be,
I'll never be you.

I sat in bed and read both entries a few more times, though
I knew them by heart now. Despite the hot water bottle and
extra blankets Lily had given me, I couldn't stop shivering.
There were things about Jim that I never understood. Maybe
the other entries yet to come had answers. Or better yet,
maybe Steele would tell me where Jim was so I could go and
ask him for myself. I could wipe his brow and help him heal.
Maybe, I could finally tell him how I really felt.

I set the pages on my nightstand and snuffed the candle
stub, but I wouldn't sleep. I couldn't. A part of me was still on
the *Empress*. Trapped. Drowning. Sinking deeper and deeper
in regrets. And so I lay awake as I had each night for the past
three weeks, listening as the house creaked and moaned, an
empty shell settling in the darkness around me.

∞ THE FIRST INTERVIEW ∞

June 1914
Strandview Manor, Liverpool

༜ *Chapter Eight* ༜

THE NEXT MORNING, I sat in front of the breakfast I wouldn't eat and grudgingly read Steele's Rimouski and *Titanic* articles. I skimmed the Rimouski piece. He'd captured the details and facts. But more than that, the people. I could hear Gracie in his retelling. Even the *Titanic* articles were top-notch. Clearly he'd interviewed dozens of survivors from third class. Heart-wrenching accounts. The man could write, I'd give him that. But that didn't mean I wanted to be his next headline. *I wasn't really going through with it—was I?* Just thinking about it made my stomach twist even tighter.

As promised, Steele arrived at ten sharp, eyes bright and keen. He seemed excited to be here. Lily sat him across from me at the dining table. I'd had her remove the drape cloth and polish the table before Steele arrived. It seemed more formal, but the truth was, I felt safer, less exposed, with the solid mahogany between us. Clutching the curved armrests in my white-knuckled grip, I anchored myself to weather whatever he'd throw at me.

"Let's get started," he said, flipping his notebook to a fresh page. I felt hunted—no, worse than that. I felt trapped, about to be skinned and dissected.

Can I do this? Am I really going to talk about that night?

I'd put so much energy into staunching those memories as they bubbled up these past few weeks. Yet here I was, baring their very arteries to a stranger.

"So, Miss Ellen," he said, looking at me as though I were a specimen. His pencil, ready for the first incision. "Tell me about the *Empress of Ireland*. When did you first meet?"

He spoke of her as the crew did—as though the ship were a woman and not steel and rivets. I released the breath I didn't realize I'd been holding. Though it had some pain of its own, that memory came easy.

"It was the summer of 1906, the year I turned ten. I spent time with Aunt Geraldine. My mother had been ill—she was dying, actually. And I suppose my parents felt it best that I be spared that goodbye. I was sent from my home in Ireland here to Liverpool, to Strandview Manor, which I hated, and to Aunt Geraldine, whom I liked even less." I cleared my throat and focused on what I meant to say. "That was when I first saw the *Empress*. Mr. Gaade, the chief steward, was an old friend of my aunt's and had invited us to see the ship off on her maiden voyage. Just a short one, across the Irish Sea to Ireland."

I was back there, then, looking at the *Empress* through my ten-year-old eyes. I could almost hear the band playing beneath the bunting, almost feel the long blast of her horn shake my heart as she pulled away. From her red-bottomed hull, up her sleek, black sides, past her white upper decks to her black-rimmed golden funnels, she was a beauty. But I didn't care about all that, I didn't want to wave my hankie at a ship bound for Ireland—I wanted to take it. I wanted to go home.

I paused, but Steele, seemingly comfortable with the uncomfortable silence, waited for me to fill it.

"That's the first time I saw her," I finally added, pulling away from the memory. "I never thought I'd sail, much less serve, aboard her."

"What did you think when you boarded her for the first time as crew?" Steele prompted. He glanced at a side note. "In January 1914."

It seemed like such a long time ago. Was it really only five months? "I didn't know what to think, really. I'd only recently recovered that winter from … an illness. I was tired and overwhelmed."

He jotted something in the margin. "And Meg Bates, you joined together, didn't you? What was her first impression?"

"Honestly, you'd think she'd won a first-class ticket." I smiled, remembering Meg's excitement. "She loved it. Meg loved every minute of that job."

I SPENT THE BETTER PART of the morning educating Steele on the life of a stewardess. Hardly newsworthy. But he'd asked, and so as we sat at the table in the front room, I told him all about it: league after league of making beds, cleaning cabins and alleyways, scrubbing toilets, drawing baths at the right time and temperature. Stewards and stewardesses existed for the comfort of the upper-class passengers. We were to be out of sight and within call, summoned like trained dogs. Run my bath. Fetch my tea. Hang my clothes. Arrange these flowers. Each stewardess was assigned to about a dozen cabins— enough to keep you hopping, all right. And we worked six straight sailing days from five thirty in the morning till eleven at night, squeezing in our meals when we could, second-class leftovers hastily scarfed where we stood in the corners of the steamy pantry. If we were awake, we were on duty one way or another, and always under the watchful eyes of Gaade and Matron Jones. Nothing roused their fury more than stupidity. As a stewardess with absolutely no experience, I had more than my fair share of stupid mistakes on that first voyage: dropping teapots, constantly getting lost in the maze of halls, botching the errands I did remember. I'll never forget the look on old Colonel Ripper's face when I mixed up his laundry delivery with Lady Featherton's extra-large unmentionables. My eyes smiled even now as I recounted the incident to Steele.

"There he was, standing in his dinner uniform in the middle of his cabin intent upon the large white flag he held in one hand. With the other, he scratched his bald head, confounded by what was, in fact, an enormous brassiere dangling on the tip of his cane. 'Good Lord, Ellen,' he'd finally said, red-faced and wide-eyed, when it dawned on him what he'd retrieved from the laundry bag I'd left him, the one that was clearly not his. 'It's like the billowing sail of a double-masted brig!'"

Steele laughed.

"And whenever Meg and I saw Lady Featherton's great girth coming down the deck, I'd only to lean in and whisper, 'Thar she blows!' to send poor Meg into a fit of giggles. Oh,

Meg." I shook my head and smiled, lost in the mist of a good memory. "I wouldn't have survived it all without her."

The truth of my words echoed in the dining room, tolling through my fog like a ship's bell. I *survived* because of Meg. That horrible night, she'd given me her life vest. Insisted upon it. Her last great act of service to me.

A dry lump lodged in my throat as I took my hankie and dabbed my stinging eyes, uncomfortable under Steele's scrutiny. I swallowed and shifted in my seat. "I'm sorry."

He nodded, but the apology was not for him. Not really.

"Take your time." He scanned his questions. For a man who made a profit on words, he was surprisingly stingy. Had he any words of comfort, he kept them to himself.

Unready to continue, and unwilling to sit still, I stood and rang for Lily. Twice. Where was that girl? My throat was parched. I turned to stare out the window while I waited.

In all the weeks that I'd been at Aunt Geraldine's before we sailed, I'd never truly appreciated all that Meg did. Or how well. To be honest, I hardly noticed her at all. My aunt had hired Meg the year before, I believe. Most of the time a cup of tea would appear on the end table before I'd even realized I wanted it. Earl Grey, milk and two sugars. My bed was always turned down and warmed up no matter what hours I kept. My clothes neatly pressed. Meg was simply a part of the house, really. If I rang a bell, I knew Meg would run as surely as I knew water did when I turned the tap. "You just have to get to know them, is all," she'd said, when I'd returned to the second-class galley a third time because Lady Featherton's soup was too cold, then too hot, and eventually too late. "They're people just the same as you and me, Miss Ellen."

I had my doubts about Lady Featherton, but for the most part, the passengers were patient with me, and I improved over the winter as we crossed the Atlantic from Liverpool to New Brunswick and back each month. Six days at sea, serving passengers from dawn to dark; six days at dock to clear them out, clean her up, and board again; and six days back to Liverpool. With Meg's help, I learned how to serve hot soup, steep strong tea, and carry five plates at one time just as well as she could, though I never got the ten-shilling tips Meg did when the passengers docked. Many even offered to hire her for their personal staff. But she never even considered it. "I couldn't leave you, Miss Ellen. I made a promise to Lady Hardy, so I did. And I don't break my promises."

I wasn't too keen about having my aunt's spy watching me day and night; still, you couldn't help but like Meg. She lived to please, and it seemed to please her to live that way. Getting paid for it was a bonus. Though, truth be told, we weren't paid all that much; we relied on those tips. Once we paid for our uniforms and our laundry bills, not to mention all my broken dishes, there wasn't much left. But there was always enough for us to treat ourselves when we docked in Saint John, New Brunswick. Freed from the rule of Aunt Geraldine, the demands of Gaade, and the disapproving eye of Matron Jones, we'd kick up our heels in Saint John, sharing a pilfered bottle of stout on the pier, sharing the adventures of stealing it, the recent melodrama of the passengers, and the longing for that look from those two young men we fancied. Just two girls having fun. I didn't realize it then, but not only was she by far the best maid, Meg Bates was the best friend I ever had.

∽ *Chapter Nine* ∾

STEELE SAT IN HUNGRY SILENCE at the table behind me, waiting to feed on whatever I might reveal next: more of my life aboard the *Empress*, more about Meg, more about all that I had lost. I'm not sure how long I stood staring out the front window at Aunt Geraldine's garden, lost in thought as I watched Bates putter around in his rubber boots.

My mother brought me here a few summers before she died. She always made time for Aunt Geraldine, her husband's aunt who never seemed to have time for us. But Bates always had time for me. I'd often sit on the garden wall and watch him prune or weed or water. Ask him a million questions about why he plucked at the plants. *Oh, just making a space for the new buds.* He'd always been so gentle with the flowers, so patient with my many questions. Back then, he'd answered every *but why, Bates?* Yet even Bates couldn't answer that question now.

I looked at him now, the stoop of his back, the tremble of his wrinkled hands as he reached his shears into the white rose bush. He seemed so old. So frail. What would become of him, of us, without Aunt Geraldine's direction and Meg's help? He snipped a rose, dropped it beside the other two on the ground. They'd be on Aunt Geraldine's grave within the hour. She would have liked that. Then Bates turned his attention to the foxglove by the gate. Its vibrant purple bells rustled in the breeze, carrying its sweet scent through the open window. Meg loved foxglove. No doubt her grandfather would have cut her some, would have brought a bouquet to her grave, had he known where she lay. Like Jim, her body had never been recovered. I never saw either of them in a rough-hewn coffin, lined up among the hundreds of others. Husbands. Wives. Children. I closed my eyes.

No.

I never saw them because they weren't there. Jim and Meg were listed as "lost at sea." *Lost* ... not dead, and something lost might still be found. For weeks now, I had clung to the withering hope that there had been some kind of mistake. That one day I'd see Jim on the docks, see Meg coming through that gate. Bates had told me it was time to let go, but I just couldn't. I saw her struggle and gasp. No matter how my numbed hands tried to hold her up, no matter how I kicked my leaden legs, she kept slipping away, and all I could do was watch her terrified eyes disappear beneath the black water.

I wouldn't let go of her. Not again.

"—as a stewardess? ... Miss Ellen?" Steele's voice bobbed on the edges of my darkness and I gripped it like a lifeline, letting him reel me back to here and now.

"Sorry?" Once again, I found myself apologizing to the very man who was keelhauling me through the depths.

"Well ..." He scanned the pages, flipping back through the many notes he'd made this morning. "We've got when you started, what you did, where, and with whom. Mainly Meg, right?"

I nodded, in slight shock at his callousness. Bloody journalist. His cold detachment contrasted with my wild emotions. He was calm and rational while my mind galloped and my heart bucked. Yet somehow he tethered me to the present. Gentled me, I suppose. I didn't know whether to be angry or grateful.

"This is good. Really good stuff." He put his pencil to his lips. "But one thing I don't understand is *why*."

"That's the question, isn't it, Mr. Steele?" I returned to my seat, drawn by his sympathy. "Why? Why do these tragedies happen? Why do we lose people we care about?"

He flipped the page. "No, I mean why were you even on the ship?"

Once again, his bluntness caught me off guard.

"You're Ellen Hardy," he continued. "Daughter of Joseph Hardy—sole heir of Hardy Estates, one of the richest stables in County Wicklow."

My face burned and I shut my mouth, only just noticing it was hanging open. Clearly, he'd done his homework. Any gratitude or connection he'd evoked in me were gone. How dare he? How dare he bring up my father! I wondered how much he already knew. Not all of it, not if he was asking.

"I don't see what any of that has to do with the *Empress*." I tried to keep my voice neutral, though I knew my face betrayed me. My very thoughts flushed up my neck and across my cheeks. I'd never been a good liar.

"Why would someone like you be living a second-class servant's life?" He squinted as if trying to read me more clearly. "What made you do it? Now, *that's* exactly the kind of story that sells."

My mind raced. "It was for a story, of course." I scrambled for an answer to stop up the truth I didn't want to spill. If I let it out, even a little, I knew the whole of it would gush forth. "That's exactly it. Aunt Geraldine needed some research."

His eyes darkened as a frown settled over them. He wasn't buying it.

"For her new book," I added. "About a stewardess. Who works on a steamship."

He tapped the pencil on his lips, sounding my story for truth. "It's just, I can't see G.B. writing about something that mundane. A stewardess adventure—I mean, come on, who'd want to read that?"

I arched my eyebrow and clenched my jaw. "Indeed."

He smirked at the irony, and his eyes brightened once again. He relaxed into his chair. "So why not just send the maid, Meg? Why both of you?"

"Have you met my aunt, Mr. Steele?"

"I wish I had."

"She was a perfectionist who lived and breathed her books. Her characters were more real to her than … than I was." The words came easier the less he doubted. Plus I spoke the truth. Aunt Geraldine simply wanted to write my life. To control me like some secondary character in her bloody novels. "I wanted to get away from her overbearing ways. I wanted … an *adventure* of my own." I chose my words carefully, using what little I knew about the man before me. If we were going to play this game, I needed to know more about him, a lot more. "Besides, surely a writer such as yourself would know that two sources are better than one."

Lily knocked and entered with tea. I'd made it clear before he came that Mr. Steele would not be staying. I'd given him the whole morning, enough for one day. She seemed embarrassed when he noticed the tray held tea, soup, and buttered soda bread for one. Aunt Geraldine would've been disgusted by my actions. But my lack of hospitality was the least of the many ways I'd disappointed her.

He caught Lily's eye and winked as he flipped his notebook shut. "Well, I guess that's my cue."

Lily blushed and set the tray on the table before me. I don't know why, but her obvious adoration of him irritated me. He was toying with her. Didn't she know?

"I'd stay," he continued, as if he'd been invited, "but I want to get back to my boarding house and pound out a bit of this while it's still fresh in my mind. My editor said he wants a draft as soon as possible." He shoved his pencil and pad inside his leather satchel before standing and shrugging it over his broad shoulder. "Same time Monday?"

"Aren't you forgetting something?" He was going to make me ask, make me beg again. But I wouldn't. He couldn't play me as easily as Lily.

"Oh, right." He pulled out Jim's journal and ripped out another few pages. He tossed them on my tray.

His indifference infuriated me and I bolted to my feet, driven forward by emotion. "Damn you, Steele. Can't you just give me the whole story?"

He held my stare. "Can't you?"

The tension crackled blue fire between us, hot and electric like a Tesla-coil globe. I'd seen it at London's 1912 World's Fair, a great orb of electricity exploding into a hundred blue veins when the scientist brought the wand closer. As Steele's intensity was somehow doing now. It lasted seconds, but in that moment I knew. I knew he held the wand and all its power. I knew he could, and would, draw whatever he wanted from me and I could do nothing to stop him. We both knew it. Without a word, he left, and my energy went with him. All my anger and outrage. My fury and purpose.

All drained away, leaving nothing but a transparent globe, empty, ready to shatter.

June 14, 1913

I hear it gurgle in the dark, spilling under my bedroom door. It's come for me again. The sea. Even back home in Liverpool, in my own bed, it stalks me. Water swirls around my boots in the corner, dragging one toward my bed in its growing current. In truth, it's no deeper than a puddle in the back lane after a storm. But I know what's coming.

"Da!" I call to the bed on the other side of my room. His dark form doesn't move from where he lies, as always, facing the wall. There isn't much time. Already the water is lapping round our mattresses, tugging our blankets. "Da, please! We have to go!"

I want to get up, to shake him, to get us the hell out of here, but I can't move as the freezing water breaches my bed. It surges under my back and around my legs, rising farther and farther up my pounding chest. A steady stream spurts from the keyhole and the door groans in defeat before exploding in a gush of whitewater and splinters that floods the room. Water swirls around my head, fills my ears, and climbs my cheeks. I can't breathe even though I know I've only moments left to take that final gasp.

And then it's too late.

As the surface closes over my face, I sink deeper and deeper into its darkness. I'm not afraid of dying. In fact, I want to. I wish for it every day. I deserve this. And so I make myself look at what I can't bear to see.

My heart hammers and my lungs burn, yet I am numb to everything but the sight of my father, in the darkness, just out of reach. He drifts closer, the strings of his life vest trailing behind. His steward uniform is torn, his brow still cut. But it's his eyes, always the eyes, milky, vacant in his bloated white face that make me scream as my father drifts over me in a dead man's float.

"Jim! Jim!" Strong hands shake my shoulders. "Wake up! That's enough!"

I'm back in my bed. Mam is rattling me something fierce.

"Stop your screaming, boy. Must you wake the whole of Liverpool?" She stands and pulls her shawl close. "Enough now. You're upsetting the girls."

My heart is thudding like a steam engine and I'm sweating like I've shovelled two tons of coal. Libby is behind her, candle in hand. In its dim light I see the door is sound, the room is dry, and the spare bed is empty.

Once again, I'd woken the house.

"Just another bad dream." Mam nods at Libby, who takes Penny's hand and leads her back to their bed.

But it isn't a dream. Da is dead.

"I'm sorry, Mam," I say, sitting up and holding my head in my hands. It's my fault he's gone. My fault.

She strokes my hair like she did when I was a lad. "I know, Jimmy. I know, love. I miss him, too."

But she doesn't know the half of it. And she never can.

I wipe my nose on the back of my hand. I can't stop trembling.

"Things will look better in the morning, son." She doesn't sound convincing or convinced of the lies she tells herself each night. "You've been having more nightmares lately. Are you nervous about sailing? Is that it, do you think?"

Maybe. Or maybe it's being home again. Seeing how much they need Da's pay. As the only son, now it's up to me—and a stoker's wage is nothing compared to a top steward's. It doesn't matter how I feel about the work or that I am only seventeen. I owe it to my family.

"I'll be fine once I'm on board ... once I'm working again."

"Would you not rather work here on the docks?" she says. "I'm sure we could find you something. Maybe Mr. Carroll might need—"

"No, Mam. It's already set." I can't stay. Can't see her pining for Da day after day, her sighing, the way her eyes linger on his empty chair.

"Why him? Why my Davey?" she often whispers. And I know what it means: Why Davey ... and not you, instead?

I haven't got an answer for her. Lord knows, I've asked the same question every day.

"I like the work," I lie, as she turns to leave. I'd already done one voyage from Liverpool to Quebec and back. Hot. Noisy. Endless shifts shovelling coal until my body and mind were numb with exhaustion.

Only then can I escape the nightmares.

∞ FOUR MONTHS BEFORE ∞

February 1914
The Empress of Ireland,
somewhere on the Atlantic

∽ *Chapter Ten* ∽

I DIDN'T SEE MUCH OF JIM after Dr. Grant gave his burn the
all-clear. I don't know what I expected, really. That he would
come with gifts, knocking on my cabin door like Timothy
Hughes?

Most nights, we'd hear Timothy clear his throat, the soft
rap of his knuckles. "It's for you, Meg," Kate would chide as
Gwen and I laughed at Meg's feigned surprise, the pinking
of her freckled cheeks. She'd open the door to find him,
arms laden with the books he'd deliver to passengers. Yet, no
matter how many runs he had to make each day, somehow
his route always brought him by our door at the end of it.
He'd hold out the latest *Woman's Weekly* paper, not a word out
of him. Mind you, he didn't have to speak. His face said it all.
Smitten, he was, since they met on our first voyage. And Meg,
too, as she thanked him with her slight smile, face rose red.
She'd always give the papers to Gwen or Kate, shrug, and say
she was too busy to read. But eventually I realized the truth

of it. She'd broken down when I asked her alone in our cabin, and Meg didn't cry easily.

"I can't tell him I can't read! What would he think?" She blew her nose. "He's a library steward, for godsakes. He adores books."

"No," I assured her. "He adores you."

Her eyes brimmed with hopefulness. "You think so, Miss Ellen? You really do?"

"I can teach you to read, Meg. If you want me to." It felt good to finally be able to offer her something in return. "It's the least I can do after all your help."

She waved me away.

"You're smart, Meg. You'll pick it up in no time. Before you know it, you'll be writing as well—'My darling Timothy.'" I clasped my hands and brought them to my heart, like a film star. "'How I love your ginger hair, the way it parts right down the middle like an open book, the way your cowlick juts out like a bookmark. Just the sight of you makes me want to rip off your dust jacket and run my fingers down your spine.'"

"Miss Ellen!" she scolded, and hit me with her pillow.

I laughed. She was so easy to tease. "In all seriousness, Meg. I'll help you. But only on one condition."

"Anything, Miss Ellen. I'll do anything."

I smiled. "You have to call me Ellie."

She did learn to call me Ellie, and to read and write. Though she never did write that letter. And with a tip from me, Timothy started bringing her *Tatler* magazines, full of gossip and photos. It was easier for them. Simpler, I suppose. They were simpler. But right from the start, Jim and I were so—complicated.

No, I didn't expect him to come knocking at my door. What would he bring me anyway—a shovelful of coal? Yet, I never could get his face from my mind. Never stopped hoping that I'd see him again.

Each night at the end of my shift, while the girls caught up on the day's gossip and news, I'd slip on my woollen coat and, keeping an eye out for Gaade on his night rounds, sneak down the hall and outside to the right, to the spot on the rail. The only place that was mine. I'd gone there the first night out of desperation. Maybe even to jump, had I the nerve. But every night since, just being there was enough to calm me. I'd breathe in that cold night air, breathe in the broad sky of speckled stars, breathe in the limitless horizon and start to believe there was more to life than what I'd been doing all that long day. There, in the cold dark as the wind whipped the strands of my unravelling braid from my face, I could finally breathe.

And it was there that I saw him again.

He stood in the shadows not four feet from me, a dark shadow himself but for the red tip of his cigarette that moved to his mouth, glowed bright for an instant before arcing down to rest where he leaned on the rail. I'd never noticed him here before. And yet, he seemed like part of the landscape.

He took another drag. In its red glow I saw his soot-covered face, his iceberg eyes watching me. We held each other's gaze, neither of us moving or speaking. Unsure of what to do next. I turned and faced the water, trying to pretend I'd known he was there all along.

"Are you even allowed to be up here?" I asked, knowing he wasn't.

"Are you?" His deep voice was calm, almost teasing.

"Well, I won't tell if you won't." I leaned on the wood rail and took a deep breath.

"Deal." He flicked his cigarette over the railing into the dark sea. "There's still a problem, however. You appear to be leaning on *my* rail."

"Yours, is it?" I looked at him sideways, unsure if he was joking or not. "Has it got your name on it, then?"

Without a word, he came closer and took my hand in his. His fingers like weathered steel, hard, coarse, yet surprisingly warm. A tingle of electricity passed between us and he paused. I wondered if he felt it too. He rubbed my fingertips along the rail's edge near where he stood, and I felt small gouges in the wood's smooth finish. Letters carved into it: J.I.M.

I smiled. "You've got me there. Looks like you've been here a few times." Had he been here all those nights I'd thought myself alone? Was he watching me then?

He clicked open his penknife. The blade glinted in the dim moonlight, and he pulled an apple from his pocket, slicing a piece and eating it off the back of the knife.

"Gaade would lay an egg if he saw me out here after curfew." I glanced over at him. "Especially with a knife-wielding scrapper from the Black Gang."

"In your nightdress ..." Jim added between bites.

"I have a coat on, thank you very much!" The blush rushed to my cheeks. Thankfully, it was too dark to see it or my nightdress hanging below my coat. It truly was madness, me being here. At this hour. With this lad. In this state. And yet, it felt anything but.

"It's just—I've no place to call my own. You know?" I leaned onto the railing. "Sometimes, I feel like I might explode if I don't get away. Like I need more air. It's always: *Get me this and bring me that. And wash this and iron that—*"

"And shovel coal. And shovel coal. And shovel coal."

"You're mocking me," I said, realizing his work in the boiler room was infinitely worse.

He shook his head. "No. I know exactly what you mean."

"And we don't even get a break to eat. Do you know how horrible it is to be always on the run, grabbing your meal where you stand in the back corner of the galley? Three minutes to gobble it down before some bloody passenger wants another bloody pot of tea."

He let me rant.

"For once, I'd like to sit and enjoy my food. You know? Like a human being and not a plow horse strapping on the feed bag in her stall."

Jim drew the blade along the apple, cutting another thick slice. Then he stopped and looked up at the wide sky. "Sometimes, it feels like the only time I can breathe, really breathe, is when I'm up here."

I wondered if I should leave. I'm sure the last thing he wanted was to stand here listening to a stewardess's tantrum, whining about having to make tea, while his long days were so much more gruelling and dangerous. I'd never seen the boiler rooms, but I'd heard about them. About how the men there nearly worked themselves to death. No wonder they drank and fought as hard as they worked. It was a tough life.

We stood in silence for a few minutes. I didn't want to leave. He didn't ask me to.

"How is your burn?" I finally asked.

He rolled up his sleeve and extended his arm to show me. In the dim light, it seemed healed and I gently touched the skin. It felt taut and smooth.

"It's healing well," I said.

He made a fist and flexed his hand. "I'll live."

"I hope so." I took my hand away and slipped it back into my pocket, but stayed beside him. "Otherwise, that was a waste of good ointment."

He laughed then. It seemed to surprise him as much as me, as if he had forgotten the sound. His smile transformed him, softening his face into dimples, melting his stare. It relaxed his shoulders, his fists, his whole demeanour. It made him glow like an ember. Warm and compelling.

"You should smile more often," I said, surprised at my boldness, but I was only speaking the truth.

Jim's face dropped and he turned from me to whip the rest of his apple into the sea.

Did I say something wrong?

We stood in silence for a few moments.

"Yeah, well, I've never had a lot to smile about," he muttered.

He glanced down at me, his last words drowned out by the blast of the ship's horn. But I read them on his lips as they tugged a smile and pinned it in with his dimple.

"Until now."

⧼ *Chapter Eleven* ⧽

AS I WENT ABOUT the next day's duties, Jim filled my thoughts. I began to wonder if maybe I'd just imagined those words. But I hadn't imagined that half-smile. A white crescent in the dark. A sliver of something that was so much more, but hidden in shadow. I couldn't tell you what it was about him that intrigued me so. Sure, he was broad chested and thick armed. Tall. Strong. Even handsome, yes, under all that soot and scowl. But it wasn't even all that. It was him. Jim Farrow drew me like the tide. Slowly. Mysteriously. Powerfully.

"What has got into you, girl?" Matron Jones chided as I stood in the galley absentmindedly holding a laden breakfast tray. "That's to go to the Smiths in 345. The tea will be cold if you don't get a move on."

I murmured an apology and set off down the long passageway to deliver the tray. And then another. And another. I made the beds and took the laundry to be cleaned. I scrubbed the sinks while the Shultz family took their morning stroll on the promenade. I pictured it, the Shultzes or some other wealthy couple standing there, their long dress coats and scarves blowing in the wind, their gloved hands gripping Jim's rail, and smiled to myself.

They think it's theirs.

But hadn't I done the same? Hadn't I barged in and rambled on about needing my own space? Telling him to smile more.

I paused, scrub brush in hand. Maybe he didn't want me there, intruding. That hadn't occurred to me before—and now I couldn't stop dwelling on it.

Maybe that was why he was so quiet. He must think me a right idiot.

I opened the porthole and took a deep breath of sea air as the ship cut through open waters at top speed of twenty knots. For me, the day just seemed to drag on. And any knots were those tightening in my stomach.

A dozen cabins to clean. A dozen families that needed serving, dressing for dinners, cups of warm milk, or hot water bottles in their freshly turned-down beds, and then my last check-in to lock up their portholes, and finally my duties were done. But the day was not my own, not yet. Kate, Gwen, Meg, and I got ready for bed. It took some shuffling in our tiny room, but we had it down to a well-timed routine, each of us slipping out of our uniforms and into our long white nightdresses. Then hanging and brushing our kit for the next day. And soon enough, we were shelved in our bunks, like books in Timothy's library: Gwen reading us the news from the latest *Tatler*; Kate tying rags in tired curls; Meg opening the door to let Emmy in for a saucer of milk and a belly rub; and me, counting the minutes until they were all asleep. With lights out, the gossip and gabbing soon ebbed in the darkness as their wakefulness wound down. But not mine. For my mind kept turning to Jim.

Is he there now? Should I go?

When their breathing settled slow and steady, I slipped out of bed and into my coat and shoes. Opening the door a crack, I peered down the dimly lit hallway. The night steward might be on his rounds, but he'd usually passed this hall by now. Seeing no sign of him, I slipped through our door, clicking it gently behind me.

I made my way to the deck, to where I'd seen him last, but he wasn't there. Not even in the shadows. It surprised me how disappointed I was to find the rail empty. I ran my fingers over it searching for his name. J.I.M. E.

E?

I stroked the grooves, straining to feel what I couldn't see. I hadn't noticed the *E* last night. To the right of it continued more etching. L.L.I.E.

"I thought you'd like a place to call your own."

I jumped at the sound of his voice as he came from behind the forward mast.

"Jim! You just about gave me a heart attack."

He smiled and the pounding of my heart increased, but not from fright.

"Close your eyes," he said, moving toward me. "I've got another surprise for you." ·

I paused.

"Come on, Ellie," he teased. "Don't you trust me?"

"Do you think I'd be here if I didn't?" The truth was, I felt completely safe with him. I covered my eyes. "What's this about?"

"Just wait. And no peeking." He stood behind me, his strong hands on my shoulders, and guided me toward the forward mast.

"You're not about to make me walk the plank or anything, are you?"

About thirty feet away, we stopped on the far side of the mast. "All right," he said. "Open them."

And there on the deck sat a table set for two. White linen. First-class china. Silverware. Flickering candles on either side of a great domed serving tray. It was as though someone had transplanted it from the first-class dining room.

"But how—"

"What? You think all my friends are boiler monkeys?" He smiled. "I have connections, you know." He lifted his hand and whispered behind it. "But you may have to tell me which fork is which." He held out his arm and I slipped my hand through it, blushing as he escorted me to my seat.

The doorway was less than fifty yards away. I glanced back. "But what if—"

"Already thought of that." He looked up and waved to the sailor in the crow's nest. "I slipped John a few chocolate bars. He said he'd keep an eye out for us. But if you hear him whistling, you're to run like the devil."

"You did all this?" I couldn't believe it. No one had ever done anything so thoughtful for me.

"Don't get too excited," he said. "The setting's first class"—he smiled at me—"and so is the company, but, sadly, the food is not."

He lifted the silver dome of the serving dish to reveal, not the *canard à l'orange* served earlier that evening, but rather a smiley face made of sliced apples, with a small pot of melted chocolate for the nose.

"I made it myself," he bragged. "Old family recipe."

The face on the tray blurred as my eyes watered and I looked away, embarrassed.

"God, I'm such a stupid arse!" His smile dropped as he looked at the tray. "Here you are wishing for a real meal and not to be eating like some horse in a stall … and what do I give you? Apples. Bloody apples. Hell, why don't I just feed you sugar cubes off my palm?"

"No, no." I gripped his arm. "It's perfect, Jim. I love it. All of it." I wiped my eyes. "I've just never … I've never had anyone do something like this for me before."

"And I daresay, you've never had anyone feed you sugar cubes either." He looked at me sideways. "But that doesn't mean you want it."

I laughed, then.

"I know it's not exactly what you pictured, Ellie. I just wanted to do something nice for you, you know, to thank you for what you did … for my arm." He shrugged and rubbed the back of his neck.

"And a bit of vandalism just didn't seem to be enough," I teased. "Larceny, then? Stolen silverware?"

"Borrowed," he corrected, and just like that, his grin was back.

"How did you know I would even be coming tonight?" I asked.

"Well, now, you've been at that rail every night since you started back in January."

I blushed. So he had been watching me.

He held out my chair and I sat. "Tuck in there, Miss Ryan. I've to get this lot back in thirty minutes."

We dipped our apples first with our forks and eventually with our fingers. What a mess we made of the linens, dripping globs of chocolate from the pot to our mouths. I'd never tasted anything so sweet. As we leaned in with the last few slices, something fell from above into the chocolate, splattering it all over the table, all over us, like a slapped mud puddle.

"Shite!" Jim whispered, looking at John, who was waving and frantically pointing behind. "Someone's coming!"

Jim grabbed my hand and pulled me from the table, up the deck and around the hatches and vents to the very front of the ship, before dragging me down behind what looked like a huge steel spool. My heart thudded in my chest.

From our darkened hiding spot we could see the electric torch beam scan the deck and stop on the table. "What the devil—? You'd better get Gaade. He's not going to like this."

The shaft of light travelled up the deck close to where we hid and we crouched lower. In the beam, I saw a great chocolate handprint from where Jim had been leaning. He saw it too and clapped a hand over his mouth to stifle a laugh, leaving yet another handprint across his face.

Maybe it was all that chocolate, or the fact that I was so overtired, maybe it was nerves—what would happen when Gaade found me like this? But even that sobering thought only made me giggle all the more.

The ray of light drew closer and so did the footsteps. And just when I thought we were done for, a thud on the far side of the deck drew them away.

"Come on!" Jim whispered, and glancing at John way up in his crow's nest waving us down the left side of the mast, we scurried from shadow to shadow.

"What is it?" Gaade's voice snapped on the other side.

The night steward stood. "A chocolate bar, sir."

"Looks like I owe John a few more," Jim whispered.

"Yes, well, I can see that, man," Gaade continued, "but the question remains, how in the blazes did it get here? And who the hell put this table—"

We bolted for the doors and slipped through them into the dimly lit hall, our chests heaving. Jim eyed me and smiled. "You're a mess."

"You should talk." His devilish grin was splattered and smeared with chocolate like a child caught licking the cake bowl.

He ran a finger down my cheek and popped it in his mouth.

"You look good in chocolate," he said. "It brings out your eyes."

I punched his shoulder.

"Well, unless you want to get caught brown-handed, you may want to get moving before Gaade is back inside."

"Thanks, Jim. For everything."

He smiled. That smile. God, my very heart felt like melting chocolate.

"I think," he said, heading for the stairs down to his quarters, "I may just stick with the sugar cube thing next time."

Next time.

I tiptoed down the hallway, careful not to touch anything

as I entered the lavatory. Jim was right, I was a mess. I cleaned my face, spot-washed my coat, and left it hanging on the back of the door. On my way back to my room, I ran into Gaade.

"Ellen?" He seemed shocked to find me in my nightgown in the hall, hair still wet from where I'd washed my face. "What are you doing up?"

"Um, upset stomach, sir. I didn't want to wake the girls." I'd been seasick a few times on our first runs. But that was weeks ago. I wasn't sure if he'd believe it, but he seemed too frazzled from the nighttime capers to be worried about my upset stomach.

He glanced down the hallway. "Did you see anything … unusual tonight?"

Like a chocolate-covered stoker?

A giggle bubbled up and I gripped my mouth in panic before running back to the lavatory. Slamming the door shut, I leaned on it, heart pumping, leaving Gaade wondering exactly what kind of a ship he was running.

Gaade never did discover who had moved a first-class table and chairs to the deck that night, but at the next muster roll, he'd given us all a warning to keep a level eye out for anything unusual and threatened us with severe conse-quences for assisting. "No tip, no bribe is worth losing your job." Clearly he'd assumed it was the work of some first-class passenger with more money than sense. Gaade made it quite clear that he ran a tight ship. "For the *Empress* is no place for shenanigans."

But our shenanigans continued.

Every night after, I'd find Jim at our rail. Or he'd find me. With Gaade's diligent watch, we had to be more cautious, settling for furniture already on the deck. Some nights we lay side by side in our deck chairs watching the stars that speckled across the dark dome of sky. It made me feel small and invisible and at the same time filled me with such awe. Most of the time we just stood at our rail. We didn't talk much about anything important. Though he did like to tell me about the *Empress*—how fast she moved, how safe she was, and all the lifesaving equipment she carried.

"Did you know she has 2100 lifebelts?" he'd say. The sound of his deep voice more of a comfort than any silly statistics. "Twenty-four collapsibles, extra lifeboats for a total of forty boats to carry 1960 people, more than we ever have aboard." He mentioned that a few times, and I was never quite sure if he said it for my comfort or his own. Or if it was, in fact, some kind of secret obsession with safety or dark fear of drowning. I didn't mind. To be honest, I just liked being near him, wrapped in the warmth of his words.

Sometimes he talked about the stoker's life. Or I vented about that of a stewardess, but never about anything before it. I let him think I was a maid—not a disowned heiress. What did it matter? Neither of them was truly me. Truth be told, Jim and I were decks and worlds apart. But none of that meant anything while we stood together those nights at the rail with darkness before and behind. Our secrets didn't matter. Neither past nor future existed for us—only those moments together seemed real.

It was enough to just be there. Together. Breathing.

Timothy and Meg shared words—but we shared silence. A knowing. A simple presence. I looked forward to just being with him, side by side at the rail as the *Empress* rushed headlong into the unknown, its wake disappearing in the dark.

And for the first time in my life I felt, I don't know, accepted. I felt known. For the first time, I felt like myself.

↬ THREE DAYS BEFORE ↫

May 26, 1914
Quebec Harbour

∞ *Chapter Twelve* ∞

"ARE YOU SURE you don't want me to come with you?" Meg asked as we stripped the bed. After the passengers disembarked, cleaning up was a huge undertaking, but at least we didn't have to be at anyone's beck and call. Meg and I found it quicker to clean the cabins together, and by now, with five months and ten crossings, our routine was as fast and efficient as an oiled engine running full steam. I shook a pillow out onto the mattress and held open the case as Meg bundled the dirty linens inside.

"I'll be fine," I reassured her, stuffing in towels and face cloths. "I'll be with Jim."

She stopped and put her hands on her hips. "In a town you don't know—with a man you shouldn't know."

I rolled my eyes. "Now you sound like Matron Jones."

On the first run of its spring–summer schedule, the *Empress* had just docked at Quebec City. Most of the year, we put in at Saint John, New Brunswick, but with the spring thaw, Quebec was our new port from May until November.

I wouldn't have thought the winter schedule ran so late in the year, but Will Sampson, the chief engineer, told Jim we'd encountered heavy ice floes in the Cabot Strait right as we entered the mouth of the St. Lawrence. The captain had even sent wireless messages warning other ships. It might be the third week of May, but the waters were still freezing, cold enough to carry ice at least.

"You're just jealous," I teased, tossing the load of washing by the door and picking up the pile of fresh bedding I'd left on the chair. "Because your bookworm hasn't asked you on a date."

We each grabbed two corners of the white sheet and moved to either side of the bed, snapping it open over the mattress. Within two minutes we'd tucked and smoothed the sheets, blanket, and coverlet. I shook the pillows into their cases and tossed her one.

"Jim didn't ask you neither," she reminded me. And he hadn't. Not really.

On our last night together before docking, as the ship sailed along the St. Lawrence to Quebec City, I'd hinted that he might show me the town. Joked that it would be nice to see each other in daylight. But he'd remained quiet. Some nights he barely spoke at all. I never knew what to expect with Jim. That night, his silence left me feeling foolish for asking. I finally said I had to get some sleep and turned to leave. Docking day was always hectic, and I knew I'd be exhausted if I stayed out late clearly making an arse of myself. But I hated to go. We wouldn't see each other once we docked. Being at port meant even more work for both of us. Rooms to clean, coal bunkers to fill. We didn't sail again for a few more days, but we'd surely spend those cleaning up from the last voyage and setting up for the next.

"Tuesday," he'd said from the rail behind me, as I reached for the doorknob. "I'll be at the *funiculaire* at noon."

I'D AGREED TO LET Meg and Kate walk me ashore. They had the afternoon off and were keen to see the city. Eager to be out of uniform, we'd all worn our best dresses. I suppose anything was better than those horrid uniforms, but I felt self-conscious and nervously fiddled with the white pleated collar rimming the scoop neck.

"That periwinkle is your colour, Ellen," Meg said. Even now, she knew just what I needed.

"Are you sure it's a date at all?" Gwen asked. I'd never told the girls about meeting Jim at the rail at night. They didn't know about Jim and me. Even I wasn't sure what we were exactly. I'd just said he'd invited me out to thank me for tending his arm. It seemed safe enough.

"What if he's there with the Black Gang?" Gwen continued. "You're not seriously going to go off gallivanting with that lot, are you?"

I had no idea what to expect. It had sounded like a question that night, like an invitation. But now, in the light of day, I wondered if I'd misheard him. My stomach twisted.

"What's a *funiculaire*, anyway?" Meg continued. "It sounds like something Dr. Grant would pull out of his doctor's bag."

I laughed nervously.

"Is it a pub? A restaurant, do you think?" Gwen added. "Someplace romantic, at least?"

"Well, whatever it is, it's right there." I nodded across the cobblestoned lane at the grey house with FUNICULAIRE in black letters above the door. An old woman dressed in black sat at a cart brimming with tulips of every colour. They reminded me of the gardens back home.

"Maybe he'll buy you a single red rose," Gwen teased. "It means true love."

"Maybe you've been reading too many *Tatler* magazines. Besides, why would he waste his hard-earned wages on something as silly as that?" I said, secretly hoping he might. I'd never had someone buy me flowers before. "Thanks for helping me find it. You can go now."

Meg hesitated, clearly uncomfortable with leaving me, until Gwen linked her arm and urged her away. I watched them go until they disappeared in the crowd, half wanting to follow.

"Ellie." His voice felt like a warm touch and I turned to find him standing behind me. He wore a white shirt tucked into his brown trousers; black suspenders ran up his wide chest and over his muscled shoulders. He wrung his cap in his hands. He'd scrubbed them clean, his face, too, for it glowed pink-cheeked like a child's on bath night. He'd even slicked his unruly curls, though they'd sprung up in the breeze. It carried his scent: soap and aftershave, faint cigarette smoke, and something else. Something fresh and strong—like the energy of a skittish horse. I met his eyes and his tentative smile spread to my face.

"You look—" we blurted at the same time and laughed.

"Sorry," he added nervously, but he couldn't stop staring. "Ellie, you look ... amazing."

"Thanks." I tucked my hair behind my ear. I'd worn it down. He'd never seen it like that. Never seen me like this. Sure, he'd seen me dozens of times with my coat thrown over my nightdress, my hair braided for bed. But somehow, standing here in the light of day, I felt more ... exposed.

He scratched the back of his neck, slightly embarrassed as my eyes looked him over—up his long legs, across the breadth of his chest and the width of his raised arm. His sleeve tightened across the flexed muscle. In the sickbed of Dr. Grant's office, dirtied from the soot of the day, or hidden in the shadows of night, I'd never truly realized how handsome he was. How vibrant. How strong.

"Jim," I whispered. "You're ... you're—"

"Clean?"

I grinned and his eyes shone with amusement. "Ma always said I clean up good, though it does take some time," he admitted, "and an awful lot of soap."

We laughed again and the awkwardness left us. It was going to be all right. Day or night, dirty or not, he was still the same Jim.

I slipped my hand through the crook of his elbow, falling in step with him as we headed to the grey house. "I always knew there was a man under all that soot."

∽ *Chapter Thirteen* ∽

IT WASN'T A PUB OR A RESTAURANT AT ALL. Turns out, the *funiculaire* is a train of sorts or a lift that runs straight up and down the steep cliff overlooking the town. Jim bought our tickets and we stepped into a small car that seemed to magically slide up the hill, taking us from Lower Town to Upper Town. We walked to the cliff edge and stopped at the palisade running alongside the boardwalk. The view was breathtaking. The St. Lawrence sparkled in the sunlight as it meandered past the cliff and out to the open sea miles away. Thick wooded hills edged the far side of the river, their green pierced here and there by church spires, each pinpointing another small town. Ships of all shapes and sizes sat moored in the harbour beneath us. I wondered which one was the *Empress*—they all seemed so small from here—and I gripped the rail and leaned over for a better look.

A cool breeze circled me and I teetered a bit, but Jim grabbed me even before I could steady myself.

"Careful, now."

His broad hands felt sure and strong on my small waist and lingered even after I'd found my balance. I'd no fear of falling. In that moment, I felt like I might fly. Eventually, Jim let go and leaned his arms on the handrail.

"Look at us," he chided. "Finally free of that damn ship and what do we do? We stand at a railing.

"Come on," he said, like an excited child. "Today we're doing things you can't do on a bloody ship."

We walked all over the town that sunny afternoon, around the Château Frontenac, the grand hotel perched atop the cliff, and along the stretch of boardwalk. We followed the stone wall snaking its way through the city, along cobblestoned streets, past shops and cafés where couples sipped cool drinks at bistro tables.

"Ice cream?" Jim asked, nodding at the shop.

"I'd bloody kill for one," I said, fanning my face.

Jim laughed. "Well, then it's a good thing I have enough money for two."

Wisps of hair stuck to my forehead and I pushed them back with the back of my hand.

"You think this is hot?" he teased. "Try visiting the stokehold."

He moved closer to me and leaned in, bringing his face to mine. His smiling mouth puckered and, for a moment, I thought he was going to kiss me, right here, right now. I thought I could want nothing more. Until I felt the breeze as he gently blew on my face. I closed my eyes, revelling in the coolness of it on my forehead. Down my cheek. My jaw. My neck. Covering me in goosebumps that were not from the cold.

He stopped and I opened my eyes, swooning slightly.

Jim smiled, suddenly shy. "Why don't you go wait in the shade?" He nodded at the park across the road. "I'll meet you there."

The benches were full of tourists and townsfolk out enjoying the day, so I sat on the lawn in the shadow of an apple tree. I slipped off my shoes and wriggled my toes in the cool grass. Leaning back on my elbows, I breathed the air, sweet with blossom, and closed my eyes, imagining that whisper of a breeze was Jim.

When I opened my eyes, Jim was standing in the middle of the street, two ice-cream cones in his hands, just watching me. I smiled and he smiled back.

"Your ice cream is melting." I nodded at the drips running down his fist onto the cobblestones, and noticing them, he rushed over with the cones.

"I seem to have a problem with sweets, don't I?" he laughed as he wiped his sticky hands.

We laughed and ate, savouring the time together as much as the ice cream.

"It's such a pretty city. Why would they build a wall in the middle of it?" I asked.

Jim explained how it used to enclose Old Quebec, but the city had outgrown its borders, spilling out for miles beyond. And I thought for a moment about boundaries made to keep others out and how freeing it must be to break past them.

We sat in silence eating our ice cream and watching the people come and go. Mothers and children. Fathers and sons.

"Tell me about your family, Jim," I said, when I'd finished my cone.

He stiffened beside me. "Why?"

I shrugged. "I don't know. I guess, I just wanted to know about them." *About you,* I thought.

"I don't want to talk about them now."

"But is your father—"

"My father is dead," he snapped. "I'm sorry, Ellie. I just … I don't like to talk about it."

A blossom fell on my skirt, and I picked it up and twiddled it in my fingers.

Should I breach this wall?

"My mother died, too," I said, quietly. "I know how it feels."

He fidgeted, clearly agitated by the topic. Then he stood and dumped the rest of his cone in the rubbish bin. "We'd better be going if we want to get back in time."

I stood before him. "Jim, I'm sorry if I upset you. I didn't mean to pry. It's your story. I just wanted to know more about it."

He looked at me with that intensity I'd seen in the doctor's office the first day we met. "My father drowned two years ago." He clenched his jaw and looked away for a second. "End of story."

It surprised me how fresh and raw his grief still was. "That's his story, Jim. Not yours."

"It's my story," he said. "And I live it every day."

"I'm sorry," I said. "I shouldn't have asked." God knows, there were many questions I'd never want to answer. Not to him. Not to anyone. I had walls of my own. "No one has the right to make you talk about something you don't want to."

"You wouldn't understand." He took the apple blossom

from my fingers and tucked it behind my ear. "You're perfect. What dark secrets could Ellie Ryan possibly have?"

I cringed inside as he said it. Ryan wasn't even my real name. And he knew nothing of my secret shame. Jim was right. Why talk about it?

Stooping, I picked up my shoes. "You promised we'd do things you can't do on a ship. And I've got one more—race me!" I bolted barefoot across the cool grass, not caring who saw or how unladylike it truly was. My father had always scolded me for running in the fields.

It was the last thing Jim expected, and I hoped it might give me enough of a lead to reach the far side first. But Jim was all muscle. All leg. Within seconds, he was beside me, matching my stride, taunting me with that smile as we sprinted across the sprawling lawn.

Both of us running full tilt, running from the past.

"WHAT A PERFECT DAY," I sighed as we took the *funiculaire* back down and my spirits fell with it. "I don't want it to end. I don't want to go back to that horrid ship life."

Jim seemed hurt.

"I don't mean you." I took his hand, emboldened by our day together. "Jim, you're what gets me through the days—"

He looked away from me, a frown settling on his brow.

"It's just—" I continued, trying to put words on the feeling. "Don't you think there's something more?"

He stood in silence.

"No." He gently pulled his hand away and turned from me, staring out at the distant *Empress*. "Not for me."

I never understood his moodiness. But this time was worse. So absolute. So sudden. Other than the talk of his father, things seemed to be going so well.

"I can't—" He shook his head. "I'm sorry, Ellie. I can't do this." The tighter he clenched his jaw, the more his lip seemed to tremble.

He wasn't making sense. My mind couldn't grasp what he meant, but my heart somehow knew. It clenched painfully in its knowing and, for a moment, I couldn't breathe.

"I shouldn't be here," he finally said, "with you."

A numbness spread from my core, protecting me from the sting of his message. But I forced myself to move, stepping in front of him again so that he had to face me. And I forced him to tell me. "What are you saying, Jim?"

The car slid down into the shadow of the town and stopped at the bottom, but that sinking feeling continued.

"It's not right. Us." He hung his head, avoiding my eyes. "I just … I can't anymore."

The doors opened and he sidestepped past me, off the car, past the gate, and just kept walking. Stunned, I followed him for a few steps and then stopped on the curb.

Jim was a hard man to read, closed, almost secretive. But today at the top of the hill, I felt a real connection. I saw the real Jim—a man I could love. The way his strong hands gripped me tight as I leaned over the edge and lingered on my waist long after I'd stopped. The way he caressed me with his breath, held me with his eyes. I hadn't imagined all that. He wanted me, too. I knew it. I just did.

Then *why*?

I watched his broad back move through the dwindling

crowd. The *X* of his suspenders, black against his white shirt, grew smaller and smaller with the distance between us. Head down, hands in his pockets, he seemed sad, all right. Regretful. I don't know, almost ... guilty?

I'd felt more alive today than I had in months and I knew he did, too. Jim did want me—might even love me. But what did it matter? He said it wasn't right. *We* weren't right. And that was that.

There is someone else. A voice whispered inside me and wouldn't be quieted. *Another woman.*

My stomach tightened into a sailor's knot, twisting until I doubted it would ever come undone. Jim Farrow had his secrets. Deep ones. But we never talked about them. Maybe they had to do with his father. But for all I knew, his secrets could have been about his girlfriend waiting for him in Liverpool.

Or his wife.

I didn't realize I was crying until the old woman from the stall touched my arm. I looked down to see her holding out a broken flower. One she'd never sell. One no one would want. Shaking her head, she said something in French and patted my arm before hobbling back to her seat.

And when I looked back, Jim was gone.

∽ TWO DAYS BEFORE ∽

May 27, 1914
Quebec Harbour

∽ *Chapter Fourteen* ∽

THE GIRLS HAD HOUNDED ME for details when I got back yesterday. I sloughed it off, made them think it was nothing. He was nothing. Said I was too tired to talk about it. But Meg saw through my facade. She knew how I looked when my heart had been broken. She'd seen it before at Strandview Manor. But even if I had wanted to talk, the next day we simply hadn't the time. The Wednesday before a sailing was always busy. Gaade and Matron Jones kept us running. It helped to keep my mind off things somewhat. Gaade was in total control of everyone and everything, checking the refrigerators, meeting with bakers and cooks, telling the butchers how to prepare the seven thousand pounds of fresh beef and pork and what to do with the twelve hundred chickens ready for roasting. It boggled the mind, really, and Gaade managed it all—every one of us in the stewarding department, every baker and bartender, cook and culinary expert, fell under his command and rose to his high standards.

He gathered the stewarding department in the second-class dining room, where we stood at attention as he gave us his usual spiel on what he expected of us. But this time he added that after a life of service at sea, this was to be his last sailing as chief steward. The *Empress*'s owners, Canadian Pacific Railway, had offered him a job as port steward in Liverpool, and so he wanted his last voyage to be top-notch. We owed that to him, at least. He'd dedicated himself to the *Empress,* and though he had nothing to do with what happened in the engine room or captain's wheelhouse, Gaade was the one who managed smooth sailing for all the passengers by overseeing every detail from morning to night. Gaade wasn't Captain Kendall, but to my thinking, his role was just as important.

Gaade had approached me in the galley that morning while I was having a quick cup of tea in the corner. Given the hundreds under his command, I was surprised he'd remember my name, and his words shocked me even more. "Ellen, I know you didn't start here under the best terms, but I just wanted to tell you that I'm proud of how far you've come."

"Thank you, sir." It meant a lot to me to hear him say that.

"Your aunt would be proud of you."

I doubted it. Whatever earned Aunt Geraldine's praise was something I clearly did not possess. Given what I'd put her through this past year, her lack of esteem for me was no surprise. We'd never been close, but she seemed to be more distant each time I returned to Strandview Manor between sailings, spending more time locked in her study, clacking away on her typewriter. Come to think of it, I don't even remember her getting up to say goodbye to me this last time. I guess I just didn't matter.

"How is she faring?" Gaade asked. His concern made me wonder if they were closer friends than I thought. Close enough to get me hired in the first place.

"Oh, well, you know Aunt Geraldine." I lifted my teacup to take a sip.

Gaade shook his head as he continued, "It's a wretched illness, liver cancer."

Cancer? I froze, cup midair, and looked at him in shock.

"She's an incredible person, your aunt," he hastily added. "Strongest woman I know. If anyone can beat this, it's Geraldine Hardy."

A steward called for him and Gaade left me standing alone in the corner.

Aunt Geraldine has cancer?

The first thing that hit me was anger.

Why didn't she tell me?

But why would she? She was my father's aunt. As her grandniece, I no doubt seemed a child to her. And I had been childish. Sulking about my problems, throwing temper tantrums when she made decisions for me—like signing me on with the *Empress*. Or months before, signing me into the Magdalene Asylum and, worse yet, leaving me there for so long.

Gaade didn't know it, but he had given me two truths in the galley that morning, both of which I needed to know.

One: I was a lot stronger than I thought. Looking back, I had come a long way in these past five months. And two: As strong as my aunt was, she needed me. Looking forward, I realized that if I served anyone, it should be her.

❧ *Chapter Fifteen* ❧

I LOOKED AROUND THE DINING HALL at the uniformed staff gathered for Gaade's address. No, I didn't want this servant's life, not by a long shot, but I knew I'd still be locked in the Magdalene Asylum, trapped in that hell, if it wasn't for Aunt Geraldine. How I hated that place and all it stood for. In my grief and pain, I hadn't seen Aunt Geraldine's rescue for what it was. Hadn't seen her for who she was. Even in the last few visits back, I never noticed her illness. Though it seemed obvious now. Her weight loss. Her lack of energy. Even her skin had a slight yellowish tinge. It wasn't just old age. I decided that, like Gaade, this was going to be my last trip, too. Aunt Geraldine needed me to take care of her. It's what my mother would do, but more than that, it was what I wanted to do, what I needed to do for my aunt. I'd made up my mind. And for the first time, I wasn't going to let her tell me otherwise.

Gaade handed out the saloon passenger lists, which we were to put in each room: small seven-page booklets

that included not only basic information for the passengers on our route or how to send a wireless message, but
also, more importantly, the names of who's who in first and
second class. No doubt there would be much scrambling,
as always, on that first afternoon, particularly for the first-
class stewards as their guests jostled for the best seats with
the best people for dinner. Gaade reviewed the manifest:
1057 passengers—87 in first class and 717 in third. Of the
253 in second, 170 were Salvation Army officers and their
families, heading over to a big convention at the Albert Hall
in London—or so Gaade said. I scanned my assigned rooms
and sure enough most passengers were captain, major, or
lieutenant something or other.

"Are they military?" Meg asked. I'd wondered, myself.
But Gaade told us the Salvation Army was more like an army
for God. That Salvationists were about charity, compassion,
and giving to their fellow man.

"So long as they're as generous to their stewardesses,"
Kate whispered beside me. "I'm no running meself ragged
for a bloody blessing."

"Did he say the Irvings?" Gwen grabbed my arm. "Oh,
I've read all about them, Laurence and Mabel—what a
talented couple. And glamorous, too. The *Tatler* said they've
just done a three-month tour of Canada." Her eyes were
wide with awe. "Fancy that, Ellie, having real celebrities travel
home on our ship!"

Gaade read a few more from the passenger list, of note,
Sir Henry Seton-Karr, a wealthy gentleman and sportsman;
Ethel Paton, a socialite from Sherbrooke; Major Lyman, a
millionaire from Montreal. I always noticed that the majority

of our passengers, all those Russians, Italians, Irish, Swedes, Scots, and who knows what—the hundreds of working-class immigrants—got little or no mention. They simply boarded as anonymously as they left.

THAT AFTERNOON, Captain Kendall ran the lifesaving drills we always did the day before sailing. As usual, the crew swiftly made it to their posts, swinging out and lowering the eighteen two-ton steel lifeboats that lined the decks, making ready by the extra collapsibles, or cranking closed the many watertight doors. The two in the stokehold level at the very bottom of the ship were shut by engine-room controls that dropped the huge doors like a guillotine, or so Jim had told me one time, but the other twenty-two on the ship were cranked by hand. Men raced to the deck above each door and pulled down a three-foot metal key from its brace on the bulkhead. The key, a T-bar of sorts, fit into the hole in the floor and by turning it, a man worked the gears that closed the heavy horizontal door. Timothy liked to brag that he'd made it to the Upper Deck and shut Door 86 in less than three minutes. Meg, at least, seemed impressed.

My first lifeboat drill scared me, to be honest. What with the wailing siren and everyone running to their stations. But more than that, it was the sudden realization—boats can sink. You'd think the sheer size of this gigantic contraption would make that obvious, that and the fact that steel doesn't float. *Titanic* proved that two years ago and she was supposed to be unsinkable. But maybe it was the very size of the *Empress*, the steadiness of her under my feet, the sense that we were in a small city and not a man-made boat in the middle of the ocean, for even now after a drill, denial always lulled my mind into assuming we were never really at risk.

When the siren sounded, the stewardess's job was to inform and help the passengers. Simple enough, I suppose. In the drills, Matron Jones had us knock on our assigned cabins and go in and touch the life vests in the closets while saying to the empty room, "Please put on your life vest and proceed to the Upper Deck. Captain's orders." It seemed a ridiculous thing to practise, really. A waste of time, given all we had to get ready for the next day's sailing. Kate and I often met in the hallway between cabins and rolled our eyes.

By the day's end—with beds made, drills run, store-rooms stocked, menus printed, tables set, linens pressed, brass polished, and crew spent—the *Empress* sat secure in her moorings and in the knowledge that she was shipshape for another leg of the journey. With no passengers to serve, I stole away to the railing, eager for some time to think. Jim was somewhere on the ship. I figured he was among the blackened lads calling to each other as they ran the last barrows of coal up the lowermost gangway. Perhaps he was with the same gang staggering in later that night, falling-down drunk from their last binge. Their bawdy songs and colourful cursing drifted up to where I still stood, alone at the rail. One of them stopped and looked up at me. Or maybe I just wished he did. Either way, Jim never showed up that night.

I leaned on the rail and looked at the glowing lights of Quebec City's cafés and restaurants lining its cobbled streets. Beneath the shadow of the Château Frontenac, two tiny lights drifted together and I realized they were probably the illuminated cars of the *funiculaire* on their last run. They came together seemingly as one for a brief moment and then moved on to settle at opposite ends. Upper and Lower Town—such different worlds.

I took one last look at the cityscape, knowing I'd probably never see it again. Wondering if I'd ever see Jim again, either.

∞ THE SECOND INTERVIEW ∞

June 1914
Strandview Manor, Liverpool

∽ *Chapter Sixteen* ∽

MONDAY CAME AND WENT, and Steele never showed up for our second interview. Instead, I got a note saying he had to do an interview up north. This whole deal with Steele was a bad idea, especially if he was going to be bringing my father into it. Wasn't it enough that I told him about the ship? What did it matter how I ended up on it? Or why? Those were my secrets, a shame I never wanted to revisit, let alone speak about. My gut told me to quit, to have nothing more to do with this manipulative man. But my heart told me Steele knew something more about Jim, and in truth, I'd do anything to find it out.

Steele knew that, too.

I'd already learned some of Jim's secrets in the few entries I'd read—how he felt about his nickname, about his father, and a bit about me. The last passage was different, though, for he'd written about nightmares. About drowning and feeling stalked by the sea. I wondered why he'd put it down on paper if it scared him so.

I picked up the other entry Steele had left on his last visit.

October 23, 1913

I can't get her out of my mind.

I'd read it a million times since Steele left it with me, but even now it was hard to read. Not just because they were Jim's words, but because the entry had come from near the start of his journal, before we'd even met. Whoever he was writing about, it wasn't me.

I didn't want to know about *her*. Why torture myself? Why read Jim's private thoughts about someone else? But there had to be something in there, some answers to all my questions. Something I'd missed. I gripped the page with both hands, forcing myself to read it once more.

I close my eyes and there she is—her hair a thick rope hanging over her shoulder, black against the white of her nightdress. She had a red ribbon knotted at the end. I remember how a few curls stuck to her cheek, framed her haunting eyes. They never left me. Not for a second that night. I still feel them on me. Pleading with me.

The yellowed sheet trembled in my hand. I thought I might be sick. Had I eaten anything, I probably would have retched. But this was sickness of the heart, really. Not the stomach.

I flipped the page, feeling that familar sense of dismay and relief to see that was all he had written.

Who was she? Was he with her now? Was he thinking of her then, on our last night together?

Was he thinking of her when he kissed me?

I SPENT THOSE LONG DAYS waiting for Steele's return from Ireland with both hope and dread, swinging between extremes like the brass pendulum of the mantel clock. I did not care to go out—for where would I go? And no one cared to come over—for who had I left? And so I sat in my chair listening to the tick of the clock until I thought I might explode. Lily and Bates went about their usual routines, structuring their days by duties. Dusting. Driving to market. Dinners. Dishes. Delivering me cup after cup of tea that sat unsipped on the side table until it was stone cold. I envied them their chores, actually. As mundane and monotonous as servants' duties were, they provided purpose. Something to occupy the hands and mind, at least for a little while. A reason to get up in the morning, even if only to grumble about it. I missed that.

"Would you like to come to market with Lily and me?" Bates asked from the hall. "It's a fine afternoon. Perhaps a stroll around the park after?"

"No, you go on ahead. I have some things to do here," I lied, for the only thing I could do was wait. Wait and worry.

WHEN STEELE FINALLY ARRIVED on Thursday, a week since our last interview, I made him wait. I sat at the vanity table in my bedroom as Lily showed him to the front room. She told me he was waiting downstairs. Truth be told, I wanted to rush down and get the door myself, I was that eager to have someone else to talk to, even if it was Steele. But on the other hand, my stomach churned over what he would ask today—about why I was on that ship, about how I survived, about that night. It amazed me how the man could both pull and repel me. And how I was starting to feel the same way about information on Jim. I wanted to know everything Steele knew about Jim, I wanted more journal entries, I wanted the truth—and yet, it terrified me.

I stroked my hair a few more times before setting the silver-handled brush on the vanity. A part of me wondered if Steele left me waiting on purpose. Was it part of his plan? Some American swagger.

He's a journalist, I said to myself. *You are a source. Nothing more.*

I stared at myself in the mirror, the dark circles under my grey eyes, the lines worry had etched into my stony face, like dates on a headstone—a marker to commemorate that someone under here had lived, once. Eighteen years old—I nearly laughed. More like eighty. What did I have but solitary days rambling around in this empty old house like Aunt Geraldine? At least she had her writing.

I pulled back my thick curls and twisted them into a bun, tightly pinning it down. If only I could restrain my anxious mind as easily.

The music caught me by surprise. It bounced up the stairwell like an unruly child, lively, full of rabble-rousing fun—a foreign sound in this house.

Is that the piano?

I'd quite forgotten we even had one under that dust cover.

But who—

Steele!

I bolted to my feet and marched down the stairs and into the room where, sure enough, there he sat at the piano bench. Playing with fervour. His thick brown hair fell over his brow, tousled from bobbing. Lily stood at his side clapping in time, eyes aglow.

"What are you doing?" I demanded, though it was obvious.

"Ragtime." He closed his eyes, smiled as he said it. "Joplin's 'Ragtime Dance.' Ain't it something?"

"Are you … are you playing my piano?" I blurted, realizing the ridiculousness of my question as soon as it had left my lips. Lily froze and scurried away, but Steele only glanced up at me with that half-smile of his as his hands continued to jump around the keys. He played with strength and precision from note to note, thrumming a bass line that felt as vibrant as a heartbeat. I never knew that old piano had it in her. Aunt Geraldine had only ever played classical, though not very well or very often. And all I ever got out of it were those godawful scales. Up and down and up and down from one end of the keyboard to the other. I always saw this piano as a punishment. But this ragtime Steele played on it was loose and bold, almost sensual in its teasing pace. It invited me to saunter along with it. With him. I could lose myself in it and that unnerved me. Instead, I folded my arms.

"I don't know how they do things in America," I said as his fingers found the final chords. My raised voice seemed too loud, too forced. Good Lord, I was even sounding like Aunt Geraldine. "But here in England we don't lift up someone else's dust skirt and just … fiddle about." I blushed at my choice of words and his delight in my discomfort.

He grinned and ran his hand over the glossy black top, admiring the instrument's smooth surface, its solidness, its shine. His strong fingers seemed to flow over the wood's curves. "This one is a beaut. I just couldn't help myself."

"Well, it seems as if you did." I meant to sound accusing, but my words only made him smile.

Steele drummed his fingers in the air. "I love to hear my typewriter clacking out a story—it's like the sound of my mind. But there's nothing like striking piano keys." He stood and moved closer to me, face flushed and eyes alive. "That's all heart. Do you know what I mean?"

I didn't. Not really. Though my heart was still pounding from the drive of his tune. He moved toward me. I stepped back a bit, unsure of his intentions. Or mine. He'd flustered me, so he had, with all his playful nonsense. His hand reached around me and grabbed his satchel from where it lay atop the piano.

"I'm sorry," he said, like a scolded schoolboy. His eyes still sparkling with the fun of his misdemeanour. "You're right. I should have asked first." He sighed. "It just seemed a shame, really, to leave it hidden away in the corner of this old house." He slipped the bag over his shoulder and put his hands in his pockets as he surveyed the room, letting his eyes drift from one dust-covered shape to another. Ghosts of themselves. "I dunno." He shrugged. "What was she saving it all for?"

I knew what he meant, but it annoyed me that he'd voiced it. That in some way, he'd disparaged the way of things.

Slighted my aunt. Insulted me. Even worse, that he was right. I looked away.

"Listen," he continued, eagerly. "Why don't we get out of here for a bit? It'll do you good to get some air and I'd love to see a bit of the town. We can—"

"I don't think so." My words came short. Was he seriously asking me on a date? Now? "The deal was a trade of stories, Mr. Steele. Not to be your tour guide." I sat on the edge of my chair by the fireplace, spine as rigid as a poker. I had no desire to talk about that night, but I knew I had to if I wanted to learn what he knew about Jim. Was he alive? Injured? Dying?

As if I'd tripped a switch, that boyishness shut off and he became a reporter again. "Yes, I suppose we each have our deadlines."

I cringed a bit at the literalness of the word, hoping it wasn't too late for me. Too late for Jim.

"My editor said he'd like the article for the July supplement," he continued. "That gives me just a few weeks to pull this together *and* get him the bit on the British army."

"Yes," I agreed, less enthusiastically. Wishing I could "pull this together" as easily as he seemed to think he could. Mine was just another story, one of many he juggled. Mind you, he just had to write it. I had to carry it. To bear it. To live with it.

I sighed. "The sooner we finish, the sooner you can be on your way."

Though truth be told, deep down, some small part of me wanted neither.

"TAKE ME BACK TO HER LAST SAILING," Steele said once we'd settled ourselves in our seats.

I paused. "Where do I start?"

He could see I was reluctant to go back. To remember.

"She's docked at Quebec City," he said. "The passengers are all aboard now and the captain's given the order to ready the ship."

I closed my eyes for a moment, the sound of the bugle echoing in my memory. The sound of the start of another voyage.

Only this one would be our last.

❧ SAILING DAY ❧

May 28, 1914
Quebec Harbour

∽ *Chapter Seventeen* ∽

4:00 P.M.

"ALL ASHORE THAT'S GOING ASHORE!"

The bugle blew once more, alerting the passengers that the *Empress* was readying to cast off. The stewards busied themselves with the mounds of baggage stacked high on deck, still to be sorted. There were trunks and crates, boxes and luggage of all shapes and sizes, for the upper class did not travel light. Granted, they tagged much of their baggage as "unwanted," meaning it had to be moved to the bottom of the ship for storage in the cargo hold. But you may bet they'd want something or other out of it during the voyage, and the poor stewards would have to lug it all the way back up to their staterooms.

"Are we being raided by the Royal Canadian Mounted Police?" an elderly woman beside me asked, confounded by all the men milling around the deck in red tunics and Mountie-style stetsons.

"They're Salvation Army, ma'am," I explained.

She didn't seem convinced, at least not until the band members, about forty of them, collected their instruments from the luggage pile and gathered round the bandmaster. They raised them to their lips, the brass glinting in the afternoon light. Bandmaster Hanagan threw out his arms and with a flourish launched the men in a perfect rendition of "O Canada." The old lady next to me sang along, even more thrilled when they followed up with "Auld Lang Syne."

Maybe it was the loud music, or maybe it was some other sixth sense about her ninth life, but Emmy, our ship's cat, deserted us then. Billy left his bundle of baggage and ran down the gangway after her, but as soon as he dropped her on deck, she bolted again. Before anyone could follow, Captain Kendall gave the order for all lines to be cast off.

The flags snapped in the breeze as the ship pulled away to the cheer of the crowds waving from decks and docks. Bandmaster Hanagan raised his arms one more time, cuing his men for another serenade. This time the air was wistful, almost sad.

God be with you till we meet again … the people sang.

It might have been the song, or Emmy leaving, the fear of losing Aunt Geraldine, or of having lost Jim's affections. Perhaps it was the fact that I knew this would be my last voyage, though not for the reasons I'd expected. But despite the sun and celebrating, despite all the reasons to smile, I felt a chill run through me as they sang the last few lines.

Keep love's banner floating o'er you,
Smite death's threat'ning wave before you,
God be with you till we meet again.

The *Empress*'s whistle sounded low and loud, making me jump as it drowned out their singing.

The foreboding lasted only a moment; I hadn't the time to give it a second thought. Mrs. Hanagan, the bandmaster's wife, needed help finding her room. She laughed as I told her about my first time following Matron Jones through the maze of corridors. Had that really been only five months back? It seemed so long ago. A small hand slipped into mine and I looked down to find Mrs. Hanagan's daughter walking beside me. She looked about seven years old.

"You must be Gracie," I said, much to her surprise.

"How did you know?"

"Oh, it's my job to know my passengers." I slipped a toffee from my apron pocket and held it out to her. "I'll bet you like these, too."

Gracie smiled as she took it, tucking it inside her cheek.

We navigated our way through the ship to the starboard side of the Upper Deck, near the back, travelling down the fanned staircase and up a side alleyway. "Here we are. Cabin 442. This is you." I opened the door to the room I'd cleaned in preparation for them. A pair of bunk beds hid behind the green curtains on the left. On the right was a sofa bed. Directly across from us stood a dark wooden armoire. Gracie pulled on the handles and the doors opened down to reveal a pair of sink-sized porcelain bowls.

"It's a double lavatory," I explained.

"Inside the cupboard?" Her eyes widened and her mother and I laughed at her shocked expression.

"A ship has to find ways to make the most of the space. That sofa is also a bed, and look here." I pulled back the curtain, revealing the top bunk. "You can sleep here."

Her eyes flickered to the porthole in the wall beside it. I could tell the space made her feel uncomfortable. Trapped. Even many adults got that same expression. I know I did at first.

"Can you build sandcastles?" I asked, changing the subject. She nodded. "Well, why don't we let your mother get settled in while I take you to see the children's playground."

"Here on the ship?" She took my hand.

"A great big sand playground, wait until you see it. On the way, I'll show you the barber shop and library, and the lovely dining room where you'll be eating."

Mrs. Hanagan smiled in gratitude. If only all passengers were as easy to please as young Gracie.

⊙ *Chapter Eighteen* ⊙

7:00 P.M.

THE BUGLE CALLED FOR DINNER, inviting all first and second class to their allotted dining rooms. And though second class lacked the rich mouldings and gilded accents, the domed ceiling, and the Moroccan leather seats of first class, the *Empress* bragged of the high standards offered to all. The second-class menu boasted boiled halibut, followed by veal cutlets, beef ribs, roast fowl, and ox tongue. Finished off with Devonshire tarts and jam puffs with ice cream. High-class dining. Even those in third class, who did not get dinners, were offered smoked herring, cold meat, pickles, and bread and jam at tea time. They'd also received another impromptu concert by the Salvation Army band, which to my mind was every bit as wonderful as the five-piece string orchestra of first class. More so, I'd say, for they did it out of the goodness of their hearts. Then after eating, many passengers strolled the decks, bundled against the cold night air. Others lounged in the music room, or stopped by the library to dash off a quick postcard before the bags left on the midnight mail tender.

10:00 P.M.

AFTER SUCH A BUSY DAY, most passengers had retired to their cabins, except for the few men in the smoking room who lingered with their cigars, Scotch, and another round of cards.

My passengers had settled in for the night, thankfully, though it had taken some convincing to get Gracie to quiet. That porthole spooked her something awful.

"I don't want to sleep there."

"What? Sure that's the best bed in the place, Gracie," I'd said, picking her up and peering out the porthole. "You can lie in your bed and watch the night stars. You can make a wish for every one."

She'd squirmed as we drew nearer to the open window. "No, Ellie. No! That's where the water will come in."

"You're just overtired," Mrs. Hanagan explained. "You've had a big day today." In the end, she settled her young daughter in the lower bunk farthest from the window and, spent from all the excitement of her first day aboard, Gracie gave in.

I closed the porthole slightly. Like most people in the outside cabins, her parents enjoyed having a bit of fresh air. Technically, the stewards were supposed to lock up every porthole that ran in long rows down the *Empress*'s steel sides. But when we appeared with our brass keys, many passengers protested, and, in the end, many portholes were left open. It wasn't a big deal. It happened all the time. We'd report the open portholes to the night watchmen, who simply made note of it.

The girls were in their bunks by the time I reached our cabin, Gwen nose deep in an article about the Irvings, Kate rolling her hair in the curls that would frizz before breakfast, Meg reading the latest magazine from Timothy. I changed into my long white nightdress and hopped into my bunk just below Gwen's. The girls chattered a bit, and after the lights went out I heard each one's breathing grow long and steady as she sank deeper in sleep. But I bobbed around in the same uneasiness I'd felt that afternoon, my mind tossing from one thing to another yet settling on nothing.

Something just wasn't right.

12:45 A.M.

I COULDN'T SLEEP. After what seemed like hours of restlessness, I couldn't take it anymore. I needed air. I got up and slipped on my shoes and woollen coat and, with a quick glance at the three sleeping shadows behind me, slipped out into the darkness.

The ship seemed deserted at this late hour. Though a few night stewards were on duty, even Gaade would have turned in. The *Empress* had stopped—probably to meet the mailboat from Rimouski. Men's voices called to one another from down the side, and looking over the rail, I could just make out the dark outline of the dwarfed steamship *Lady Evelyn* slowing to a stop. A ray of light shone on the *Lady Evelyn*'s deck as a door opened in our hull and mailbags were thrown across from our ship to the other. Within minutes, mail delivered and hatch closed, we were underway. The lights of *Lady Evelyn* faded into the night as we parted.

I gripped the rail, hoping the nip of the night air might settle me, or at least numb my mind as it did my fingers. But the cold only seeped into my bones, chilling me to the marrow with an unease that left me all the more anxious. After another fifteen or twenty minutes, the *Empress* stopped again. We must have been near Father Point. After navigating the two hundred miles of river from Quebec, this was where the river pilot's trip ended and he disembarked onto the cutter that had met us alongside. From here, Captain Kendall took over and we gathered steam. Next stop, Liverpool.

I flipped up my collar and took a deep breath, the cold air pinching my nostrils and piercing my lungs. Poor John. I glanced up at his post high in the darkness where he manned the crow's nest on the foremast. It was from there he had spotted the night steward approaching Jim and me during our first-class dinner, and from where he'd seen the ice floes on our way in to Quebec a few days ago. I hoped he'd have as keen an eye at night on our way out—for there was surely ice in the air. And for all we knew, in the water too.

As my gaze fell from the mast, I noticed him farther down the rail. Jim stood, motionless, in the misty rays of light that fell from the windows, hunched over his journal. Writing. So intent upon it, in fact, that he never noticed me standing there. I wondered what had riveted him so.

Or who.

I watched him for a while, the tilt of his head, pencil at his lips, the eagerness of his scribbling when the thoughts flowed. For a man of few words, he certainly had a lot to write.

A low bank of fog crept in over the water, blurring the lights of another ship in the distance. I'd often wondered how the captains navigated in conditions like these, with neither sight nor star to guide. Jim had told me once as we passed ships before, something about the lights—I squinted in the darkness. Green, I thought. We'd pass green to green on the right side. But then as suddenly as it had appeared, the vessel vanished in the fog.

The *Empress* gave three short blasts. The signal that we were reversing engines and slowing down. Captain Kendall wasn't taking any chances, thankfully. The horn of the other ship echoed eerily in the darkness and I shivered as the fog draped my shoulders like a damp shawl, making me sneeze.

Jim looked in my direction, and as our eyes met, I felt everything at once. Embarrassed at being caught spying, anger for how he'd left me in Quebec, confusion about why, exactly, and, under it all ... desire. A yearning, a great longing for him to look at me the way he did at the top of the hill. I felt torn, like I wanted both to be seen and at the same time to disappear completely in the fog, and so I stood frozen on the spot, unsure of whether to run to, or from, him.

The *Empress*'s horn gave two short blasts. We were at a dead stop. Lost in the fog.

Jim closed his journal and slipped it in his pocket as he stepped toward me. "Ellie?"

Don't let him in, a voice said. *Don't let him hurt you again.* I clenched my jaw. He'd never even apologized or explained his actions in Quebec. I didn't want any more games. He'd said it wasn't right—*we* weren't right.

But as he moved closer, I knew the truth. Every part of my being did, and my resolve crumbled.

Jim stood before me and lifted his hands, cupping them gently around my face. Like a sheltered flame, I felt suddenly stronger, warmer, brighter. His thumbs brushed my cheeks one at a time, clearing the two tears I hadn't realized I'd shed.

"Oh, Ellie," he whispered, his eyes locked on mine, reading me with the same intensity that he had his journal. "I am so sorry." He lowered his face to mine, put his mouth on mine, and I melted into him. My hands slipped inside his open jacket, up his chest, and spanned the width of his broad back as he pulled me to him, the heat of him drawing me as surely as his strong arms.

I didn't know what he was sorry for—for hurting me, for leaving me, for what sadness he saw in my eyes, or perhaps for what sad news he had yet to tell. I didn't want to know.

I just wanted him. Here. Now.

∽ *Chapter Nineteen* ∽

"THE BAND, THE LAUNCH, THE CAT." Steele sat across from me in the wing chair by the fireplace, ticking off the details like a shopping list as he scanned his notes. "The dinner, and settling Gracie in her room."

I hadn't told him all I remembered. Some memories were mine to treasure. And many were mine to forget.

As if I could.

"Were you sleeping when the *Empress* was hit?" he asked, urging me to see what I'd shied away from these long weeks. I had never talked about it to anyone.

We'd come to it, then. The accident. That night.

"No." I took a deep breath and gripped the armrests, trying to hold myself here in the present even as the memories of that night pulled me back. "I was at the rail. With Jim. Starboard side on the Lower Promenade Deck."

His mouth dropped as he raised his eyebrows. "So you *felt* the *Storstad* hit?"

"Worse," I said. "I saw it."

1:55 A.M.

I DON'T KNOW HOW LONG our kiss lasted, minutes I suppose, but your whole life can change in an instant. Mine did. One second Jim and I were lost in each other, and the next we were caught in the white glare of the *Storstad*'s masthead lights. It burst from the fog and barrelled toward us. There was no time for it to turn or reverse its engines. All it could do was shriek its horn as it rammed the *Empress* midship. I braced myself for the impact, sure it might throw us from where we stood farther up along the rail, but there was no bone-jarring collision, no screeching or horrendous crash, just the spark of metal on metal as it knifed her deep between her ribs.

"Christ Almighty!" Jim shouted and ran down the deck.

I caught up to where he stood near the middle of the ship and, gripping the rail, looked over it, horrified to see what should not be there. Another ship—jutting out of her side.

"It's in at least fourteen feet," Jim said, panicking as he leaned over for a better look. "She's breached from Shelter Deck to well beneath the waterline. Maybe even down to her boilers."

I held my breath. That had to be four or five decks down.

"Keep your engines ahead," someone yelled from our wheelhouse on the deck above us. 'Twas basic first aid, really. The impaling ship itself might cork our hull, might staunch the wound it had just caused if its engines propelled it to keep the pressure. But even as the man's voice called, the *Storstad* twisted astern and with a groan of metal pulled free, disappearing back into the fog.

My pulse rushed in my ears, a gushing *shwoosh* making my head spin.

This can't be happening!

My vision tunnelled and the ground seemed to tilt beneath me, making me swoon.

Jim's hands were on my arms, shaking me as he yelled. The strength of his grip hurt but it dragged me back to reality. "—do you hear me, Ellie?"

I focused on his face, saw the urgency in his eyes. The panic. His fear sobered me, and I realized it wasn't my lifeblood I heard, but the gush of the St. Lawrence, gallons of it, surging through the hole, the *hole* in our ship.

He yelled it again. "You have to get to a lifeboat."

"What?" A lifeboat? Surely it wasn't that bad.

"Listen to me!" He shook me again. "She's listing, Ellie. Even as we speak. Do you not feel her?"

I looked down at my feet, steady on the teak deck, and realized it wasn't the shock that left me unbalanced. Jim was right. The *Empress* had rolled slightly toward her injured right side. As she listed, more of the gash in her side slipped under the waterline, and more water thundered in.

"But—" How could this be happening? The hole was probably a dozen feet wide and who knew how deep, but there was no way it breached even three of the eleven compartments. Once the crew closed the watertight doors, we'd be fine. Wouldn't we? She'd been designed with that precaution. I looked back at Jim. "But you said she'd float even with two compartments flooded."

"It's like the *Titanic*," he said, his greatest fears realized.

"This is not the same, Jim," I said reassuringly. He had to

be overreacting. "The iceberg punctured her many times, but there's only the one hole in the *Empress*."

He turned and pointed the length of the ship, down the hundreds of portholes row upon row. A few shone like torchlights on the water but most were in darkness as over a thousand passengers slept within. True, portholes are water-tight, even when submerged. *If* they are closed. I realized with horror—most were not. The night had been calm. We weren't even out on the open seas yet. Even I had left most portholes open for my passengers to get a bit of air.

The ship tilted a fraction lower and the dark water lapped the lowest row of portholes, drawing her down a little further as it burst through.

"Dear God, Jim." I turned back to him, mirroring the terror in his face as the horrible truth rushed in. "Her hull—it's riddled with holes!"

The emergency horn gave a single blast, making us both jump. *All hands to the boats*. This was no drill. Jim looked over his shoulder as crew members, some half-dressed, burst from the doors and ran to their stations. Within seconds, two men had climbed in the lifeboat while the team swung the davits, the huge pair of cranes that suspended the lifeboat over the Boat Deck. Another four men gritted their teeth as they pushed the boat clear of the rail, where it hung over the dark water seventy feet below.

They'd done this drill hundreds of times, but never on a tilting ship, and even the slightest list had an enormous effect on the two-and-a-half-ton steel lifeboats. Though it looked as if the men might get three or four free, most of the other lifeboats sat jammed against their davits, and no matter how the men had practised or how they scrambled and bellowed now, the fact of it was, those boats were stuck.

Jim looked over his shoulder and then back at me, torn. "Promise me, Ellie, promise me you'll get to a boat."

"Come with me!" I gripped his dark coat, not wanting to let him go. A great trembling ran through me and wouldn't stop.

He took my hands and held them tight. He'd somehow calmed himself, even as the ship rolled another few degrees. As though he'd resigned himself to her fate.

Or his.

"Go now," he pleaded. "Warn your passengers. And then get yourself to a boat. It's your only hope."

"But—but what about you?"

He drew me in his arms and I felt safe. Stronger. "You are my hope ... and I won't lose you, Ellie. I won't." His mouth trembled as he said it, but his resolve was firm. Contagious. Even I believed him. He kissed me, hard. Then suddenly he was gone. Running for the stairs to the engine room, running toward the flooding hold of a sinking ship.

And I never saw him again.

∽ *Chapter Twenty* ∽

2:00 A.M.

I WANTED TO RUN AFTER JIM. My heart screamed to follow him, but my head overruled, mindful of the passengers, the families still abed, who had no idea of the danger they were in. Suddenly all those drills kicked in and I knew what I had to do.

I fled down the deck to the back stairs and down the alleyway, passing pyjama'd crew mustering to their tasks. A few passengers milled about the hallways; others poked their sleepy heads out their doors as Gaade's voice belted through the halls, "Please put on your life vest and proceed to the Boat Deck."

"What did he say?" they murmured.

"Have we hit an iceberg?" someone asked.

"Where are life vests?"

"Boat Deck, good heavens … which way is that?"

Their voices grew in panic. At two in the morning, on the

first night of the voyage aboard a ship they didn't yet know, it was no surprise the passengers were so disoriented. A few frantic women clung to Gaade's arms, begging to be helped.

"No one will be saved," he said, pulling himself free, "unless you give us a chance to get on deck and get the boats out." His abruptness said it all. Things were bad, very bad.

"Hurry." I reached the first of my passengers' cabins and pulled the life vests from the cupboards. "Put these on and get up on deck."

They stared at me, bewildered, as though I'd been into the barman's booze. But they felt the list. They'd only to stand up out of bed to realize something had gone terribly wrong. The floor was slanted enough to send furniture sliding, spilling cups and perfume bottles from the shelves. They staggered about in the small rooms, trying to find their balance as they pulled on coats and shoes and dithered with the long strings of their white cork vests.

"Just go!" I shoved them out the door. A buttoned coat and knotted vest would do them no good if they never made it on deck. The ship listed further to the right, and by the time I'd reached the Hanagans' room, water exploded through the portholes like a full-on firehose, its foot-wide stream blasting through the small cabins and into the hallways. Passengers screamed as they burst from their cabins, sodden from where they'd been doused in their beds, woken from their dreams to this nightmare. The frigid water gushed up my calves; already my feet were numb. If the water had reached these portholes, what about those hundreds of poor souls in the many decks below—in third class? In the engine room?

The Hanagan family joined the throng of panicked people filling the tilting alleyway, desperately pulling themselves along by the handrail, pushing and shoving their way to the staircase that went up to a landing before fanning left and right. Or at this point, up to open air or down into the water. The pitch of the ship had sloped the stairs so much that the passengers had to crawl up them on their hands and knees, and even with several young Salvationist men lifting and pulling people up the incline, I realized that most people would not make it in time.

"Ellie, where's Meg?" Kate called to me from the crowd, her face as white as her nightdress, hair still in rags. She held a screaming toddler in one arm and his hysterical mother in the other.

I glanced around the panicked mob. She would have done her duty to her passengers, and then … I knew. I knew exactly where she'd gone.

I shoved through the surging crowd, trudging in the water rushing against my knees. Finally saw them both working on the watertight door, Timothy pushing on one side of the T-crank as Meg pulled on the other. They'd managed to jam the crank in the hole in the floor beneath them, but even with both of them trying, it was not moving. Neither was the watertight door in the deck below.

"Leave it!" I yelled, pulling Meg back. Like me, she'd thrown her coat over her nightdress. Timothy's hung from the bulkhead. And we hadn't a life vest between the three of us. In her nightie with her hair matted about her shoulders and stuck to her sweating forehead, she looked like a child after having a nightmare. I suppose we all did, really. It was a nightmare—and, truth be told, we were too young for this. Too young to be responsible for the lives of so many.

"But we have to close it!" Timothy said through gritted teeth as he took both sides of the T and cranked again, veins bulging blue on his red forehead. He'd prided himself on the fact that he'd been assigned Door 86—one crucial to the safety of the ship—bragged that he could close it in under three minutes in every drill. And he had. But that was under perfect conditions. And these were anything but perfect.

The lights flickered and the ship rolled a little more. She was easily at a fifty-degree angle and falling faster. Freezing water rushed around our thighs, rising quickly. Time was running out.

"It's too late, Timothy," I said, gripping his trembling arm. Jim had told me all about the watertight doors in one of his life-saving-equipment rants. "The door closes toward the *centre* of the ship. At this angle, that's practically upwards. It's solid steel, you'll not move it."

The truth of it weighed on his shoulders. He'd failed. Failed them all. All the souls in the decks below whose very lives depended on that door closing.

"It all happened so—so fast," he mumbled.

"I doubt any of the lads got theirs closed either," I said. Small comfort, really. But at least it was a burden shared.

"Come on," Meg urged, shoving his coat at him and grabbing his free hand. She wasn't giving up on him, even if he had. "We have to get out of here." Turning, she pulled him back toward the crowded stairs and I followed behind. Hands clasped, they stumbled numb-legged down the hall toward the terrified mob surging and falling at the bottom of the stairwell, each desperate soul grasping at that last glimmer of hope.

I still see them all crammed in the tilted alleyway, their wet nightclothes sticking to their thighs, the sodden tails of her woollen coat dragging in their wake, people screaming and crying as they scrambled frantically for an exit that had tilted out of reach. The lights flared for a moment like a photographer's flash, burning the image forever in my mind.

And then the darkness swallowed us.

∾ *Chapter Twenty-One* ∾

2:09 A.M.

"ELLIE!" MEG'S VOICE CRIED in front of me and I reached out in the pitch-black. The *Empress* groaned as if in pain and the tilted floor slipped out from under my feet as the ship rolled completely on her side. The force of it threw me against the bulkhead and a wave of water washed over me, filling my nose and mouth. I gasped for air and kicked, scrabbling hands and feet for something solid.

So this is how it ends.

I thought the deck had been totally submerged but my feet touched wood, and as I stood in the darkness, the water sloshed side to side and eventually settled waist high. It wasn't over. Not yet.

I stretched out my hands to get my bearings, feeling carpet on my left where there should have been wall. Voices cried in blind terror as families desperately tried to reach one another, all of us completely disoriented.

She's on her side, I told myself, and though I could see nothing, I tried to envision the alleyway I knew so well, turned it ninety degrees in my mind's eye and realized that I now walked on what had been the right-hand wall.

"Meg!" I shouted into the shrieking mayhem. "Meg, where are you?"

"Here!" Her voice was not far from me. "Over here!"

I let it lead me through the frenzied hall. But as I walked along the wall, I stepped on a door that gave way beneath me. It opened suddenly, plunging me into the flooded room underneath. I dropped deep into the middle of the submerged cabin, banging my arms and legs against the flotsam of furniture. Terrified, I kicked hard, not sure which way was up. My hand flailed and grasped at something, a fabric—*someone's dress?* But before I let go in horror, I recognized the feel. *Not a dress—bunk curtains*. I'd been heading in the wrong direction. Holding my panic with the last of my breath, I felt along the curtain to the rod and the wooden bunk rail. Hand over hand I finally touched the door frame and, lungs bursting, heaved myself through it.

"Ellie? Ellie!"

I retched and gasped. Trying to get my breath and bearings.

Careful to skirt the doorways, I found my way over to Meg. We clung to each other, crying both in terror that all was lost and relief at being found.

"We're trapped!" I said, thinking of the stairs. "Oh God, Meg, there's no way out! If we'd closed the portholes—"

"The portholes!" Timothy's voice shouted beside me. I felt him leap and hang from the bulkhead above. Heard him kicking a few times before the wood splintered and fell upon us. Then he splashed down. "Climb up. I'll give you a boost through the door."

He linked his fingers and took my foot, heaving me upwards into the room. Thankfully, this one was dry, and I clung to whatever solid handholds and footholds I could find as I dragged myself inside. Meg and Timothy followed behind. In the cabin's darkness, a glimmer of stars a million miles away shone through the open porthole and, though it seemed just as far, I moved inch by inch toward it. Toward a way out.

Finally, I reached the round window and, stepping on the bunk rail, pushed my arms and head through. I barely fit and the metal frame scraped my shoulders and chest as I desperately wriggled. Leaning on my forearms, I wrenched and kicked, hauling my body through, sure I'd shed my skin to do it.

I flopped onto the cold steel and lay there for a second, drained from the effort and dazed at the sight. The *Empress* lay on her right side, like a dying animal. She gasped through her gold funnels, now almost level with the water, hissing and sputtering as she drowned. Her right half was totally submerged and her left, all 550 feet of it, stretched like a black sandbar, sloping into the lapping waves.

Like a beach. A steel beach, I thought, my head trying to make sense of a shoreline of portholes. Hundreds of people clambered along the hull that stretched three football fields long. Some sat. Others staggered around in their tattered, sodden pyjamas, shivering from cold and shock. Many desperately clung to the white rail of the upper decks, as though that might save them.

Meg called to me and I got to my knees, guiding her through the narrow passage, like a midwife pulling her to her life. Once free, she collapsed beside me. "Timothy ... help Timothy ..."

He'd already pushed his head and right arm through the porthole, but there was no way his shoulders would ever fit. "Hold on," he said, disappearing inside. He took off his coat and shoved it through the window. Meg grabbed it and slipped it on over hers, keeping both hands free to reach for him again.

Meg and I heaved on Timothy's arm like a tug-of-war rope and just when I thought he might wrench through the narrow window, something snapped and, with a cry, Timothy fell back inside the cabin.

"Timothy!" Meg shrieked, and I grabbed her by the waist, holding her from diving in after him. I wouldn't have the strength to get her out again.

A roar sounded from the ship's two tall funnels as the river rushed down their hot throats and into her belly. I peered into the porthole where Timothy gazed up at us from the shadowy room. He stood straddling the door frame, cradling his right arm like a load of library books.

"Try again," Meg begged, her voice frantic. "Please, Timothy. Please. It will work this time."

I knew by his face it wouldn't. We both knew.

"I'm not leaving you." Meg dropped to her knees, leaning over the porthole.

"Don't worry, Meggie," he said, trying to be braver than he must have felt. "I'll find another way out. Go ahead now to the lifeboats. I'll meet you there."

I didn't want to tell them there were no lifeboats. That

hardly any had been launched, and of those, the two or three I could see had pulled away, fleeing the dangers of a sinking ship. Fleeing the suck of its undertow and the desperation of the hundreds thrashing in the waters around us—passengers who'd made it up those alleyways and stairs only to be flung from the deck into the open water as the *Empress* rolled. Some still fought for survival, splashing frantically. Others bobbed in silence, their life vests white in the dark.

I looked back at Timothy. His face, pale in the dim cabin, framed by the round window that was wide enough to sink a ship, yet narrow enough to trap him inside. With a small step, Timothy dropped through the doorway and splashed back into the dark hall beneath. Meg screamed after him, but it was no use. He had gone.

A wild-eyed man ran by us, his feet thundering on the ship's side. "She's run aground!" he yelled. "We're saved."

But somehow, I doubted it. There were no shoals. Not here. There was nothing below us but black, freezing water. About a hundred and fifty miles of it. And though land was only six miles away on either side, it might as well have been six hundred.

A few lone swimmers staggered bloody and dazed, having dragged themselves onto our metal shore, where a woman stood, calling hysterically for someone who no longer answered. Water lapped at our feet as though the tide were coming in, as though we were all of us lounging on a strand and not clinging to a sinking ship. It felt surreal.

"Come on, Meg." I urged her away from the porthole, away from the water, for now. "We have to get to higher ground."

Stepping over steel seams and rivets, we walked up the black hull and slumped, soaked and shivering, in the frigid night air. Our breath came in misty puffs as I put my arm around Meg and we huddled together. Already the tide had crept past our porthole. With every lap it drew nearer, swallowing more. I looked out past the water's edge, past the floundering souls, past the distant few lifeboats to the lights of the *Storstad* flickering in the fading fog. I wondered how long she'd take to get back here.

And if we'd still be here when she did.

∽ *Chapter Twenty-Two* ∽

2:10 A.M.

WE'D ONLY SAT THERE FOR A MOMENT OR TWO. The *Storstad* seemed no closer, but I could tell that the *Empress*'s hull and our time on it were quickly disappearing as the water's edge crept closer. A corpse floating face down drifted nearby, and I left our perch to wade over and take the vest the poor man clearly had no use for anymore. I tried not to look at his face, or the waves lapping up his legs, swallowing him one piece at a time. I could do nothing for him. I turned and, vest in hand, climbed the last few feet of slippery hull to where Meg waited. One vest between us. Still, it was better than what most had. We were young, uninjured. We had the hope of seeing our men again. It might be enough to buoy us up, to carry us on. Maybe.

I wrapped the belt around my right wrist twice and gripped it, making her do the same. "We'll have to swim for it, Meg."

She looked at me, horrified.

I pointed at the *Storstad*. "It's not far," I lied. "We can do it." I hoped. "Just don't let go. And kick your legs."

But before we could move, the hull disappeared from under our feet. A mere fourteen minutes after she'd been hit, the *Empress* sank beneath the water's surface and we along with her. A great cry arose like the roar at a football match as the seven hundred souls clinging to her side screamed in terror before going under. The freezing water gripped and shook us in the suck and drag of the ship's wake, violently tossing us like rag dolls in a washer full of wood and metal debris. Deeper and deeper it drew us until I thought my lungs might burst. I'd no idea which way was up as my right arm yanked me forward. I'd given up all hope, when suddenly my head broke the surface and I gasped. Meg breached next to me, retching and coughing. Bodies bobbed up around us, and those still living floundered, grasping for anything and anyone within reach. Some used the dead to stay afloat. Others died fighting off the desperate grip of a drowning stranger. A moustached man flailed beside me. His hand closed in a death grip on my collar and dragged me under a few times. Letting go of the life vest, I dove down, finally shrugging him off with my coat. I gasped as I broke the surface again.

"Kick your legs," I yelled through gulps of air as I grabbed the vest's strap. We needed to break away from the desperate mob. But from the dark below, a hand grabbed my ankle, its partner clutching further up my calf. I thrashed and kicked, desperate to break free, but they only grasped tighter, climbed higher, dragging me to my death as they scratched and scrabbled for life.

I wouldn't let them drag Meg down, too. Letting go of the belt again, I sank under the water. My lungs burned and my kicking slowed. And just as I was about to give in to the sinking darkness, the hands suddenly went limp and let go.

I broke the surface once more, exhausted, and reached for the vest, but my numb fingers couldn't close around the string. Ice floes still drifted in these waters, even in May. It had to be below freezing. Meg shifted her weight off the vest, two flaps of six cork blocks in canvas the only thing keeping us afloat, even though it couldn't carry us both at the same time. She pushed it toward me.

I wanted to protest, to insist that she stay on it. I was the stronger of the two, but I could barely even catch my breath. The *Storstad* seemed motionless in the distance, a mile or two away. I dropped my head. There was no way we'd make it. Voices still cried out in the dark, but there were fewer now. Perhaps they were saving what little energy they had left. Perhaps they had none.

Meg and I took turns resting on the jacket and kicking along beside it; if nothing else, it kept us moving. It made us feel like we were doing something. It separated us from the frosty corpses that drifted at the mercy of the current. 'Twas as though a whole village had drowned. I don't know how long we struggled in the water. But as the cold numbed our limbs and despair numbed our hearts, I looked at Meg and knew she'd reached the point where she didn't want to struggle anymore.

"Meg," I gasped, reaching for her as her face dipped below the surface. "The lifeboats … just hold on."

I pulled her to me and the life vest sank beneath us, both

of us floundering for a breath, both of us choking in the dark. "Link your arm through the neck of it," I said, coughing. "Float on your back."

But she couldn't. The two coats, hers and Timothy's, weighed her down and neither of us had the strength to remove them.

She went under again.

"I can't," Meg said as her face resurfaced. "I'm so tired, Ellie."

"Don't give up," I pleaded.

"I promised your aunt I'd take care of you"—her voice came in short breaths—"and that I'd never tell you the truth. But at least I can keep one of those promises. Take the vest." She shoved away from me, from it, from all that might have saved her.

I lunged for her, clutched her collar in my failing fingers, grasping it again and again as she slipped from me. "Meg ... don't ... I can't hold you."

"Barnardo's," she gurgled as she floundered.

Then her head went under for the last time.

☙ *Chapter Twenty-Three* ☙

2:30 A.M.

IT SHOULD HAVE BEEN MEG. She should have been the one prodded with a lifeboat oar and dragged from the water. It should have been her bundled in the sling and hoisted up the side of the *Storstad*. And as long as I live, I'll never understand why it was me.

I shivered from shock as much as hypothermia as Mrs. Andersen wrapped a long shirt around me. I didn't realize I was practically naked. Most of us were, as we huddled in the wet remains of whatever we'd had time to throw on. Mainly nightgowns and pyjama pants, flimsy items that had ripped asunder in our harrowing escape, in our fight to live. The first few survivors donned the extra clothes of the *Storstad*'s thirty-six-man crew. The small working vessel was not equipped for passengers, let alone the hundreds of survivors it hauled aboard. As more and more arrived, Captain Andersen and his wife wrapped them in whatever they could find: tablecloths, pillowcases, and curtains. One man had even resorted to wrapping himself in sheets of newspaper—we were that desperate for warmth.

Mrs. Andersen rubbed my numb arms through the flannel shirt and then closed my frozen fingers around a mug of whiskey, but I felt nothing. I didn't want to feel anything ever again. "Drink." She lifted my hands to my mouth.

The whiskey burned a path down my gullet.

"Ellie?"

I blinked as he came into focus. Not Jim—Dr. Grant. He was wearing only a pair of trousers, large ones he had tied up with a bit of rope. He gently touched my shoulder. "Are you hurt?"

My reddened limbs tingled and ached as they thawed. I'd been grazed, battered, and bruised. But I was alive. I shook my head.

"I could use your help—if you're able," he added.

"Are you the master of this ship?" Captain Kendall's voice bellowed and he rushed at Captain Andersen. "You sank my ship—you were going full speed ahead in that dense fog!"

He raved like a madman and rightly so, as Dr. Grant intervened to hold Kendall back.

"*I* wasn't going full speed," Captain Andersen blurted, outraged by the ridiculous accusation. "*You* were!"

Two crewmen drew the men apart and Captain Kendall staggered, supported by the doctor's arms. His ship lay at the bottom of the St. Lawrence. Two-thirds of his passengers and crew were dead. His worst nightmare.

"Why didn't they let me drown?" the captain cried. "Why didn't they just let me drown?"

He voiced the pain so many of us felt. The question we'd never get answered.

The *Storstad* crew and a few sound passengers continued to help survivors on board. Almost five hundred of us in all. Most, like me, suffered from shock; many had broken limbs and bloody wounds; a few had gone completely mad and needed restraining as they called out names and tried to jump over the rail. Dr. Grant worked tirelessly with me at his side—splinting, bandaging, staunching, breathing life back into the seemingly dead. Nearly two dozen died after being saved, but there was nothing any doctor could do for them. And by the time the few *Empress* and *Storstad* lifeboats went out on their third trip in search of survivors among the debris, they found nothing but drifting corpses. Hundreds of them.

3:15 A.M.

THE *EUREKA* ARRIVED almost forty-five minutes after the *Empress*'s distress signal and the *Lady Evelyn* after that. They quartered the river in a vain search, and in the end, I heard they found five of our crew on an upturned lifeboat. And many more dead.

But we knew the death toll was much higher. For how many, like Timothy, had gone down with the ship, trapped in tilted alleyways and unable to escape? I hadn't seen Gwen or Kate, Matron Jones or Gaade. Did they make it out? And what about all those passengers who drowned where they slept? Where they now slept forever.

And Jim? And Meg?

I couldn't let my mind go there. I just couldn't.

Shivering, I threw myself into the work at hand, thankful

that Dr. Grant kept me focused on the living, on helping those I could.

At dawn, all the *Empress* passengers pulled from the St. Lawrence, both living and dead, were transferred aboard the other two steamers that would take us to Rimouski, the nearest town.

I stood at the *Lady Evelyn*'s rail and took one last look at the *Storstad* as she made ready to continue upstream. In the light of dawn, her bow seemed so much smaller than it had coming out of the fog. The steel was mangled, twisted to port and crumpled in. Bits of *Empress* debris still stuck to it like blood on a blade. Crewmen had laid out the corpses in long rows on the deck of the two steamers. My gaze passed over the hundreds of dead but I didn't let it linger.

They aren't there. They can't be.

I hadn't seen either of them on the *Storstad* as Dr. Grant and I did our rounds. Given the odds, it didn't make sense that Jim or Meg survived. But it made even less sense to accept that they were gone.

I stepped into the crowd of survivors along the rail as the *Lady Evelyn* and the *Eureka* gathered steam. Huddled aboard, we shivered in the frostbitten wind, holding tight to one another, holding on to the hope that our lost loved ones were doing the same on the other small ship.

∞ *Chapter Twenty-Four* ∞

"DRINK THIS." Steele handed me a crystal glass of amber liquid. Whiskey, I think. Aunt Geraldine's private stock. He must have poured it from the sideboard where she kept her good pinwheel crystal. I'd never even noticed him getting up. The memories had so completely taken over, I was surprised to find my clothes were dry. I brought the cup to my lips, steadying it with both hands as I sipped. Horrible stuff, just like what Mrs. Andersen had given me, but already I felt its warmth radiating in my core. My heart throbbed in my ears, as though I'd just run ten miles.

"Better?"

I nodded.

He didn't take a drink himself. Didn't pick up his notepad.

I swirled the liquid in the glass. Sipped again. "That night was the last time I saw either of them, Meg or Jim."

I'd seen Meg take her last breath, heard her last word, even though I'd no idea what she meant. As far as I knew, there were passengers by that name aboard. Retelling those last moments together made me face that horrible truth— Meg was gone. My heart knew it, too. The hope had turned to grief.

But Jim was strong, sound when I last saw him. I wanted Steele to tell me that he'd seen Jim since. That he knew something more. But he said nothing.

"It's funny," I continued almost to myself, "you never know it's the last time ... until it's too late." I paused. "Like with my aunt, I didn't even know she was ill. I can't remember what I last said to her. Or even know what I would have said, really." I shook my head. "But the things I never should have said—those are the ones that I'll always remember."

We sat in silence for a few moments.

"I've interviewed a lot of sad stories over the years and if it's taught me anything, Miss Ellen, it's this: regret is an insatiable sonofabitch. No matter how sorry you feel, it's never enough, and the more you feed into regret, the hungrier it gets."

He spoke like a man who'd done his share of feeding. I wondered what his story was.

"The way I see it," he continued, "a card laid is played. There's no sense second-guessing. We do what we can with the hand that we have. And sometimes we make stupid moves. And, yes, sometimes we have terrible hands, so grim we just want to fold."

"Wait—" The ridiculousness, the futility of it all, struck me. "You're comparing my life to a—a poker game?"

He leaned forward, elbows on his knees. "I just think we gotta keep on playing, you know? We're still in. Who knows what might come on the next flip from the deck."

His optimism seemed slightly forced and I wondered if he was advising me or himself.

"What do you regret?" I asked, curious. The question caught him off guard and I saw the shadow of his answer ripple behind his eyes.

"This isn't about me—"

"I'm asking. I'm making it about you."

He looked away for a few seconds, then, seemingly resolved, sat back in his seat. He met my eyes. "Nothing. I don't regret anything."

I studied him for a moment, the jut of his chin, the glint in his eye. "You're bluffing."

He smiled slightly and I knew I was right.

"You play your cards very close to your chest, Mr. Steele. Always the one asking the questions. Never revealing anything. But I bet of all the sad stories you've interviewed, yours is equally tragic. I've read your work." The man wrote with detailed description, but also great passion. In few words, he got to the heart of it. Though he played the objective reporter, the cold and detached journalist, somehow I knew he wasn't.

"No one could write the way you do and not *feel* deeply," I concluded.

"Maybe I'm just that good of a writer."

"Maybe." I finished off my drink and set the glass on the mahogany end table. "But I doubt it."

Steele's half-smile crept up his cheek, making him look almost bashful, like a young scamp caught doing something right. "You have a way with words, Miss Ellen. I'm not sure if you are paying me an insult or a compliment."

"That depends—do you think compassion is a virtue or a flaw?" I paused a moment before asking what I really wanted to know. "Do you care about anyone, really, or are we just article fodder?"

For a second, he seemed stung by my question but he spoke with conviction. "I report the truth. The facts. I learned long ago not to let my feelings get involved. If my mother taught me anything before she took off, it was that."

He bent and rummaged through his bag, making it clear this conversation was over. As he pulled out Jim's journal, I hoped that, given all I'd said about the sinking and the rescue, he might tear out a few extra pages for me. I'd given him the story. He owed me more than a scrap of Jim's. Instead, he handed me the book.

I looked at him in wonder as I took it. "The whole thing?"

He shrugged. "You earned it."

My heart thudded as I held it in my hands.

Jim's journal.

I stroked the worn leather cover, now rippled with water damage, and pulled the red ribbon's frayed end through my fingers. Finally, I'd get Jim's story. The spine cracked as I opened to the first few pages. But these entries were too blurred, too ruined by the river, to read. I turned to the next. And the next. Only to see they were, all of them, washed out. In a few places, ragged remains of a page jutted from the crease, remnants of entries Steele had torn out. I flipped to the end of the book and my heart sank. Every yellowed page was either illegible or empty. I traced my finger down the blurry entries, skimming through smeared ink and faded lead. Ghosts of Jim. Words lost forever. I'd get no answers in here.

"You knew." I glared up at Steele. "All this time, you knew there were no more entries and yet you sat there and let me tell my story. How dare you play me like that!" My lip trembled. I was done. With Steele. With hoping. With all of it. Frustrated, I flung the book at him. It hit him in the chest and fell to the floor. "You used me."

"I promised you the journal," he said, but he seemed deflated. "And now you have it."

"You bastard!" I stood and rested both hands on the mantel. I could barely breathe. It felt like I'd lost Jim all over again. I closed my eyes and gripped the wood, inhaling deeply.

"Did you … did you ever even see Jim?" I swallowed and made myself say it. "The body, I mean." My heart pounded in the silence as I waited for the answer.

"No."

I let out the breath I didn't realize I'd been holding.

Steele's voice continued behind me. "I've checked and rechecked my sources. His name isn't on any list of deceased. But you have to realize, Miss Ellen, many were never identified."

"I know," I whispered.

"I know you think me cold-hearted—just out for a story. But it's not like that." He paused and his voice sounded distant when he continued. "I saw them."

I turned to see him staring into the fire at the memory burned into his brain.

"The *Times* sent me to be the eyes of the world," he continued. "And so I went. And I saw. In the Rimouski shed, and again at Quebec's Pier 27. I walked those long silent rows of open coffins. I looked at every battered body lying half-naked, bloated, and broken in its pine box. Every one of them had a number scribbled on a scrap of paper lying on their chest. Men. Women. Children. Just a number—until some loved one claimed them. Many never were.

"So many mothers," he said, eyes unblinking, and I knew he saw them still, "corpses still clutching their babies even in death." He closed his eyes. "I saw what no one should ever see."

I didn't remember reading that in his Rimouski article. He hadn't mentioned those details. Maybe there was some humanity in him.

He looked at me, his eyes slowly returning to here and now.

"I saw them, too," I said. "In the water, lying on the steamer decks. Jesus, Steele. I *knew* them. I served them tea. I worked with them. Lived with them. Laughed with them." I thought of Kate and Gwen, of Matron Jones and Gaade, of Timothy. All gone. I choked out the words. "They were my friends."

I never did go into the makeshift morgue they'd set up at Pier 27 for people to identify the bodies. I just couldn't. That day by the pier, I heard two men arguing just outside the door. They were fighting over a child's body. I remember thinking, *How could you?*

But I understood it now. Each father needed it to be his son. Because the winner at least got the body, a chance to say goodbye. And the loser was left with nothing but questions and grief.

I looked at Steele. "I need to know what happened to him.

You said you'd give me his story." I gestured at the journal by the foot of the chair. "And you give me this."

He stood. "I think we're done for today."

"For *today?*" I scoffed at him. I marched to the dining-room door and held it open. "We are done. *Period.*"

He slowly walked over, stopped in front of me, and hitched his satchel up his shoulder. "Not quite," he said. "You still have not told me why you were on that ship. You have not told me your whole story."

He had some nerve. As if I was going to tell him any of my secrets. Of what I'd done. Of where I was sent. Of all that I'd lost. "Why should I tell you anything more?" I raised my chin. "I have the journal."

"And I have the story of the man who gave it to me. William Sampson, the chief engineer." He paused. "I know what happened to Jim that night."

∞ *Chapter Twenty-Five* ∞

"WILL YOU BE WANTING ANYTHING ELSE, MISS?" Lily asked, setting the tea tray beside me. I had no appetite and no matter how I protested, Bates insisted that she make me something after Steele left.

I felt angry at Steele for manipulating me with this journal, for witholding information. But wasn't I doing the same—each of us playing the other to get what we wanted? Steele and I, we were more alike than I cared to admit. I didn't want to see him again, but the truth was, I had to if I wanted to learn what he knew about Jim. He'd said he'd be back in three days' time to continue our interview.

I picked up Jim's journal from the floor, absentmindedly fiddling with the ribbon. How unfair that after all I'd said to Steele, the book gave me nothing more, no other insights into the many questions I had about Jim. Not just if he lived—but if he loved. Had there been another woman in his life? Did I mean anything to him? It felt real to me when we were together, but maybe I just wanted it to. Maybe I just remembered it that way.

Jim was like the tide. One look would rush at me so intense and powerful, so overwhelming. Yet, just as I was about to give in or give voice to the feelings he'd stirred in me, I'd feel him pulling back. Retreating to the depths inside himself once more. I never knew whether I was coming or going with him. And even when he seemed withdrawn, on those nights when he wouldn't say a word, his unspoken need of me pulled fiercely, like an undertow that might sweep me away.

I tugged on the ribbon and was surprised to feel it jam between the two pages. Curious, I slipped my thumb between the stuck papers and carefully wedged them apart. They tore a bit as the book fell open to the ribboned page, each leaving remnants on the other. But through the patches I saw Jim's writing as clear as the night he wrote it. That night as he stood in the misty light, lost in his words. The last night I saw him.

May 28, 1914

I have to tell her the truth. I can't keep it any longer. It terrifies me, so it does, because in telling her, I might lose her.

What if she wants nothing to do with me? I don't think I could live with it.

But I can't live with this secret between us anymore.

I paused and looked up, my heart throbbing in my chest. *So this is it. He is going to tell her the truth.*

I wondered who she was. What dark secret he had—

Was I that secret?

His strong feelings for me always ebbed away in guilt. As though being with me made him feel bad. I flipped the book over on the side table and stood, rubbing my forehead with my palm as I paced the room.

Wouldn't it be better just to remember things as they were?

I looked back at the upturned journal.

Wouldn't it be better to have questions than answers I didn't want to know?

No.

I grabbed the book and turned it over, chewing on my thumbnail as I read his words.

I know she suspects something. How couldn't she? I've been acting a right madman. Hot and cold. Moody. I keep telling myself that she deserves someone better than me. But her eyes. The way she looks at me—into me—makes me feel something I've never felt before. A calmness. A hope. She's the anchor, steadying me when I feel tossed and torn asunder. She's the lighthouse guiding me home.

Listen to me, going on—she's making a bloody poet of me!

She's all I think about. Ever since I first saw her, I've just wanted to be with her. To hear her voice. To feel her hands on me. I want to hold her and protect her.

I love her.

That's the truth of it. I love her, so I do.

So what, you blathering eejit. So what if you love her?

What does it matter? She won't love you.

Not after all you've done.

No, I don't deserve her and she, she deserves someone so much better than me. Someone who'll treat her like the fine girl she is. Someone who'll give her the life a stoker's wage can never provide. What the hell do I have to offer?

Nothing, that's what.

—1:30 a.m. —

I can't sleep. Again. Thought I'd get some air on deck— maybe a smoke or two will settle me. But it's not the nightmares tonight. I've finally made up my mind. I know what I have to do, and so help me God, I'm going to do it.

As soon as we dock in Liverpool, I'm going to go to her and finally tell her the truth. Every dark secret. And if she can still bear to look at me, and I hardly blame her if she can't, I'm going to get my wages and go into Boland's and buy her a ring. I'm going to ask her to be mine, so I will.

If she'll have me.

That last night, he'd said he was sorry. But for what— leaving me in Quebec? Sorry for being a right arse? Or sorry for what he was about to tell me?

I touched my lips, and remembered the passion in that first kiss. The fire. The feeling.

Was he really kissing me goodbye?

I closed the book and set it on the mantel. However he meant it, the truth of it was, our first kiss was also our last.

∞ *Chapter Twenty-Six* ∞

BATES TOOK ME FOR A DRIVE THE NEXT DAY. Said I needed to get out, that the air might do me some good. I had to admit, I did feel the better for it. Sea air does it for me every time. Scours the soul, Mam used to say. I can see why she came to Liverpool those Julys long ago. It is lovely this time of year with the gardens in full bloom and the sun sparkling on the sea. We drove to the harbour and stopped at the market where farmers' wives and fishmongers hawked their wares in raspy calls, like seabirds themselves.

Bates loaded our bags into the boot of the car. "Shall we walk in the park a bit, miss?"

I nodded.

The path meandered through lush gardens, veering around statues and fountains. It felt peaceful here. A green oasis, hidden in the heart of the bustling town.

"Did Aunt Geraldine know this place?" I asked, looking up at the archway of limbs and leaves. I'd never been here with her, but it seemed familiar, somehow.

"Your aunt ..." He hesitated. "She didn't like to go out much."

"It's funny, isn't it, Bates? She wrote about such exciting adventures on the far side of the world and yet wouldn't venture out to a park just a few blocks away." She barely left her study.

He sighed and shook his head.

We crested a small hill as the footpath ran alongside a pond nestled like a large blue egg in the green grass. A paper boat scudded across the water's surface, caught in the summer breeze. I stepped off the path to stand at the water's edge, my feet sinking in the thick grass.

"I *have* been here before." And I knew I had stood in that very same spot, though I was much smaller then. I looked back up the hillside and, in my mind's eye, saw a tartan blanket, a picnic, spread on the slope just ahead. I saw Mam there under the oak, laughing at the state of my wet skirt.

"My mother took me here," I whispered, "those summers when we came to Liverpool, back when I was very young. Before she got sick. Before Father sent me away."

"My Meggie loved this place, too." He joined me at the edge of the pond. "I often used to bring her here when she was a girl. She was forever wanting to feed the ducks."

He pulled a small paper bag from his pocket and opened it. Bread crumbs. He tossed a handful on the water and an emerald-headed mallard paddled over and snapped them up in his rounded beak.

"Even as a child, she had a tender heart, she did." He threw another fistful, like a sower with seed. "Always worrying about everyone else." He sniffed.

Bates had no idea how true that was. I wondered if I should tell him that she'd given me the life vest. That I'd been with her when she drowned. That she'd sacrificed herself for me.

He drew out a hankie the size of a small tablecloth and blew his nose, two great honks and a quick swipe of either side, before tucking it back in his pocket.

"You've never asked about … that night." I hesitated, unsure how to proceed. Or even if I should. I stared at the water, at the way the ripples reflected a distorted truth. "Did you want to know about Meg?"

He shrugged beside me. "It wouldn't bring her back, would it?" he said wistfully. "No." He dumped the last of the bag on the water's edge and crumpled it before shoving it inside his pocket. "No sense in filling my head with how she died." He cleared his throat and brushed his hands. "I'd rather remember how she lived. That's what Meggie would want. Don't you think, miss?"

"Yes," I agreed. Bates was right. It's what anyone would want.

I survived because of Meg. But at what cost? And for what good? She deserved to be here. Not me. No, the waters didn't take me that night, but I was drowning, still, in survivor's guilt.

BATES LEFT ME IN THE PARK and I sat on the bench overlooking the pond and the rolling green beyond. He would be back in an hour, and to be honest, I dreaded the thought of sitting cooped up in that empty house with nothing but the ticking clock to pass the time. Two young boys in short pants laughed as they ran with a kite, the red diamond bouncing and flopping on the ground behind. Though the breeze had died down, their fun had not. I smiled and turned my face to the sun. Closed my eyes for a moment.

"Lovely day, isn't it?" A shadow fell over me.

I looked up to find Steele standing in front of me, a little smile tugging at his lips. "It was."

"Oh, come on now. Don't be like that." He sat beside me without bothering to wait for an invitation.

I glared, still angry at him for playing games, for rationing out whatever he knew about Jim. Even though I was as stingy with my story. "Don't you have somewhere else to be?"

He leaned back, crossing his arms and stretching his long legs. "I don't, actually."

"So you're following me now?"

"No," he argued. "My B&B is right across the street. I come here all the time."

I rolled my eyes. "Oh please. I doubt you've ever even been—"

"Wyatt!" the boys yelled and thundered toward us, their bright eyes dancing. "Can you launch us again?"

He glanced at me, face smug. "You were saying?"

I clenched my jaw. Would I never be free of this insufferable man?

The youngest of the freckle-faced boys handed Steele the kite and the three of them trotted out onto the green. As if on cue, a wind picked up, tousling Steele's slicked hair as he stopped and turned. He seemed like a great big child himself with that goofy grin and messy hair as he yelled over to the boys at the bobbin end of the line.

"Okay, guys—on three." Steele lifted the kite by the crossbar high over his head. "One ... two ..."

On three the boys bolted with Steele jogging behind, pacing himself to keep the string taut. He moved smooth and strong, with the confidence and steady stride of a thorough-bred horse. The red sheeting billowed slightly behind the kite's frame. As it caught the wind, Steele thrust it upwards, stopping his canter to stare up at the sky. He stood, hand on his hip, the other shading his brow. I didn't have to see his eyes to know they sparkled as he watched the kite swooping and soaring, its knotted tail waving behind as the boys raced over the knoll.

Steele grinned at me as he sauntered back to the bench. Mosey—that was the word. He moseyed over like the cocky cowboy he was.

"They only asked because you're tall," I snapped.

He smiled as he sat back down beside me. "Height has nothing to do with it. It's sheer technique."

I snorted. "How hard can it be?"

"Don't tell me you've never flown a kite before."

I paused.

"Seriously?" He faced me. "You've never flown a kite?"

I folded my arms and jutted my chin. "I've never felt the need."

Steele laughed then, a sound as warm as the sun, but it burned me, it did. For I knew he was laughing *at* me.

"What?" I demanded, sitting up and challenging him. "What's so bloody funny?"

He shook his head as he rubbed the back of his neck, chuckles still bubbling up. "If you've never felt the need, then, Miss Ellen, you don't know what you're missing." He stood and put his fingers to his lips, whistling once and waving the boys over. Within seconds they'd circled back to us, kite in hand. Steele took a small box or something from his bag and traded Harry for the kite. Then he turned to me.

"I'm not—" I blustered. "You can't just—"

Ignoring me, he took my elbow and raised me from the bench. Led me onto the grass. "Come on. Just give it a go."

Halfway up the knoll, I shrugged him off and straightened my shirt. "You think I can't do this? I can do this. Any idiot can fly a kite. Give me that." I snatched the bobbin of string from him and wound it out as he backed away, grinning. The thin line grew tense between us. I waited on the gentle slope as he stood wide-legged a little ways up it. A cool breeze blew the hairs from the back of my neck, flapped my skirt against my legs, and I turned to face it. Steele's voice carried on it, urging me. Making my heart race.

One … two … three!

And I ran, legs pumping beneath my skirts, hands up, gripping the reel. My hat flew off as I gained speed, my hair falling out of its carefully pinned bun, but I didn't care. The wind, the sun, the rush of it all—I felt like I did as a young girl riding Sugar in the green fields back home.

The line pulled and I glanced over my shoulder to see the diamond swooping up and up and up. I stopped and gazed into the sky, mesmerized by its freedom, as the spool spun wildly in my hands.

Suddenly, I felt him behind me, felt his strong hand on mine, slowing the bobbin even as my heart raced. His other arm reached around me, hot and solid. It flexed as he tugged on the string. Once. Twice. Just enough to make it soar even higher.

"Do you feel it now, Ellen?" he said into my dishevelled hair, his words warmed by a knowing smile. "Do you feel the need?"

⤜ THE THIRD INTERVIEW ⤛

July 1914
Strandview Manor, Liverpool

∞ *Chapter Twenty-Seven* ∞

THAT DAY IN THE PARK woke something in me. A memory. A rush. I didn't know what it was exactly, only that Steele had stirred it up. Before Steele entered my sad life, things were stagnant but they were clear. But for the past few days I'd found that grief now clouded by other feelings. Murky with hope. A few times, I even caught myself anticipating our next interview. When I would see him again. And that feeling confused me even more.

At first I thought my eagerness was because he was going to tell me about Jim. I'd finally get my answers. But in my heart, I knew they were not going to make me feel any better. No, I wasn't looking forward to that pain.

Was it simply having someone to talk to? Was it feeling heard? Was it being known?

Or was it perhaps Steele himself?

I didn't know.

As the meeting time approached, I fussed with my hair

and changed into my lavender dress. Not for him, though. I'd finally had enough of black.

He seemed hesitant when I met him at the front door, satchel slung across his chest. I wondered if he'd been thinking of me these past two days. Of my article, I mean.

He took off his hat and even before we left the entryway blurted, "Ellen, I'm going to ask you something ... and I want you to feel free to say no." He paused and shut the front door behind him. "It's been on my mind since the first day I came here and, well, I just have to ask."

My heart quickened. Was it excitement? Nervousness? Panic? I didn't know what he wanted. And worse still, what I wanted.

He glanced up the stairwell. "Can I see your aunt's study?"

I breathed out. Relieved, actually.

"It's just, I'm a huge fan," he continued, eagerly. "And I'd love to see where she wrote all those stories."

"Of course." I smiled. "Follow me."

We climbed the carpeted stairs and travelled the long hall to the far turret.

"So this is where it all happened," Steele whispered in awe as we entered the study. He slowly walked the circular room, stopping to read a title or two from the hundreds of books shelved from ceiling to floor. They lined the turret like a wall of bricks, broken here and there for a window or a door. Aunt Geraldine had books on everything from *The Flora and Fauna of the African Veldt* to *Tribal Customs and Warfare*. She may never have gone there, but she knew everything a person could know about Africa.

Her great mahogany desk stood in the middle of the room atop an exotic-looking rug. As a child, I'd thought it a magic carpet, one that carried her off on her many adventures. But it was faded now, frayed and unravelled around the edges. Her black typewriter sat, as always, front and centre on her desk. The gold letters had worn off most of her black keys. It didn't surprise me. Given the way she pounded them, I was surprised it had never jackhammered through the desk. It seemed strange to find it so silent. To know it would never tap another word.

Beside the typewriter lay a stack of paper. Thirty or so typed pages, face down. I ran my fingers along the white bumps of embossed letters. A braille I'd never know. This was Aunt Geraldine's latest novel—the one she would never finish.

"I can't believe I'm actually standing in G.B. Hardy's study." Steele stopped behind her chair and rested his hands on its back, but he wouldn't sit in it, any more than I'd sit on the King's throne.

I hadn't planned on ever coming in this room again, really. Not that I'd ever been allowed in it much before. I'd always felt that I was intruding, trespassing on some sacred space of Aunt Geraldine's. And though her creative mind always intrigued me, her sharp tongue and keen eye made me steer clear. As a young child, I did sneak in a few times and sat on the bay window ledge watching her work, watching the people on the street, making up stories of my own. There was always a fairy queen—a beautiful young woman disguised by the drab clothes she wore, burdened by a basket of laundry. She walked in the crowd, her secret strength unknown to all but me.

I moved from the desk and shifted the thick curtain to look out the latticed window into the empty street.

Where was she now—that fairy queen? Where was that little girl?

Aunt Geraldine never acknowledged my coming or going, but I remember finding a striped yellow pillow left on the sill for me. I glanced down, surprised to see the pillow, faded but still there. Even more surprised to see an envelope with my name written upon it in her hand.

"What's that?" Steele asked.

"Nothing." I slipped it into my pocket. I had promised him some memories, but not this one.

I suggested we go back to the front room downstairs. I knew what I had to tell him and I couldn't do it in this room. A whisper of Aunt Geraldine's lilac perfume hung in the air, as if she were still at her desk or pulling books down from her shelves. I couldn't tell that story here—feeling her this close. It was hard enough living through it with her once.

Back in the front room, we took our usual seats. Steele smiled to see the dust covers had all been removed and the furniture beneath polished to a shine. "Doing some spring cleaning?"

I shrugged. "Lily and I freshened things up. Something to do. Plus I figured when the house goes up for sale it might help if it doesn't look like a dusty warehouse."

"Oh, so you're selling?"

"I don't know what is happening. The solicitors are still going through all her papers now. They said her estate would take longer to settle than most because of her writing career." I knew I couldn't stay here forever, but where could I go? It scared me to think about all that. But it was nothing compared to the fear I now felt—was I really going to tell him my story?

"All right, let's get down to it." He flipped open his black notebook, rifling through my many memories, stopping at a fresh page for this last one that I did not want to tell. My face burned at the thought. "So, Ellen. I'm guessing you weren't there to research the life of a stewardess for your aunt."

He looked up expectantly.

I didn't want to tell him. Didn't want to remember. What did it matter *why* I was on the ship? Wasn't living through that tragedy enough? Did he have to make me relive all my losses?

But to learn Jim's story, I needed to hear Sampson's. And to get that, I needed to tell mine.

I swallowed. "My aunt didn't send me to the *Empress* because of her book."

He smiled. "I figured as much."

I paused and let my gaze flit around the room, settling on nothing.

"So," he coaxed, "what really brought you to the *Empress* in the first place?"

I met his gaze and held my breath. "A baby."

Steele raised his eyebrows. This wasn't what he'd expected, and yet, it was exactly what he wanted. He leaned forward, eyes intense. "Whose baby?"

And with one word, my secret was out.

"Mine."

∽ *Chapter Twenty-Eight* ∽

I COULD TELL YOU it was my aunt's fault for signing me up on the ship, or my father's fault for kicking me out of his home, but I'd say my life was ruined the day Declan Moore rode into it two years ago.

Tall, handsome, powerful—he was every young girl's dream. All the girls envied me, that Declan Moore had chosen Hardy Estates to visit. He was purchasing six teams of horses for his father's business, and everyone in Wicklow knew we had the best stock. The best by far. Normally, I had nothing to do with my father's business dealings, but as I was out riding Spirit, Father waved me over and introduced us. Said he wanted to show Spirit to Mr. Moore, bragged about her beauty and strong lines. As Father rounded the horse, stroking and assessing her proudly, Declan agreed whole-heartedly—and when his eyes met mine, I realized it wasn't Spirit that had caught his attention. It was me.

I was sixteen. Never even been kissed. I'd only just had my first dance and that was with Michael Devitt—a great oaf of a thing who didn't know one foot from another. Declan might have been just three or four years older than me, but in my eyes, he was a man. A man who told me I was beautiful. I wanted his attention and the more he toyed with me, the more I flirted, completely ignorant to the danger of the fire I was stoking. If my father saw what was going on, he did nothing to stop it. In fact, I remember him inviting me to join them at dinner, encouraging us to go riding together.

"Bring Declan up to the meadow and give him a good run," Father had said, taking me aside. "This deal will make the difference for Hardy Estates. He needs to really see the quality I'm offering." I think he meant the filly—but now I'm not so sure. A match between Declan and me would have been in my best interests—he was, after all, the son of Colonel Moore, owner of the most successful carriage company in Dublin, and I, the sole heir of Hardy Stables and Estates. But looking back, it's almost as if my father had trotted me out along with the horses to sweeten the deal.

Who does that to their sixteen-year-old daughter?

Led on by Declan's experienced ways that knew when to spur my infatuation and when to gentle my doubts, 'twas as though I had blinders on and saw nothing but him. His love for me. Our future together. He made promises, saying all the right things to do all that was wrong. Kissing me, touching me, reassuring me when I pulled away, undressing me in the meadow where we lay on a blanket. I told him to stop, that we should wait, but by the time I realized how far we'd gone, the danger of it all, it was too late. Is it rape, really, if I've followed him, kissed him, if I'm lying half-dressed underneath him?

"YES." STEELE'S VOICE CUT INTO my story, pulling me back to the present.

I couldn't look at him. Couldn't believe I'd just told him all of that—my dark secret. Good Lord, would it be in the paper?

"What he did was wrong, Ellen. Even if you were eighteen or were in a relationship, nothing gives a man the right to ignore your 'no.'"

I looked at him then, surprised at the casualness of this conversation. People just didn't talk about this kind of thing. Especially not in mixed company. But he was, as he said, a man focused on fact. The truth of the story. Even as he heard mine, there was no judgment in his eyes.

"Let me guess," he continued, "he never did sign that deal with your father."

"No." I snorted. "No, he left the next day. And when my father didn't hear from him and went up to Dublin himself weeks later, he learned Colonel Moore's youngest son was notorious for fleecing breeders, for getting down payments on deals he had no business making. That his father had, in fact, disowned him six months before. And that the last he'd heard, Declan was on a boat to America."

MY FATHER RANTED FOR WEEKS at the outrage of being swindled, of being stupid enough to fall for that whelp's smooth talking. And just when his embarrassed outbursts seemed to subside, I realized why I had been feeling so poorly. It wasn't a young girl's broken heart, or a daughter's guilty conscience—it was a pregnant woman's shame. I'd been around horse breeding long enough to know the truth of it. I was carrying Declan Moore's unwanted child. I was due in July. And worse than all of that, I had to tell my father.

I had hoped there might be a sliver of sympathy in him—hadn't he, too, been conned by Moore? But as I stood before him in his study, as he glared at me, I could see in his eyes—the sin was entirely mine.

"You've brought shame on this house!" he railed, looming over me. "Blackened the good Hardy name."

I lowered my head and said nothing. He was right. Father was always right.

He pointed his finger at me. "Your mother must be rolling in her grave to see the … the harlot her daughter's become."

I cowered as he christened me. *So, that's who I am.*

"It's just as well she'd dead," he continued, harshly. "This would surely have killed her."

Was he right about that, too? Maybe, but I couldn't see Mam's face, couldn't call her to mind. His wrath had burned any trace of a father's love and taken with it the true memory of my mother.

What could I say? He was right. Even if I'd known my mind then, I wasn't allowed to speak it. All I knew for sure was that things would only get worse once I started to show—my sin, his shame, growing bigger every day. How would I ever make it right?

I cringed at the judgment in his hard eyes, the contempt. "I can't even look at you." He turned to the window and stood, his back to me, in silence. "Get out."

I paused, unsure of what he meant. Was he sending me to my room? "I'm sorry, Father. I never meant for—"

"Get out of my house!" He slammed his hand on the desk beside him.

Surely he didn't mean that. "But where—"

"I don't care!" he yelled. And I knew that he didn't. "I don't care where you go. But you are not welcome here. Get from my sight."

I don't remember running out of the room or packing a few things in a bag, emptying my piggy bank for my fare. I don't even really remember the ship over to Liverpool or why I came here. I hadn't seen her in years, not since my mother died. I suppose I had nowhere else. No one else but Aunt Geraldine. I don't remember much of what happened after I told my father, but I'll never forget the face of Aunt Geraldine when she opened the door to see me clutching my bag on her step, soaked from my walk from the pier in the December rain. I'll never forget her eyes, the disappointment in them when I told her what neither of us ever thought I'd say:

I'm expecting.

∞ *Chapter Twenty-Nine* ∞

IF I WAS HOPING FOR SYMPATHY from Aunt Geraldine, I was sorely disappointed. She did take me in, she even left me blanketed in my sorrow while I burrowed in bed—hiding for days from the truth. But after a week or two, she'd had enough, I suppose, and she took me to Liverpool's Magdalene Asylum, a four-storey building of looming stone and slate. Home for troubled girls.

And it was anything but a home.

'Twas a slave house, a jail, really, run by nuns. They had them in England and Ireland, these asylums. I'd heard of them before. But never in my wildest dreams did I ever think I'd end up in one. Magdalene Asylums locked away all manner of family secrets. Some daughters were abused; many, pregnant; others were simpletons, not *with* child, but seemingly with the mind of one. A few were even locked away, not because they were promiscuous, but because their beauty tempted others to it. Trouble, plain and simple. That's all we were. The family shame, one more easily ignored or denied when hidden behind stone walls.

I supposed we deserved no better.

Some of the girls were very far along, their big bellies pushing out their aprons. They'd stop their chores from time to time to stretch their aching backs, but their delicate condition didn't seem to matter to the nuns. Every one of us had to do our share, be it scrubbing the dormitory floors with a wire brush, washing corridors, or preparing the meals—though we barely ate. A bit of bread and oatmeal, that was it. And we all did laundry. Load after load after bloody load of it. The upper class paid to have their washing done, but we never saw a penny.

Those days were terribly hard. Lonely—for we weren't allowed to talk. Not that any of us wanted to, really. We didn't even know one another's names. For whatever one the sisters called us was not our own. They stripped us of ourselves, berated us, shamed us, sure this penance was for our own good. The days were long, but so were the nights as we slept in our bunks in the dark dormitory. Silently crying for home. For the lives we'd lost.

Each day started with mass and then chores in silence. Then we were marched up to the laundry to scrub in our wash basins until our knuckles were raw, as though it were our sins we were washing away and not someone else's filth. We prayed. We scrubbed. We wrung and starched and ironed. We starved.

And yet despite it all, our babies grew.

I remember the night I felt it move for the first time, the tiny fluttering, even as I lay still. I put my hand on my stomach, and in the darkness it dawned on me that this wasn't a sin—this was a baby. *My* baby. My own. Declan didn't even know it existed. And never would. This baby was truly all I had in this world.

And I was all it had, too. A small hope flickered inside me.

Things changed after that. Or maybe I had. And as the spring months passed and summer came, I knew I was ready to be a mother. Whatever that meant. I'd do it. I'd do what I had to for my child.

Though I'd grown up around stables and seen many a foaling, my labour terrified me. I cried for my mother, and as the pains racked me, I truly thought I was dying. The midwife gave me no comfort or reassurance, and after what seemed an eternity, my daughter was born. Her fierce cry filled the stone room. Filled my heart.

"Can I see her?" I asked the sister wrapping her in a blanket. But she only turned from me, her dark robes swishing on the floor as she left with my child. The cry grew distant as it echoed down the hall.

"My baby—" I tried to get up from the bed, but I'd no ounce of strength left. "Can I hold her? Please, I need to hold her—"

But they didn't answer. They never even let me see her.

Later that day, Aunt Geraldine came and sat in the wooden chair next to me. She told me the baby had died. Her words clanged in my hot head like a stone in a pot but made no sense.

She couldn't have died. She was alive. I heard her. Her voice was so strong.

When I looked back, Aunt Geraldine was gone.

After the fever passed and I'd my wits about me, I felt I might lose them forever. Many of the young women had their babes in arms or toddling about their skirts. But not all of us. Not me. And the more I saw them, the crazier I felt. I feared I'd end up like one of those simpleton girls, staring into the dirty water until one of us nudged her to keep scrubbing. I wondered if they came here in that state. Or if what happened here did it to them.

By November, four months after my daughter died, and nearly a year since she'd committed me, Aunt Geraldine sent for me. As he drove me back to Strandview Manor, Bates chit-chatted to me from the front seat as though I'd been on a vacation these long months and not in a living hell. His newly hired granddaughter, Meg, met me at the door and showed me to my room. She fussed over me, but I didn't want her pity.

Though it was midday, I took to the bed, burrowing under the covers, never wanting to get up again. But Aunt Geraldine had other plans for me again—only this time as a stewardess aboard the *Empress of Ireland.*

STEELE HANDED ME A HANKIE. I didn't realize I'd been crying. Or that someone was knocking on the front door.

"Would you mind answering it?" I asked. "Lily and Bates are out and I don't think I can—" I dabbed my eyes.

"Of course, of course." He stood and left the room. His voice mumbled at the front door as another man's replied.

I'd never told anyone about my experiences at the Magdalene Asylum. Not my aunt. Not even Meg. I never wanted to talk about it, not that they asked. It was my burden to carry, my unspeakable shame. And though I was spent from the telling, somehow there was a lightening, of sorts, in sharing it. Still, I hadn't meant to go into such detail. I hadn't meant to tell him so much.

What if it all ended up in his newspaper story, a headline two weeks from now? I should never have trusted him with it.

"Who was it?" I asked, pressing the handkerchief to my eyes as he returned.

"Oh, just another reporter looking for Ellie Ryan." He waved his hand in dismissal and rolled his eyes. "Relentless bastards, aren't they?"

I laughed through my tears. Surprised that I could. Surprised at the range of emotions this man drew out of me. But if Wyatt Steele did anything well, it was that.

∞ *Chapter Thirty* ∞

STEELE MADE US SOME TEA, gave me time to compose myself. He carried the tray back into the front room and set it on the coffee table. I poured.

"Are you sure you want to do this now?" he asked.

"Yes." Why delay? It had been a long road to this point, and I just wanted to reach the end. To know for sure what happened to Jim. I braced myself for the truth.

He hesitated, and I feared that I'd been duped into telling my story. What if all this time he really had nothing more than the diary?

"I found him," he continued, "in Ireland."

"Jim?" I interrupted, a volt of hope surging through me.

"No, Sampson," he said, almost apologetically. "William Sampson, the chief engineer. I'd tried to get an interview with him while he was in the hospital in Quebec, but security wasn't letting any reporters in. Sampson had been on every one of the *Empress of Ireland* voyages, a tough old guy, in his eighties. I knew he had a story to tell."

He pulled out a different notebook and flipped through it. "Here we are." He smoothed the page and held it out to me. "I pretty much transcribed word for word. The guy was a natural storyteller."

I took it from him, and as I read the old man's words, his voice filled my head.

Eight years I've been sailing with the Empress. She was a sound ship, a tight one, and don't let anyone say any different. We were about nine and three-quarter hours out of Quebec, just past Father Point. I'd just gone off duty, barely reached my cabin astern of the engine room. Not a great jarring or nothing, but I felt it in my own bones. I knew she'd been hit. And let me tell you, there's nothing as terrifying. So off I run to the control platform yelling at the men to close the bulkhead doors. But sure, I needn't have bothered, didn't the lads see the water themselves? A great swirling gush of it running from the after boiler room. If the ice cold of it didn't chill you to the core, the sight of it surely would.

I clattered down the ladder, but even before my feet hit the bottom, the watertight door to the boiler-room door thundered down, narrowly missing Farrow as he slid through from the stokehold. He was Lucky, all right, that Lucky Farrow.

I thought that one watertight door was enough. True, she was pitching badly starboard side, but most of the water had drained into the bilges below. Surely the danger was over. Then I see the face of Farrow beside me. He's black with coal dust from the stokehold and I can tell by the look on him, it's bad. Very bad.

"She's pierced amidships," says he. "From Shelter Deck to her double bottom."

I prayed to God the rest of her belly was sound, but O'Donovan rushes in to tell us both stokeholds and boiler rooms were flooding. We're talking a space the size of St. Patrick's Church. A hundred and seventy-five feet of it.

As if on cue, down go the needles on all my steam gauges—every bloody one of them dropping to a stop. I rang up to the captain, "For heaven's sake, try and beach her." She hadn't much left—he had to run her aground on the Gaspé shore, for a ship with no steam is dead in the water.

He told me to do the best I can. And I did. Gave him all I could. We got the cranks turned over a few more times, but you can get neither blood from a stone nor steam from wet coal. There was no two ways about it. I called the bridge again with the news, "The steam is gone."

The lights dimmed as I hung up the phone, the dynamos were winding down, the Empress was dying, and we along with her if we didn't act soon. There wasn't much time.

Where I should have heard engines there came a deep roar, and sure enough a flood of water came rushing in. A great wave of it. So there we were on the bottom of the ship, eight levels down, well below the waterline, and she is listing something fierce as the water's surging in.

"Clear out!" I yelled at the lads. "You've done all you can. Save yourselves!"

I tell you, there's no harder order to give than that, but if you're not man enough to give it, you've sealed the fate of every young lad that relies on you. And there were about forty of us down there that night. Engineers, firemen, trimmers, and greasers. All of them bravely standing at their posts. They scrambled for the leering ladders and hauled themselves up. Already, the water swirling at the bottom rungs and rising fast, so fast I can hardly stay ahead of it.

Now, my mind is as sharp as ever—but I'd not be behind the door in telling you that this ol' body has seen better days. By the second platform, I hadn't the strength to haul up and I'd a long way to go yet. And as the water climbed the ladder below me, all I could do was sit gasping for a bit of air, sure my heart was going to give out.

"This is it, Will," says I. "This is how it ends." And I thought of my wife I'd never kiss again. And my children.

Then he appeared beside me, Lucky. "Come on, Chief," he said, taking my arm and lifting me up. "You can do this. We're getting out."

"Go," I said, pushing him away. "Save yourself, lad. While there's still time ... That's an order." But he wouldn't hear of it.

"I'm sorry, sir. I can't. I won't. I'm not leaving you." And I knew by the look of him, he meant it. He had heart enough for the both of us, that lad. I'd lived my life, and a good long one at that, but there was no way I'd let him lose his. Not if I could help it. He gave me the strength to keep going.

We finally made it out of the hold, up the five floors to the Boat Deck, but by now she's rolled a good forty-five degrees. And we, along with every other soul who'd made it to top deck, had to grab whatever we could get our hands on just to stay on board. Clinging like spiders on the wall, we were all of us crawling up the tilting floor to the rail rising high overhead. Most passengers were in their nightclothes and I gathered they must have been from the upper decks, from the left side of the ship. It all happened so fast, I doubt the others even had the time to get out of their beds before the river rushed in upon them. Still, making it deckside was no guarantee of survival for any of us.

A few women and wee ones clung to a gate by me; I'll never forget the terror in their eyes. Jesus. And even as I saw their fingers slipping, even as I reached out, away they dropped. Their bodies slid down the deck and smashed into the capstan before they flung out into the night lost in the black river. 'Twas horrific.

Anything and everything that wasn't bolted down hurtled as the Empress tipped: cargo boom, gear, all manner of metal contraptions, including a few portside lifeboats. Two tons each they were, the lifeboats thundered carnage down the sloping deck toward us like a runaway train. Lucky pulled me from their path just in time. But others, many others were not so fortunate. There one minute and gone the next. Imagine that—being killed by a lifeboat, the very thing that's meant to save you. Word has it that many of the corpses later found were dead of their injuries, not of drowning. And every one of them a story that will never be told.

One of the last things I remember on the ship was a young lad giving his mother his lifebelt. Leonard was his name. I'll never forget how she called after him when he

jumped in the water. I don't know if either of them survived.
I don't know how any of us did.

Then the Empress keeled over, her great twin stacks
crashing down in the water, and we were tossed out into the
dark by the force of it, like peas flicked off a spoon. As I came
up for air, I found myself lashed to the wreckage by wires,
a web of it dragging me under. Lucky pulled me free. I can't
kick, says I. My leg, I think it's broken. And he told me to float
on my back while he swam us both to the nearest lifeboat.
Honestly, I never thought we'd make it. But we did. Finally,
we gripped the gunwale, but we were not saved yet. Not by a
long shot.

"You'll drown us all!" a man aboard the lifeboat shouted
hysterically. He swung the oar like a great flyswatter. For
here he was, the only hope in a swarm of desperate souls
pulling and scrabbling from all sides.

I suppose you can't blame him for trying to save himself.
For weren't we trying to do the very same? And maybe his
wife was on board—or his child.

Water lapped over my hand and into the boat. I had to
let go. So did Lucky, but he wasn't giving up. Not yet. He
pulled me away from the horde and after swimming and
dragging me behind for a bit, he finally heaved me onto
a deck chair floating by. I flopped onto it like a load of wet
laundry, completely wrung out.

"They'll come," says I, my breath in foggy gasps. In the
distance, I saw the lights of a ship. "They'll come for us."

Lucky shrugged off his coat and flung it across me. "We
can't wait," says he, grunting and kicking in the water.

I remember the cold. The pain in my leg. The waves lapping against the wood. And I remember his voice.

"Hold on," he said, as he pushed me toward the light. "Just hold on, Da."

The next thing I know, I'm on the deck of the Storstad, Lucky's coat gripped in my fist, and a woman is splinting my leg.

I never saw him again. I never got to thank him. But I'm sitting here talking to you today because of Lucky Farrow. He saved my life, so he did.

I'm the lucky one, broken leg and all.

⤛ *Chapter Thirty-One* ⤜

I LOOKED AT STEELE. But I couldn't ask.

"When he heard I was returning to research in Liverpool," he said, "Sampson gave me Jim's coat and asked me to see it safe home to Jim's family along with Sampson's story and gratitude." He pulled the coat from his satchel and handed it to me. A woollen, double-breasted navy peacoat. No different from the hundreds roaming the Liverpool dockyard, really. Except this one was Jim's.

"I found the journal in the pocket," he added. "And I knew then he was the man you asked me about on the train."

I ran my fingers down the coarse wool. Speechless.

Steele flipped back through his notes. "The Farrows live at number six Gerrard Street. I was going to take it there tomorrow."

"Let me do it," I said. I wasn't sure who I'd find at number six. His mother. His wife. But I'd come too far not to see it to the end. And whoever opened the door deserved to be given such grief by someone who loved him, too. Not Steele.

He hesitated. Probably thinking of a lost interview opportunity.

"You can't use any of Jim's story in your article anyway." I raised my brow at him. "That was our deal."

Eventually, he agreed. With all I'd said these past days together, he had more than enough for his damned article. Jim was always so private, so secretive, I wouldn't let Steele turn him into a headline.

"Well, I guess that's it then." He seemed reluctant to leave. "Are you sure you're going to be all right?"

I nodded.

"I can stay if you want ... until Bates comes back."

"I'm fine. I'll be fine."

He seemed unsure. Almost deflated, somewhat. He was not the cocksure journalist who'd hounded me on the train, who'd bribed me with a dead man's diary, who was about to sell my story, my secrets, for a chance to make the front page and score a promotion to editor.

"Don't you have an article to write?" It seemed harsh, but I just wanted him to go. I needed to be alone. To grieve.

"I suppose I do."

We'd fulfilled the terms of our deal, traded our stories, and yet in a way, I felt emptier for it. I wondered if he did, too.

Jim's coat in hand, I followed Steele to the hall. He stopped on the threshold. "I'm sorry, Ellen."

For all he'd made me say? For all he was about to write?

He looked at me, his dark eyes sincere. "I'm so sorry for all you've lost."

"Thanks," I whispered, my chin trembling. "You know,

you are the only person who has ever said that to me." I only realized then how much I needed to hear it.

Unsure of what else to say or do, Steele nodded and left.

I shut the door behind him and rested my head on the wood. The last of the dying day's light spilled through the transom window in a skewed rectangle down the hall. Stepping into it, I slipped Jim's coat around a hanger and hung it on the empty coat stand. The broad shoulders spanned at eye level and it felt as if Jim himself were standing before me. I'd pictured him here a thousand times. How he'd look. How he'd feel. How he'd take me in his arms.

I slipped my hands along the coarse woollen shoulders and rested my face on the lapel. Closing my eyes, I breathed deeply. But it didn't smell of him anymore. The memory of Jim was long washed from it by the waters of the St. Lawrence. I ran my fingers down the arms and up the chest, its emptiness making me ache all the more.

This isn't Jim. He isn't here.

And will never be.

I saw myself in that instant, clinging to an empty coat in the dim hall of a house that wasn't mine to own, pining for a love I'd lost, a love that was truly never mine to keep. The absurdity of it, the unfairness, welled inside. As I stroked the fabric, a button came loose in my fingers and I looked at it sitting in my palm. A disc of blue-black pierced with four small holes. It had survived that dreadful night, ships colliding, boiler rooms flooding, men scrambling. It had clung to this coat through the madness of sinking and saving only to fall off at the slightest touch in this shadowy hall. Here in this moment, it let loose.

And so did I.

I cried for Jim. For Meg. For Aunt Geraldine. For my mother and father. For all our time that I'd wasted, for all I hadn't told them. That I loved them. That I needed them. That I missed them terribly. I cried for my daughter. For the time we never got to have. The tears finally came, unrelenting like a winter storm, and I buried my face in the lapel, wetting the wool of Jim's jacket with wave after wave of loss.

I don't know how long I stood there. But by the time I lifted my head, the day's light had died. In the dark of the cold hall, I turned my back into Jim's coat and wrapped the arms around me.

Both of us nothing but empty shells.

⊙ *Chapter Thirty-Two* ⊙

EXHAUSTED, I WENT TO THE KITCHEN to make myself some tea. Ever since I could remember, tea was how we welcomed, celebrated, or sympathized. For in any situation, even when we had no idea what to do, the best response was always: *I'll put on the kettle.*

I suppose there was something to be said for the ritual of it, that sense of doing something: boiling, steeping, pouring. I stirred in the sugar, tapped the silver spoon on the rim twice. Even now—the heat cupped in my hands, the fragrant steam, the sweetness and radiating warmth as I swallowed—it was far more than a hot drink, it was a cupful of comfort.

I took another sip and sighed, resting against the counter. As my hip touched it, something rustled in my pocket and I pulled out Aunt Geraldine's letter. In all the drama of the interview, what with telling of Declan and my daughter, and then reading about Jim's last night, not to mention the rush of emotion at touching his coat, I'd completely forgotten about the envelope I'd found on the windowsill.

As I opened it, I was surprised to see that she hadn't typed it. She rarely wrote anything by hand but our to-do lists, long inventories of orders and expectations for Bates and Meg. For me. God knows I'd been given enough of those. I'd know her flourish and strong slant anywhere. Her double lines under things for emphasis. It figured that even death couldn't keep her from ordering me about. I sighed.

My dearest Ellen,

This was different. Not a list, no, but a letter. 'Twas by her hand all right, yet even the loops and list seemed smaller, somehow. Feeble and frail.

I don't know how to begin. Imagine that.
After all the words I've penned, all the novels I've
written, I have writer's block ... now that it
matters most.

This wasn't the aunt I knew. She was never at a loss for words—and if she was, she'd never let it be known. My heart pounded as I read on, unsure of what I might find.

Before I say anything, I have to tell you that
everything I did, I did with your best interests at heart.
Please believe that. I know right now that might not
seem true. Perhaps you think me a heartless old witch,
and rightfully so, given all that I've put you through.

But I do have a heart and you've always had a special place in it.

I never told you I was ill. I didn't see the point in burdening you, but the doctor tells me I've only a few weeks left, if that. I had hoped to finish this blasted novel (you know how I hate leaving plots unresolved, and now I've left poor Garrett in the worst kind of peril), but more than that, I had hoped to resolve things between us. When you left this morning, I should have got up and seen you off, I should have told you all of this in person. I owed you that. But I am a weak old woman, Ellen. I am sorry. I just couldn't say goodbye knowing it was our last.

I watched you from the study window, saw you and Meg walking arm in arm down the path. It pained me to watch you go, but you were smiling. You seemed happier. I took comfort in knowing you'd changed.

I paused. So I had meant something to her. More than I realized. It warmed me to know it and I was thankful she'd voiced it—even if it came in a letter long after the fact.

You are not the same girl who stood shivering and desperate on my doorstep. Not the same one who came back raging from the asylum last November.

You are no victim.

If only she knew. That now I was also a victim of a shipwreck. Of a broken heart.

Every character learns his true strengths by facing those things that might kill him. And if he doesn't die at the hands of those dragons, he emerges stronger.

I made you face your dragons, Ellen. Even as I shied from my own. Hidden away in my tower, I wrote the adventures I longed to have. And though I know I'm no lion hunter like Garrett Dean, I do wish I'd had the courage to go there—to feel the hot African sun on my cheeks, to run my fingers through the red earth, to taste the sweetness of a fresh-picked mango and let its juice run down my chin. Things I read about. Things I imagined. Stories I never lived.

Yes, I made decisions for you—but they were not made lightly. The Magdalene Asylum. The Empress of Ireland. After much discerning, I put you into those situations because I believed you had the inner strength to face them. I knew you would overcome because you have not only your father's grit but also your mother's spirit. Her resilience. Her ability to find a glimmer of hope in a thick fog. You do have your mother in you. And I am so sorry if I ever let you think otherwise.

I thought of our argument the day she told me I was going on the *Empress*. Of the way we'd both used the memory of my mother to hurt each other; it would've saddened my mother to see it. But I took comfort, now, in knowing that I did carry her spirit with me.

I know you may have felt somewhat like a character that I manipulated and, in truth, I did, to some degree. But I want you to know that I do not write your story, Ellen. Neither does your father, nor the men you will love. You and only you write it.

And Steele, I thought, frustrated that I'd given so much of it to him. Who knew how he'd spin it—what level of detail he'd include. He had the power over how the world saw me now. And there was nothing I could do about it. The deal had cost me everything—and given me nothing, really. It had given me some answers, some details, but it hadn't given me what I really wanted. It hadn't given me Jim.

And now, it comes to this.
My solicitor, Mr. Cronin, will take care of my estate business, but I have one more thing I must do before my strength fails. I ask your forgiveness, Ellen. Yes, I took away your freedom when I put you in the asylum and again when I put you on the ship. For that I do not apologize. But I should not have taken your child.
She didn't die, Ellen. Your daughter lived.

My heart pounded as I lifted my eyes from the page. I reread it, just to be sure.

Your daughter lived.

I held her for a while the day she was born. She looked just like you did, with her thick, dark hair soft about her head, her tiny fists ready to take on the world. Maybe your mother would have made a different choice for you, but not ever having had children, I did what I thought best. I sent her to an orphanage. I wanted a fresh start for you both. Good Lord, you were only a child yourself. But I always wondered if I did the right thing. Even now, I don't know.

Hers is a story you are not a part of and will never know, so imagine one that gives you peace—that she is happy and healthy. That she is loved.

I debated whether or not I should tell you any of this. I feared knowing might make things worse for you. But after a long life dedicated to fiction, I now know the value of fact. Of truths. It's hard to tell and often difficult to hear, but it's part of your story and you deserve to know it.

You've grown into a strong woman, Ellen. Your father may not see it, but I do. You've made me proud. Your mother, too. And even though you've changed, somehow, you are the same little Ellie who perched on my windowsill, head full of dreams.

Write your story, Ellen, but more than that—live it, live every chapter. Don't be afraid to turn the page to new adventures. There are sure to be more dragons ahead, but as you face them, remember the ones you've

already overcome. Know that you are so much stronger
than you think. And years from now, when you reach
my age, when you reach your life's satisfying conclusion,
may it be with no regrets.

> *With much love,*
> *Aunt Geraldine*

I looked up from the pages into a different world. For
now, it was a world where hope and my daughter lived.

MY HEAD WAS ABUZZ the next few days. I could hardly think
straight as I sifted through all I had learned and sorted out
what to do next.

I had a daughter! She lived—but where? Aunt Geraldine
had neglected to tell me which orphanage. And even if I
knew, my daughter might well have been adopted by now.
How would I ever find her? Where did I even start?

And then there was Jim.

Knowing that he hadn't gone down with the ship rekin-
dled the flicker of hope that he'd survived. My greatest fear
had been that he went into the hold that night and never
came out. Now I feared that he had drowned after saving
William Sampson. But there was still a chance, a slim one,
that he had survived, that he had lived. Dare I hope that he
loved me, too?

I wandered the silent rooms, sat in front of meals but
didn't eat, lay in bed but didn't sleep. Poor Bates and Lily
didn't know what to do with me or for me. Though I hated

our deal at first, I had to admit I missed Steele, I missed his analytical mind. He knew how to ask those incisive questions. Surely he would've been able to help me figure this out, to find the answers within me.

And then put them in his article.

Who was I fooling? Steele had used me. He wrung my story from me. He wasn't coming back. He didn't care about me. All that mattered now was his article. His byline. His promotion. I'd traded my story for what—more questions?

I still didn't know where Jim was, whether he'd lived or died, or who he loved. No answers, really, just Sampson's transcript, a diary, and a coat.

I looked at it hanging where I'd left it in the front hall. At the button I'd left sitting on the end table next to me. And my aunt's dying words beside it.

What now? I wondered. *What now?*

∞ *Chapter Thirty-Three* ∞

"HERE WE ARE, GERRARD STREET. That's number six there."
Bates stopped the car in front of a housing row, a great long
stretch of brick broken up by a door, a window, a door, a
window, all the way down to the corner. A low wall ran the
length of them, with wrought-iron gates rusted half-shut.
The yards were dirt, no scrap of grass, never mind gardens.
Battered by the sea and the cost of life eked out upon its swells
and shore, everything this side of town seemed weatherworn
and tired, even the people walking past. An old man eyeballed
the car that clearly was not from around here.

Bates turned to me, resting his arm across the front seat.
"Are you sure you don't want me to go, miss? These are the
dockyards. The place, the people … they're a bit sketchy, if
you don't mind my saying."

The old me would have cowered in the car, but after life
on the *Empress*, I saw them for what they were. People. Sure,
they'd been roughened by hard work and hard times. Coarse,
perhaps, but sturdy and purposeful. Like the coat I held in

my hands. I knew these strangers, for they were stokers and firemen, like Jim, sailors and stewards, like Timothy.

"I'll be fine," I reassured him, sliding out of the car. "Wait here. I won't be long."

I stepped through the gate and up the stone path, forcing myself to reach the front door. To raise my knuckles to it. It had taken me a few days just to get the nerve to come. But I had no idea what to say. What was there to say, really? I hoped it was his mother I'd find here and not his wife. But either way, that woman deserved his story. Not my part in it, perhaps, but at least what he did for Sampson.

I knocked, then gripped my hands together under his coat draped over my arm. I'd put the journal back in its pocket, along with all the pages Steele had torn and the copy of Sampson's interview tucked between its warped covers. None of it was mine to keep. I'd even sewn the button back on this morning. It helped me keep my mind off Aunt Geraldine's letter and my daughter and the ache of wondering where she was—what she looked like. If she was all right.

"Yes?" A young woman my age opened the door. Tendrils of russet hair hung by her face from where they'd fallen free of her faded head scarf. She held a toddler on her hip, a girl whose chubby legs straddled the woman's apron. The girl peeked at me shyly from behind her blanket and my breath caught, for she had Jim's dark curls. His ice-blue eyes.

"Is this ..." I swallowed. "Is this the home of Jim Farrow?" I asked, hoping it wasn't, yet knowing it was.

"It is." The young woman's eyes searched mine, curious. "I'm Elizabeth."

"And I'm Penny," the toddler added. "Penny Farrow."

My heart sank. So it was true.

Elizabeth continued, "But he's—"

"I know," I cut in. I wouldn't make her say it. Bad enough she had to live with the loss. And I wouldn't steal what memory she had of him either. She could read the journal herself. Know that she was on his heart and mind that last night. "I worked—" She wouldn't have believed me a stewardess, not in these fine clothes, with my driver and car at the bottom of her lane. "I was on the *Empress*. They asked me to give you this." I handed her the coat and all its contents. "We just thought you'd want it. That you'd want to know."

"Oh, all right then." She took it in the crook of her arm, seemingly confused.

I stood awkwardly on the step of Jim's house.

"Umm ..." She looked at me expectantly. Then stood aside, opening the door a bit more. "Did you want to come in for some tea? Jimmy—"

"No, no," I interrupted. "Thank you ... but I can't stay." A part of me longed to sit at his table, in the heart of his home. To touch the things that mattered most to him. To hear her tell me of the man she knew. But I knew I couldn't do that to her. To me. I peered over her shoulder into Jim Farrow's life one last time, stopping my gaze at the toddler. I reached out and stroked her round cheek with the back of my fingers. "You have such a lovely smile."

Her eyes sparkled as her cheeks dimpled. So like Jim.

"Oh, she's the spit of her father, aren't you, poppet?" Elizabeth said. Then her voice dropped. "We lost him. At sea."

I nodded, surprised she was telling me what we both

knew. But grief had its ways. Perhaps she had to say it aloud, as I did to Steele. Perhaps this was the first time.

"How old are you, Penny?" I asked, changing the subject.

She held up two fingers. A year older than my daughter. I wondered what she looked like.

Does she have my eyes?

I don't even know her name.

"Do you have children, ma'am?" Elizabeth asked, noticing my expression.

I pulled my hand away and cleared my throat. I'd done what I'd come to do. There was no point in lingering.

"It was nice to meet you, Elizabeth," I lied as I turned away.

"I didn't catch your name," she called after me.

"Ellen," I said at the gate. "Ellen ... Ryan." It surprised me that I gave Elizabeth my ship pseudonym. Though I suppose it was the name of the stewardess who loved Jim. Of the girl I was before ships and lives and loves collided.

I stumbled into the car and Bates eagerly drove away.

It's what you wanted—to know for sure, I told myself as I leaned my head on the window. *Well, now you know.*

But finding out had hurt me more than I thought possible. Reality had, like the *Storstad*, burst through my fog. It pierced me at the heart, driving deep in my chest as the ache of cold truth rushed in.

He never loved you. No matter what you thought you felt or knew about Jim—it wasn't true. It wasn't real.

You are such a fool.

The only thing I knew for certain was that I never wanted to feel this way ever again. And as we drove down Gerrard

Street past the long row of anonymous doors, moving farther and farther from number six, I forced myself to let go of a lot of things. Jim's coat. His journal. His story. I'd left them all behind.

And Ellen Ryan, the girl I was, along with them.

∽ *Chapter Thirty-Four* ∽

BATES DROPPED ME AT THE PARK. I needed air. I needed to think. I needed answers.

My feet followed the footpath winding through the green fields, going around in circles as my thoughts did the same. Finally, I could walk no farther. I only wished my mind exhausted as easily. I veered off the path toward the bench overlooking the pond, still lost in worries when a voice interrupted me.

"I swear, you've done more laps than a racehorse." Steele. Both hands were clasped behind his head, his ankles crossed. Clearly he'd been sitting there just watching me running rings around him.

"I delivered the coat today," I said, wearily sitting beside him. It felt good to talk about it, even if it was with Steele. "Actually, I gave it to the *mother* of his *child*."

"Really?" He paused. "Sorry, I didn't know about that. Honestly. I would have brought it myself—"

"There's something else I have to tell you."

I thought of my daughter alive. Somewhere. Tomorrow was July 8. Her first birthday. I'd already missed so much. I looked at Steele. If anyone could find her, it would be him.

Did I really want him involved? We'd finally finished with all the *Empress* business. Our deal was done. Was there any point in telling him any more? Knowing him, he'd probably want a picture to go with his article, a great big eight-by-ten of the mother and child reunited.

Reunited.

The truth was, I'd do anything to find her, and what harm was there, really, in telling him about Aunt Geraldine's letter? He already knew the worst of it, that I'd lost my virginity to a scoundrel and my self-worth in the asylum. Why not tell him the rest?

"My daughter is alive." It felt so wonderful to say, I had to repeat it. "She's alive! My aunt told me in a letter. She didn't die, Steele."

"Really? That's great news, Ellen." He saw the expression on my face. "Or … is it good news?"

I told him what Aunt Geraldine had written, that they'd taken the baby and I'd no idea where. "I know our deal is done"—I turned to face him—"but if anyone can find information on my child, it's you."

Flattery, yes, and I hoped it might sway him, but I believed it, too. Steele was like a bloodhound. And I would know. Hadn't he tracked me across the ocean? Hadn't he dug up things I'd buried long ago? There was no misleading this dog once he had a whiff of something.

He stared off, lost in his thoughts. Perhaps he was wondering if he had the time. He must have had other stories on the go, other deadlines looming.

I gave him the scent of a reward. "We can ask her adoptive parents to let you take a picture of her and me together ... for your story. Imagine that, Steele."

A glimmer of something lit behind his eyes.

"'Surviving Stewardess Finds Her Long-Lost Child,'" I added, not caring if he told the world my sins and plastered my face all over the paper. Not if it meant finding my daughter. I just wanted to see her. To hold her, even once. To know that she was all right.

He hadn't answered me and I thought that perhaps he'd had enough of my story. Maybe he just wanted to be done with it. Maybe he had other women—other stories—to pursue.

"That night"—he turned, his eyes vivid—"what was the last thing Meg said to you in the water?"

"I don't know," I stammered, trying to switch tracks. "Something about promises she'd made to my aunt. About taking care of me—"

He nodded, leading me to it. "She kept that one. But what was the promise she broke?"

I closed my eyes and went back to that horrible moment when Meg slipped from me. Her voice echoing in my mind. "She'd promised to never tell me the truth. But then she said, 'Barnardo's'." I opened my eyes and looked at him.

"I'll bet your daughter is with the Barnardo family. Do you know them?"

Barnardo's. Of course! Not a passenger, not even a family, as Steele thought. But he was right. My daughter was there. I never made the connection before. Losing Meg like that had upset me. I didn't want to think about her last words. Her last breath. But with it, she'd been telling me where they'd taken my child.

"It's not a family," I said, my smile fading as the memory of the children surfaced. "It's an orphanage. Dr. Barnardo's Home."

I remembered seeing the Barnardo orphans standing on the Liverpool quay waiting for passage aboard the *Empress* during one of our crossings. It wasn't that they were so young, only nine or ten, if that. Or even that there were dozens waiting. Fifty at least. It was the white tags secured to their coats. I'll never forget the sight of them, labelled and left like luggage on the dock. It was only after that Kate told me how Barnardo's Home children often crossed aboard the *Empress*. And why.

"They are sent to work on farms in Canada," I explained to Steele.

"Like slaves?" he asked, incredulous. "This is 1914. Didn't we abolish that back in the 1800s?"

"They're more like indentured servants, really. They work to earn their freedom. But I suppose they haven't a say in it, do they?"

It had broken my heart to see the orphans. But it was nothing compared to the pain I felt now, knowing that, one day, my daughter would be standing dockside with her tag fluttering in the wind.

"Leave it with me," Steele said. "Give me a couple of days to do some digging. I'll find her."

Steele knew me, more than anyone else, even more than the man I'd loved. At that moment, the truth was that my only confidant, my only friend in all the world, was Wyatt Steele.

But I never quite knew what I was to him.

ᴓ *Chapter Thirty-Five* ᴓ

IT HAD BEEN A WEEK since I'd seen Steele and still there was no word. Bates told me I'd wear out the carpets with all my pacing, but what else could I do?

The knocker rapped and I bolted to the hall, sure it was him as Lily took an envelope and closed the door. Still, maybe he'd written me. Maybe he'd found her. But the message wasn't from Steele. Just a letter from Mr. Cronin, my aunt's solicitor, requesting my presence the following week.

THE HOURS DRAGGED ON AND ON, an endless vigil of waiting dawn to dusk for answers that never came. Day after day. Then finally, he called. "I've found her." Three small words and everything changed. All my pent-up worry, my deepest fears, all the anxiety that had been simmering all week bubbled over in tears. I couldn't speak.

"I've pulled a few strings," he said, "but we've got a

meeting with Mrs. Winters tomorrow morning. And your daughter, Ellen. She's going to be there, too."

I gripped the phone and nodded as the truths sank in:

My daughter is alive.

I know where she is.

I'm seeing her tomorrow.

The knowing I'd wanted for so long stirred up more questions. What does she look like? What will she do when she sees me? Will she somehow recognize me—from my months of carrying her? And if so, is there a place in her little soul that knows I gave her up? I hardly slept at all that night.

THE NEXT MORNING, against Bates's protests, I took Steele up on his offer to drive me to the Barnardo Home. And though I was tempted to sit in the back and treat him like what he was, a man working for me, I gave in and, instead, climbed into the front beside him. He teased me about that, about it being my first time sitting in the front seat. As if he should talk, the way he ground the gears and bucked forward.

"What is it with you people?" He slammed on the brake and shoved the stick hard. "Gears. Wheel. Drivers. You've got everything on the wrong side."

"I assure you, we've got it on the right side." Leave it to him to assume he was right and the whole country was wrong. "Maybe you're just a terrible driver."

Bates stood in the garden, anxiously watching us lurch by.

Steele waved enthusiastically as we passed. "I don't think your butler trusts me with you."

I chuckled. "It's the car he doesn't trust you with."

We drove for half an hour and then pulled over on a long stretch of road. Steele turned off the engine.

"What are you doing?" I glanced at the rolling fields. A few cows looked up from their pastures alongside. "This isn't the place, is it?"

He held out the keys. "Here."

I paused.

"If it's your first time in the front seat," he smirked, "I'm guessing you've never driven before."

"No," I conceded. "I haven't. But now is hardly the time to learn."

"Now is the perfect time. Just give it a go." He threw the keys up so that I had to catch them. Next thing he ran around the front and pulled open the passenger door.

"Get back in your seat," I ordered, even as he shoved in, forcing me to move. He laid his arm across the back of the seat and I edged farther away, shimming my legs past the gearstick and ending up right behind the wheel. "You said you'd take me to see my daughter."

"I said I'd *find* your daughter. And I did. *You* are going to get us there."

"I'm going to get us killed," I said. He had to be joking. "I'm not doing it."

I could tell by his face he wasn't giving in on this, the stubborn jackass. Well, neither was I. "I don't know the first thing about driving."

"Sure you do." He grinned. "Where do you put the key?"

"I know where I'd like to put it," I muttered, ramming it in the ignition.

He laughed. "There's the spirit."

Steele talked me through starting the car. The engine squealed a bit as I turned it too long. Easy enough, I suppose, but getting her started wasn't the problem. Clutch, brake, gas. Three pedals—not so many. I held down the clutch and brake as instructed.

"We'll take her nice and slow, keep her in first." He wobbled the shift and jammed it upwards. "Now take your foot off the brake and ease up on the clutch."

Even as I did it, I could feel the car moving forward and I slammed my foot down, jerking us to a halt. But on the next try, I let it go and we rolled along the gravel shoulder.

"Good," he said, a little smile tugging at his lips. "Now, how about we try the road?"

I turned the wooden wheel, too far at first, and we swerved out and back and out again before I wobbled us straight.

Driving! I am driving!

"Now give her a little gas," Steele suggested. "Not too much—"

The car leapt forward as I gunned it, and I braked a little overenthusiastically, slamming us to a stop, throwing Steele against the dashboard.

"See?" I turned to him, heart punching my ribs. What the hell was I doing? "I told you I can't drive! And now look what I've done. You're bleeding."

He touched his cut lip with his fingers, pushed his tongue against it, then waved it away. "It's nothing."

"I can't." I folded my arms and we sat in the middle of the road, engine idling. "It's too dangerous."

"Think of it as an adventure."

I didn't know what twists and turns the road might take

after it disappeared over the hill ahead. "It's too risky, Steele. I just can't."

"Ellen," he said, taking a deep breath, "there's a risk in every adventure. In not knowing where you might end up, figuring it out as you go along. That's what *makes* it an adventure."

I looked out my side window at the cows in the meadow, watching us as they chewed, indifferent to the drama on the road.

"So you get a fat lip," he continued, "so you make mistakes, so what?"

I turned back to him.

Already his lip had swollen like a bee sting in his sideways grin. "I still say, it's a hell of a lot more fun than idling away in the middle of the road."

This wasn't about driving. I realized it then. It was about taking control. About making a choice and moving ahead. How many ways, how many times had I let other people tell me what road I took? I'd always been a passenger in my life, at the mercy of someone else's plans.

No more.

"All right," I said, taking the wheel, heart still pounding from the rush of it all. "But I'm only driving to the edge of the town."

"No kidding," he laughed. "I may be adventurous, but I'm not suicidal."

DRIVING WAS MUCH EASIER than I'd ever thought once I got the hang of it. As planned, Steele took over when we reached the next town. A few streets in, we came to a large, three-storey brick house. The gardens and grounds seemed lovely as we drove through the gates and I wondered if those who lived inside them saw them the same way. As we entered, we passed a front office of sorts, where a receptionist sat at a desk.

"Wyatt Steele," he said to the receptionist. "Miss Hardy and I have an appointment with Mrs. Winters."

The receptionist led us to another room, where we sat in awkward silence like a pair of guilty schoolchildren in the headmaster's office.

Mrs. Winters entered the room and shook Steele's hand and mine before sitting at her desk. I could tell by her tight hair, her impeccable skirts, and her firm nod to us that she was a no-nonsense woman, much like Matron Jones. Neither paper nor pen sat askew on the blotter before her.

"So I take it you're the mother?" she said, as though continuing our conversation. Her stern look appraised me, but it was without judgment at least.

I nodded.

"This is highly unusual, Mr. Steele," she added. "But our board members feel that, given the reach of your newspaper, this kind of coverage might boost financial support. Assuming, of course, that you portray us favourably."

Steele smiled. "Absolutely. I've already done some preliminary research on Dr. Barnardo himself for a possible sidebar. Amazing man. Quite a legacy."

Mrs. Winters checked a paper. "I have the numbers you requested." She handed it to him. "By the time he died, the charity had founded ninety-six homes. That's over eight thousand five hundred children. And we're sending over a thousand a year to Canada as domestic servants and labourers." She handed Steele the page. "For the record, we check up on the children every three months to ensure they are being educated and disciplined as one of the family."

I didn't like the sound of that. What about being loved?

"We believe every child deserves a chance, the best possible start in life," Mrs. Winters added. Her eyes held mine. "Whatever the background."

For all that she knew, I'd given up my baby. Tossed it aside. "For the record," I replied, "I thought the child had died at birth."

"Yes, well." She clasped her hands on the desk. "All that matters now is that Faith is well. In fact, I'd say she's thriving."

"Her name—it's Faith?" I said, my voice a whisper.

"It was the name registered when she was dropped off."

I swallowed. "It's just ... Faith was my mother's name." It warmed me to think that for all she'd taken, Aunt Geraldine had given her that.

Mrs. Winters took up her pen and jotted on the file. "Named ... after ... maternal grandmother." She looked up as she returned the pen to its proper place. "It's always nice to know a little something like this. It means a lot to them when they are older. Now," she said, standing to escort us out, "I thought the gardens would be the nicest backdrop for your photo."

∾ *Chapter Thirty-Six* ∾

I SUPPOSE THE GARDENS WERE BEAUTIFUL—the tulips, daffo-
dils, roses probably all in bloom. I suppose the lawn was
tightly mowed beneath and the clouds probably loose and
lazy up above. I suppose Winters and Steele were there as
well—but all I saw was her. My daughter.

Faith.

She had dark hair, like mine, but cut short in a bob
pinned aside her brow with a white ribbon. Sunlight played
on her hair, giving her a shine around her crown like a halo.
She wore a simple frock, a cardigan overtop held closed by
one button. On her feet were white socks and boots. Walking
shoes they were, stiff as boards. She toddled about on her
chubby legs, one fist clasped around the fingers of another
woman who walked along beside. With her free hand,
Faith reached for a low-hanging rose blossom, determined
to get it. Even as the woman pulled back, Faith simply let
go and took a few staggering steps before plopping down
on her bottom and crawling toward it. Everything about

her amazed me. I could hardly breathe knowing this was her.

Faith.

"Oh, don't let her get grass stains on her dress, Anna," Mrs. Winters scolded the woman, who picked up the toddler and brushed her clean. "A dirty waif. Good heavens, how would that look? Not good. Not good at all."

She pointed to a wooden chair someone had set in among the flower beds. "Please have a seat, Miss Hardy."

Anna set Faith back on her feet and, taking one hand, turned her toward me. Faith's eyes were hazel, like Mam's, and I smiled as we met for the first time. Though, in truth, it felt more like a remembering. Faith squealed in joy at being back on her feet, waving her free arm about. I slowly held out my hands to her, terrified she'd shy away, or worse, cry. I couldn't handle that. As I'd pictured this moment over the past few days, her rejection was what I feared most. But Faith's face lit up as she reached for me, as we mirrored each other's delight. She let go of Anna's hand and took three or four steps to grasp mine.

"Hello, Faith—" My words caught in my throat, but neither of us needed them. I simply lifted her into my arms and her hands went round my neck. She rested her head on my shoulder, her hair soft and sweet against my face. I rubbed her back. Breathed her in. Felt her heart beating against mine. My daughter.

Steele took more photos than he'd ever need. A part of me wondered if he was purposefully dragging it out. He even asked if Mrs. Winters and Anna had some time for more follow-up questions.

"Do you mind if we take a bit longer, Ellen?" he'd asked, knowing I wouldn't. Then he led the women back to the office, giving me precious time with my girl.

Faith and I walked around the flower beds and played in the grass. I watched her explore, happy to share in her awe, seeing everything through her eyes for the first time. We knelt down as she pointed her chubby finger at a black-and-orange caterpillar. I picked it up and let it crawl on her arm. Both of us mesmerized by its rippling body, its shuffling legs. She looked at me in amazement, eyes asparkle, and I laughed, wondering—no, knowing—this was how my mother had felt about me.

"Look at the state of her," Mrs. Winters scolded when they returned an hour later, and I saw us as we were. Me and Faith, hand in hand, both of us green-kneed and dirty-elbowed. Smudges on our face. Our fingers filthy from where we'd run them through the earth.

Steele laughed and took another picture of us smeared and rumpled.

Mrs. Winters pointed her finger at him. "*That* one does *not* go in the paper."

"No." He smiled at me. "That one is for Ellen."

"It can't be time to go already," I said, sounding like a child myself. "We only just got here."

"It's twelve o'clock," Mrs. Winters said, not even needing to check the watch that hung from a brooch on her lapel.

"Can't we just have a little longer?" I pleaded.

"It's time for Faith's lunch," she said.

"Yes," said Anna, stepping forward and slipping her hands under Faith's armpits. As she lifted Faith up and settled her on her hip, I reluctantly let go of the small hand. "We should be getting home. You'll be wanting your nap soon."

I realized then who Anna was—not a nursemaid here at the house, but the woman who was raising my daughter.

"Did—" I could hardly get the words out. "Did you … adopt Faith?"

Anna smiled. "No, love, I'm her foster mother."

The only mother my daughter had known, really. Faith rubbed her eye with her grubby fist and rested her head on that woman's shoulder. The sight of it stirred all manner of feelings—tenderness, jealousy, and mainly anger. Anger that someone had taken what should have been mine. Robbed me of motherhood. Whatever her intentions, the truth was that my aunt had stolen this from me. I wanted to rip Faith from Anna's arms and run with her, run as far as I could.

Steele moved to my side and took my elbow, reading me as easily as one of his damn columns.

"Thank you for your time, ladies," he said, with his usual charm. They clucked some reply, but I didn't hear.

He pulled me forcibly away, for I would not move myself. How could I? How could I walk away from her—now that I knew she existed? Now that I'd held her. They'd taken her from me once, and it almost killed me. I couldn't let them do that again.

But what else could I do?

Steele navigated me down the path and into the car, where I sat, numb.

This can't be happening.

Circling to the other side, he slipped into the driver's seat and started the engine.

"It's what you wanted, isn't it?" he said to me as we started to pull away. "To meet her. To hold her."

"Yes," I said, sadly.

"She's in a good home, Ellen, with foster parents and three older children. I asked about all that. I thought you'd want to know."

I didn't reply.

"Not all foster parents are kind," he continued, "but Anna is. You know now that Faith is well cared for. Isn't that enough?"

"No," I said, as I watched my daughter being carried away in the arms of another woman. For no matter what Anna might give Faith, she'd never offer a mother's love. Steele wouldn't understand. I barely understood it myself. But I'd felt it in that moment in the garden. A fierce swelling of pride and awe, of protection, a love that would do anything for her. "She's *my* daughter, Steele."

We drove on in silence as the house disappeared from view.

"Maybe your aunt was right," he finally said. "Maybe the best thing you can do for Faith—is let her go."

I didn't want to hear it. Didn't want to consider that he might be right. Didn't want to remember that I had no way to support my daughter, or even a home to give her, for that matter. I had an appointment with my aunt's lawyer tomorrow. And then what? What then?

"Give her a chance at a better life with Anna or whoever might adopt her." He paused. "She won't miss you. She won't even remember you."

"I know that," I snapped, stung by the truth of his words. "But she's my daughter, Steele. How can I ever forget about her?"

I'd only just found her. And now I was losing her all over again.

∽ *Chapter Thirty-Seven* ∽

STEELE PARKED THE CAR and walked me to the front door. I wondered if this might be the last time I'd see him.

He handed me the keys. "I guess that's it, then."

"I guess."

I hadn't wanted his company, much less his friendship, and yet now, after finding and losing Faith all over again, I didn't want to let go of the only person who knew me. Though he'd bribed it from me, wrenched it from me at times, the truth was, Steele knew my story. All of it. The truth was, he was part of it now.

What does it matter? By next week, when that article runs, the world *will know my story.*

I had hoped for so many happy endings—that Jim would have survived, that Meg would come home, that I'd find peace after meeting my daughter. But I'd been denied every one.

And now Steele was leaving. And I'd be totally alone.

"Will you be all right, Ellen?" he asked, resting his hand on my shoulder. Even now he read me like a daily.

I shrugged. "I'm just so tired of goodbyes."

"Then let's not say it tonight." He lifted my face and searched for a smile. "I've got a few meetings in London the next few days for that army piece. Can I see you after that?"

I nodded. "I'd like that."

After Steele left, I opened the door, surprised by the smell of cigars wafting from within. The smell of my father. It unsettled me like smouldering hay would a filly. I wanted to bolt.

Aunt Geraldine will have a conniption, she never lets anyone smoke inside—

And then I remembered that she was gone, that the house was his, really. Or would be soon enough. He was, after all, her only heir. I wanted to face that fact as little as I wanted to face him. But as I entered the front room, there he was reading the paper. Little did he know, I'd be in it soon. His family's shame there in black and white for all to read.

"Father?"

He lowered the newspaper and took in the state of me, rumpled and dirtied. "Lily tells me you were out with a … gentleman." Already he'd written the story. Already he'd judged me, even before he'd accused. I hadn't seen him in nearly two years, and this is how he greeted me.

But I stood my ground. I had done nothing wrong. "A reporter, yes. From the *New York Times.*"

He snapped the paper and folded it twice. His disdain clear. "So, it appears you haven't learned your lesson, then?"

Aunt Geraldine was right. I wasn't the same girl I'd been nearly two years ago when my father had kicked me out. And my father was wrong—I had learned many lessons. One just then in that moment. I didn't need it—his approval. Even as I stood there, a right mess before him, I realized that I didn't care what he thought.

"What are you doing here?" I asked. For he hadn't even come to his own aunt's funeral. And if he'd known I was on the *Empress*, he'd never sent word to see if I'd lived or died. Not to me, anyway.

"Mr. Cronin advised me to come and oversee the settling of the estate." He drew on the cigar, reddening its tip.

Wasn't it just like him, to be interested now that money was involved. He was her only nephew. The sole heir. Of course he'd be getting everything.

"I've decided to let you come home, Ellen." He seemed to be revelling in his graciousness. He took out his cigar and stared at it. "Though, I can't say I forgive you."

"Forgive *me*?" I blurted. "You were the one who put me at the mercy of that … that scoundrel. I was sixteen!"

He glared at me. "Old enough to know better."

I wouldn't shy from his stern look. I wasn't a child anymore. "You used me as bait—as a bribe to sell your damn horses!"

Whatever he'd expected, this wasn't it. He froze, stunned, his mouth slightly open beneath his broad moustache, his cheeks reddening beside the white rolled ends. Even if I'd exaggerated, clearly some of it rang true.

"I never—that's preposterous—" He blustered about, searching for his own truth. Finding it, he pointed at me with two fingers, cigar wedged between them. "Whatever I do— or have ever done—is for the good of the farm. For you and your mother."

I folded my arms. His belief in that would never make it true. Not for me. Did he even notice that the farm came first? Was he even listening to himself?

"I came to you in trouble, Father." My eyes stung as I brought myself back to that vulnerable moment, but I wouldn't break, not now. "And you … you threw me out."

"What choice had I?" he demanded, bolting to his feet. He spread his hands like a priest at prayer. "What choice did you leave me?" In his mind, he'd been the victim. His pride. His name. It was never about me. Even now, it wasn't.

We stood in silence.

What more is there to say? Let him read about it in the papers.

As if sensing my resolution, he tried another tack. "I didn't come here to fight with you," he said, trying to gain control of things. "The fact is, this house will be sold. You can't stay here. You have no choice but to come home."

"And what about my daughter—*your* granddaughter?" Even as I asked, I knew his answer.

He blanched. "Aunt Geraldine said the baby died."

So he has been in touch with her.

His eyes searched the carpet for answers.

"Yes," I said, "she told me the same thing but I assure you, Faith, Mother's namesake, is very much alive."

Hope dared to glow inside me, burning brighter the more I drew upon it. We could live on the farm, Faith and I. I could give her the childhood I'd had. I could be the mother I'd lost. The horses, the gardens, the fields. Faith would love it there.

Uncertain, I looked at my father, trying to get a sense of him. He wouldn't do it twice, would he? Turn me away? I

244   CAROLINE PIGNAT

didn't want to ask for his help. I didn't want him to reject me once more. But I thought of Faith. I had to ask, for her sake.

"If I come home"—I swallowed, afraid to put my hopes on him again—"can Faith come, too?"

It could work, if he said yes. I could go back to Barnardo's and tell them I wanted my daughter. That I had a home and the money to raise her well, that I was ready to be the mother she needed.

But it all depended on his being the father I needed.

He blinked once, twice, a sure sign he was deliberating. I'd seen him do it a thousand times when faced with a deal. He'd weigh his options, his risk, his costs, and take the measure of the man before him. One more blink and I knew, his mind would be made up. He'd commit one way or another, and like a horse with blinders, he would see no other path. There would be no going back.

If only Mam were here. She'd always known how to sway him. He may well have been the head of the family, but she was the neck that easily turned him this way or that. In my heart, I knew she would've welcomed us with open arms.

My father blinked again, blind to the grey ash falling on the carpet, blind to any love for the daughter before him as he made his choice. "Absolutely not."

⊙ *Chapter Thirty-Eight* ⊙

WE SAT IN THE LEATHER WING CHAIRS on either side of the solicitor's desk, my father and I, as Mr. Cronin shuffled through my aunt's papers. Neither of us had spoken a word since last night. What more was there to say? Even now, as Cronin settled his round spectacles on his nose and muttered as he read aloud my aunt's bequeathing this and bestowing that to her nephew, I bristled at being here.

A part of me had wondered if perhaps she might have left me the house. I'd never considered it, but as I lay awake last night fearful for my future, and that of my daughter, I did dare to hope that maybe Aunt Geraldine had changed her will in the end. Maybe she thought I had matured. Maybe she felt I'd proven myself worthy. It wasn't probable, but ... *possible*, at least.

"And to my nephew, Joseph Patrick Hardy," Cronin droned on, "I leave Strandview Manor—"

My heart dropped.

"—and all of its contents, including the Ford automobile,

the antique clock, the ..." Cronin rattled down the long list. My father seemed smug, as though he'd just called my bluff and won at poker.

Is that why I was here? To see him win? So that he could rub it in and prove once and for all that he held the power?

"And to my grandniece, Ellen Geraldine Hardy," the lawyer continued, at the very bottom of the page, "I bequeath my piano and my literary legacy." He flipped the last page over and laid the will on the desk.

So that was it. She'd left me a piano I couldn't play and books I'd never read, a whole turret stocked ceiling to floor with African non-fiction and copies of her novels. Bloody brilliant.

"Are we done here?" I stood, for I could take it no longer.

"Oh, well, yes? I suppose—" Cronin dithered about. "Just sign here."

I did as he asked. Then turning my back to both men, I walked from the room, down the stairs, through the front door, and out onto the street. Unsure of what to do next, I simply stood on the sidewalk, heedless of the stream of people spilling either side of me. I needed air. Space. I needed to think. What now? What now?

As I looked up, I saw him watching me across the street from where he stood, motionless in a blur of rushing crowds. He wore a white shirt, sleeves rolled, a black cap on his head, suspenders holding up his brown trousers. He didn't smile or wave or move. He simply stared. And I at him.

My heart stopped.

Jim?

It couldn't be … could it?

I stepped into the street toward him, stopping as a bread van trundled by. For a moment, its hand-painted side blocked him from my sight. After it passed, he was gone—not on the curb, not in the shopfront doorways. He'd disappeared. I scanned the crowds flowing up and down on the other side of the road, the faceless strangers busy getting where they had to go, but Jim was nowhere to be seen.

And I wondered if I'd really seen him at all.

I gripped my head in both hands as a sob wrenched out. I'd already lost him twice. Once from this world, when he drowned. And then again from my heart, when I stood face to face with his wife and child. Hadn't I suffered enough? Why was my mind playing such wicked tricks on me now— conjuring his phantom? Making me see what wasn't there.

He's like old Ian's leg, I thought, unsure if I was hearing the voice of insight or insanity.

Even as a little girl, I had always been fascinated by Ian's wooden leg. I watched him muck out the stable, groom a horse, or shift a bale of hay, amazed that he could do the work of any man. Once, I asked to see and he pulled up his pant leg to the knee. He undid the leather straps and detached the wooden contraption from his leg. It both intrigued and horrified me to see the stump, pink and scarred, skin flapped and melted over an ending where there shouldn't be one. I couldn't take my eyes off it.

"I feel it now and then, my leg," he said. "The hairs moving on my shin. Sometimes I get an itch on my foot or swear I feel the grass tickling my toes. In those moments, I think I'm whole and I'd never believe otherwise, if I didn't look down and see it gone—if I didn't see what I'd lost with my own two eyes. Phantom limb, that's what they call it."

I didn't understand, not then. In fact, I wondered if he'd been kicked by the mares one too many times. But there in the front of the lawyer's, in the middle of the road, at the bottom of my hope, haunted by phantom loves and legs, I wondered if I truly had gone mad.

"Miss Ellen!" Bates put his arm around me and waved his hands at the cars honking. "What are you doing out in the middle of the road? Good heavens, you'll get yourself killed."

As he led me back to the sidewalk, I looked over my shoulder for the ghost of a man. Sure I felt Jim watching, even though my eyes told me differently.

I get it now, Ian. I know how it feels.

For when a part of yourself is taken, there are a million ways your mind wishes it back.

⤫ *Chapter Thirty-Nine* ⤫

MY FATHER DIDN'T STAY LONG. We avoided each other, taking our meals at different times; it wasn't hard in a house of this size. I retreated to the study, spent my days staring out the window at the people on the street. I dreaded the day Father would give Lily and Bates their notice. Didn't want to see him hammer the for-sale sign in the garden. Before he left, he reminded me of my only choice—to come back with him, provided I came alone. Provided I never spoke of Faith again. How was that a choice?

"I've business in Coventry for a few weeks. Then I'll be back to wrap things up here. You can stay until the house sells," he offered, as though he weren't throwing me out on the street. "But it's a valuable property. I can't see it staying on the market for long. Two weeks. Maybe three."

So I had my deadline. A part of me just wanted to crawl into bed, to burrow under the covers and never come out. It's what I would have done before. But I knew better now. Knew I deserved better, too.

I took long walks along the shore, mulling things over, the answer as distant as the horizon. I thought about it as I cleared out the hundreds of books my aunt had left me, her literary legacy, now sitting in stacked boxes by the door, waiting for Bates to drop them at the library. I'd painstakingly written "Donated by G.B. Hardy" on the inside cover of every one. I thought perhaps it might inspire someone else to write or maybe even to visit Africa. Aunt Geraldine would have liked that. But I kept her novels. And her typewriter—I couldn't bear to give it away. The vacant shelves circled around me, row upon row of them. Their emptiness mirroring my own. Mocking me.

What now? What next?

Without someone to please or serve, it all came down to one question: *What did I want?*

Always my thoughts came back to her. Faith. I wanted to be in her life. To see her grow. Even if I hadn't the means to support her, I had love to give her. Surely that counted for something.

I hadn't seen Steele in a few days. Perhaps I'd never see him again. He'd gotten what he wanted—my story. Why would he be back?

No, I couldn't wait for Steele's advice or Aunt Geraldine's to-do list. Nor did I want either. I couldn't wait for Jim's ghost, though I swore I felt him watching. And, above all, I would not wait until I had nowhere to go but my father's farm.

I slipped into the kitchen and lifted the car keys from the hook. The car wasn't mine to take, but I was only borrowing it. I'd be fine on my own, as long as I took it slow.

The road to the Barnardo Home seemed longer that day

and I wondered if I was even heading in the right direction. Eventually, I recognized the long stretch of road where Steele had thrown me the keys. It wasn't much farther. After a few more miles and turns through town, I rolled up the gravel driveway. Faith wasn't here. I knew that. But this time, it wasn't my daughter I'd come to see.

Would Mrs. Winters see me? And if she did, what then?

I killed the engine and sat in the car for a few minutes.

What's the worst that can happen? I asked myself, envisioning it.

That she laughs at me?

No, Mrs. Winters was not that type. I wondered if she ever smiled.

That she tells me I can never see my daughter again?

That was what I feared most. But doing nothing to stop it, nothing to change it, only ensured it would happen.

I won't give Faith up again. The first time, I never had a choice. But I do now.

I opened the door and made myself walk the footpath to the front step. Made myself enter and ask for Mrs. Winters. I sat nervously on the edge of the waiting-room chair for what seemed like hours. With no appointment, who knew how long it might take. But I wasn't leaving until I saw her. I'd made that clear.

I still didn't know a lot of things: where I'd live, how I'd make it work. But I knew who I was and what I truly wanted—and I needed to say it.

"I'm Ellen Hardy," I said, standing as Mrs. Winters finally entered the waiting room. I held my head high. "I am Faith's mother."

"Is this about the article for the newspaper?" she asked.

"No." I cleared my throat. "I just want to see my daughter again ..." My voice drifted off. I wasn't really sure what to ask or how this wish might be possible. I just knew I wanted it.

"Come with me." She led me into the office where I'd first met her with Steele, but she was not the stern matron now; her demeanour had softened.

"I must admit, Ellen," she said, lifting the teapot from the side table and pouring the steaming liquid into two china cups, "I assumed your only interest in Faith was that Mr. Steele thought it would make a good photo opportunity. She'd been here a year and you'd never tried to contact her before. Never even asked how she was faring."

"They took her from me right after she was born. I never even got to hold her, Mrs. Winters. As I said before, they told me she'd died," I explained, ashamed to think that I'd believed their lies. But why wouldn't I? "I never knew she lived ... and now that I do, I need to be a part of her life."

Mrs. Winters considered me for a moment. "Do you have the means to care for her?" she asked, cutting to the heart of it. "A job? A home?"

I shook my head, worried she'd take the hard line. That it was all or nothing.

"I see. Well, you're not the first unwed mother, and I daresay, you won't be the last." She handed me the steaming cup. "Many, like you, want to be with their children and simply can't because of their circumstances. It's hard to raise a child on your own. Especially for a young mother like yourself."

Hard? It terrified me. I edged the trembling cup onto her

desk and looked down at my empty hands. *So this is it. This is where she tells me I can't.*

"But," she continued, "that doesn't mean it is impossible …"

I glanced up.

She paused. "I don't suppose you've had any training as a domestic servant?"

I told her of my experience as a stewardess aboard the *Empress*. I even told her of my life at the Magdalene Asylum, my aunt's passing, and my father's ultimatum. She swallowed it all with a sip of her tea, and I realized she'd probably heard similarly tragic stories from countless other women. That for her, my story had none of the sensationalism Steele craved. It simply was what it was. Backstory. What concerned her now was what happened next.

After weeks of Steele making me look back, it felt liberating to finally be looking forward.

"It is not our intention to separate mother and child. In fact, I believe that relationship is integral to both." She looked at me with such understanding. "Dr. Barnardo developed a plan for women in your exact situation. With your experience you'd have no trouble being hired by an approved employer, and there are many in the Liverpool area. We'd board Faith in a home nearby, closer to you."

I nodded in relief. The car wasn't mine to take and travelling this far to visit Faith was simply not possible.

"She'd be fostered within walking distance of your employer. You'd pay half of Faith's fostering from your wages and our benefactors would cover the rest. Five shillings a week."

"Would I see her?" I asked.

"You could visit with Faith during your time off."

I could hardly believe it. It wouldn't be easy for Faith or for me—uprooting her from Anna's home, the only home she'd ever known, labouring long days for a glimpse of her now and then—but it was something. It was a start.

"Thank you," I said, my heart and eyes brimming with hope. "For doing this."

"We're only the trellis," she said. "A support for those in need."

I took out my hankie but decided not to dab at the tears. For the first time in a long time, they'd sprung from joy and, unashamed, I let them run free.

"How your rose fares, if it grows, if it blossoms, is entirely up to you," Mrs. Winters said, reaching over and squeezing my hand. "And it's my hope that in time, you and Faith won't need us at all."

∞ *Chapter Forty* ∞

WITHIN THE WEEK, Mrs. Winters had secured both a new foster home for Faith and a new job for me. I worked as a housemaid for the Morgans, a wealthy family on the far side of town. It was a good hike from Strandview Manor, but who knew how much longer I'd be able to stay at my aunt's house? Who knew how much longer any of us had? I'd broken the news of my father's plans to Bates and Lily. I owed them that at least. Knowing Father, he'd return and toss them out with no notice at all. They were dismayed, but not surprised. Lily would be fine—a young girl like her would have no trouble starting over. But I worried about Bates. Looking back, I realized that he'd been more like family to me than my own father. When I grieved my mother and, years later, my child, it was Bates who listened, who told me things would get better. Bates who picked me up from the asylum and, most recently, from the docks. Bates who'd been my rock during Aunt Geraldine's funeral and all the aftermath. In his simple, steadfast, and quiet manner, Bates had always been there for me. How could I let Father just turn him out on the streets? But how could I stop him when I was powerless to prevent him from doing it to me, too?

As I child, I had visited the Morgans with my aunt, though I doubted they remembered me. I was not G.B. Hardy's niece to them, just the maid from Barnardo's. To Colonel Morgan, I was merely a new name on his ledger. Lady Morgan seemed far too busy planning her luncheons and fundraisers to give me more than a once-over when I appeared for the interview. She'd skimmed my letter of reference from Mrs. Winters. "I told them I'd take you on as a maid, but you can't live here." She did not remember having met me before. But I wondered if her daughter did.

Charlotte Morgan had always been a bit of a snob. It didn't matter that she had a dozen designer dresses, a concert pianist as a tutor, or a powerful father who moved in all the right political circles. What mattered most to Charlotte was that everyone knew it. I remembered meeting her just once, when we were ten, at a fundraiser for African charities held by her mother. My aunt was the guest speaker.

"Did you not know it was a formal event?" Charlotte had asked, eyeing the dress I'd found perfectly acceptable, until then. Suddenly, next to Charlotte's flounces and bows, mine seemed shabby. Even my hair felt flat and lifeless beside her crown of ringlets, each a perfect gold spiral. "Mother ordered this dress especially from Paris for today." She smoothed her hands over the skirt. "It cost over six pounds."

The ridiculousness of it struck me. "How much?"

"Almost seven pounds," she repeated, revelling in the

wonder of the girls gathered around us, their fingers itching to touch the fabric.

"Didn't your mother just say in her speech that six pounds was enough to feed a whole village for a week?"

The girls around her gasped; suddenly the dress they desired seemed frivolous and wasteful. Like wildfire, red rushed across Charlotte's cheeks and down her neck. It smouldered under her new pearl necklace and burned right up to the tips of her earlobes where the matching earrings dangled. I didn't stay long at the event. My aunt gave a short speech on her research about African culture and, in Aunt Geraldine form, excused us. No doubt she wanted to retreat to her study as soon as possible. But I'd felt Charlotte's hateful gaze on me the entire time.

I felt it on me even now as I dusted her father's hunting trophies. I wondered if she knew me. If she remembered. And all the ways she might make my life more difficult for it.

I needed this job. With only a few days left before my father kicked me out, a daughter to support, and room and board to pay once I found suitable lodgings, I had enough on my plate without Charlotte. I had no time for a foolish girl's drama. So during that first week, when she demanded I make her bed again *properly*, or re-iron her skirts, or even pay for the cup she'd broken because I'd left her tea on the wrong side table, I thought of Faith, I closed my mouth, and I did what Charlotte asked.

All the while, Kate's words to me on that first day aboard the *Empress* echoed in my mind. *First-class daughters are rich, spoiled brats who speak of nothing but clothes, hair, and dresses.* A stereotype, for sure. But one that Charlotte embodied. I'd known many first-class people on the *Empress*, and liked most. But I'd never like Charlotte. Not because of her class, but because she was simply a first-class brat.

The days of that first week were terribly long and the work was hard, but Monday was my day off and I was taking Faith for the afternoon. Our first outing together. Alone.

I knocked on the front door, the address tight in my other fist. Faith's new foster family, the Buckleys, lived down by Gerrard Street, an hour's walk from the Morgans, but the neighbourhood seemed a world away. I could hear the gulls calling from the nearby shore and planned to take Faith there, show her how to skip stones, how to find a world in a tidal pool and a kingdom in a pile of sand. The door opened and a scrawny boy of about five stood on the other side, his matted hair like an upturned nest on his head. He wiped his runny nose with the back of his hand, smearing mucus across his grubby cheek.

"Get away from the door, Daniel! Haven't I told you never to answer it?" A wiry woman gripped his ear and yanked, dragging him aside. He yelped and squirmed but her pinch held fast. No wonder the poor lad's ears stuck out like open doors on a Ford. She finally let go and he scurried down the hall. "And tell your brothers I'm still waiting on that firewood. Lazybones the lot of you! You'll get no supper if that fire goes out!" she yelled after him before rolling her eyes at me, as though I were in agreement. She dried her hands on her skirts. "Honestly, these kids'll be the death of me."

I wondered if I had the right house, and worried that I did.

"I'm Ellen? Ellen Hardy?"

"Oh right, right. Faith's mother. Is that today?" She put her head behind the door and yelled for another child before turning back to me. "Mrs. Winters did say that you would be settling your half on your visit." She forced a smile. It lacked warmth as much as teeth.

"Oh, right." I took the money from my pocket and handed it to her. As I'd walked here, wages paid, I'd felt proud of myself for working so hard, for providing even a little for my daughter. But something about this exchange with Mrs. Buckley felt sordid and tawdry. As though I were renting my own child. How much of this money was going toward Faith's care, really? Would it make any difference to that empty pot over the cold hearth? To her dirty clothes?

"How many children do you have, Mrs. Buckley?" I asked, as she counted the coins.

"Five boys," she said. "And four girls from the home." She glanced at my surprise. "But I love them all like they were my own, of course."

I thought of the way she loved Daniel.

"Get a move on, Alice. We haven't got all day!" Mrs. Buckley hollered down the hall. "And you've to get to the market for me, yet." A young girl, about ten or so, appeared at the doorway half as dirty as the lad and twice as tall. In her thin arms she carried Faith.

Faith seemed as happy as ever, if not as clean. Not that I minded the dirt of childhood—hadn't I let her get mucked up and grass stained on our last visit? But something told me this dirt was not from fun. Where Anna had tied Faith's hair in a white bow, Mrs. Buckley had left it loose, uncombed, and Faith chewed on a piece of it as she tried to pick a button off Alice's dress. She'd been fed at least, for some oatmeal had hardened in her hair and dried upon her cheek. Her white dress and cardigan were replaced with a cotton smock, grey from being washed out and handed down one too many times.

"Did you not think to clean her face, Alice?" Mrs. Buckley raised the corner of her apron to her mouth and spit on it. She wiped my daughter's cheek, much to my disgust and Faith's, who squealed in protest.

"There now, pet," Mrs. Buckley said. "Is that better?"

I'd only been a mother for a short time, really, but already the guilt of it weighed upon me. How could I have taken Faith from Anna's care only to leave her here? Mrs. Buckley probably wasn't a bad person, not if she'd passed the fostering interview; surely the Barnardo Home had their standards. But the truth of it was, she was as rough and weary as the hand-me-downs she washed. I'd spent my week's wages to give my daughter this shabby life and, sadly, it was the best I could do. I felt guilty that Faith lived here, guilty that I'd taken her from the only woman she'd known as her mother. No doubt she pined for Anna. But most of all, I felt guilty that I couldn't be the mother she needed.

But when Faith smiled and reached for me, none of that mattered.

FAITH AND I SPENT OUR FIRST AFTERNOON together on the boardwalk. All along the strand, families pitched parasols and beach blankets. Children waded, pants rolled to their knees, as they searched the shallows for shells or scooped buckets of water to fill their newly dug moats. I glanced at the other mothers calling in their little ones to gather round wicker baskets laden with sandwiches and flasks of milk. I'd come empty-handed. It hadn't even occurred to me to bring a snack, a ball, or even a blanket. The excitement of seeing Faith, of having time with my daughter, had taken over my thoughts.

Next time. I stroked her head, smiling at the thought that there would be a next time. Many more next times.

We stopped to rest on a bench and I sat as Faith toddled about picking up pebbles and putting them in a row along the faded wood.

I have my daughter. And, I've got a job. Faith and hope.

… and love?

I glanced down at the seat where lovers had carved their initials and thought of Jim. Of our names, carved together and lost forever to the murky depths.

I thought of Steele, of the article he'd no doubt finished by now. His name and mine, together in black and white. Our deal was done. I'd probably never see him again. Though the thought of seeing that article made my stomach lurch.

Jim's love. Steele's friendship. Stories that might have been.

⤫ *Chapter Forty-One* ⤫

I WORKED HARD FOR THE MORGANS over the next week. I tried to serve them as Meg had served me, efficiently, quietly, anticipating every need. I'd come far since my early stewardess days. So it surprised me when Charlotte's keen eye pointed out streaks I'd left on the front-hall mirror. I was sure I'd left it sparkling. The next day, Charlotte brought me a mud-splattered slip. "You dropped this when you took the washing off the line. Wash it again and try to be more careful."

Had I dropped it? I wasn't sure. I admit, I often got distracted by thoughts of Faith, of losing my home, of worrying about where I'd live next. But was I letting it affect my work? Whatever was going on, I couldn't lose this job. I did everything I could to keep it. But as the complaints racked up, it was becoming clear to me that Charlotte was doing everything she could to get me fired.

Ironically, the more Charlotte complained about me to her mother, the more Lady Morgan took me under her wing. She loved to pull me from my duties and brag to her tea party about how well I was doing, how far I had come, how greatly I'd improved under her direction. "I'll make something of her yet," she'd say, clearly refusing to see that I was something already. To her, I was not only a maid, but a project, of sorts.

She seemed overly committed to proving I was an exceptional maid, whereas Charlotte had fully committed to proving I wasn't.

"Ellen, will you come do my hair?" Charlotte called from her room the next morning. I wondered why she asked for me and not her lady's maid, but I obeyed, careful to curl and pin each lock perfectly so she'd have nothing to complain about. Surprisingly, she loved it. And that made me even more suspicious.

"Fetch my pearls, will you?" She spoke with the voice of a stage actor, projecting it loudly even though I stood beside her. I searched the vanity and the jewellery box, but they were nowhere to be seen. "What? They're missing? But I always leave them on my vanity," she proclaimed, yet she never even glanced at the tabletop. She waved me away, but I wasn't long at my dusting before Lady Morgan summoned me to her parlour. Charlotte stood behind her mother's chair, as always, but this time, she looked triumphant. Wickedly so.

"You sent for me, Lady Morgan?" It was only as I folded my hands in front of me that I felt something in my apron pocket. I didn't have to see it to know it was Charlotte's pearl necklace, the one she'd obviously slipped into my pocket while I did her hair. The one she was clearly about to accuse me of stealing.

"Oh, Miss Charlotte," I said, as if only just noticing her there. Before Lady Morgan could ask, before Charlotte could accuse, I reached in my pocket and pulled out the strand. "I found this under your bed when I was making it just now."

Her furious look said it all.

"There, you see, Charlotte?" her mother tut-tutted. "You've always been such a careless girl."

"*I'm* careless?" Charlotte blurted. "Don't you know who she is? Don't you know what she's done? Ellen Hardy, Miss Hardy's niece. Little miss high and mighty, and look at her now—a maid. With a *child*!" Her eyes flashed at me once more. "You don't do a very good job of hiding your dirty secrets, Ellen. Particularly, when you parade them up and down the boardwalk."

So she'd been spying on me. Let her. I had nothing to hide anymore.

"Well, of course, I know, silly girl," her mother chided. "Where do you think I hired her? She's one of those … Barnardo mothers." She said it as though the words themselves were bitter. "But I can hardly head the fundraiser and not have one in my employ, now, can I?"

Lady Morgan may have been a benefactor of Barnardo's; she no doubt gave the organization significant amounts of her money and time. A small price to pay to keep up her charitable image. Too bad she hadn't learned that compassion was free.

I bit my tongue as Lady Morgan dismissed me. Charlotte followed me out and cornered me in the hall. "You and your little bastard might be mother's favourite charity case right now, but not for long. And then you'll be out on the street.

There are a hundred other sad cases knocking on her door, just begging for her attention."

"Like you?" The words popped out before I'd even fully thought them. They shocked me almost as much as Charlotte, and I left her standing there with her mouth gaping like a fish's.

I still had a job with the Morgans—but not for long. Not if Charlotte had anything to do with it.

August 1914
Liverpool

∽ *Chapter Forty-Two* ∽

I LIVED FOR MY AFTERNOONS WITH FAITH. I could handle a hundred of Lady Morgan's lectures or Charlotte's temper tantrums if it meant I could keep having time with my daughter. I wasn't sure what would happen if, or when, Charlotte got me fired. Would Mrs. Winters give me another chance? I didn't care if I lost the job ... but would I lose Faith, too?

She stood at the water's edge throwing pebbles into the surf, cheering herself on with every *kerplunk*. It seemed she'd throw every stone upon the beach before she'd ever tire of it, but soon enough she was content to wade in the shallows, her toes like pink pebbles sinking in the sand as the water ebbed and flowed around her ankles. I wondered if this was her first time in the sea.

I'd been worried that I wouldn't know how to mother, but wanting to protect her, to care for her, to make sure she was happy and healthy, it both pleased and surprised me how natural mothering felt. Loving her took no effort.

"Faith, come eat." She toddled up the pebbled beach to where I sat on the plaid blanket a few feet away. I held out the sandwich and she leaned in to take a quick bite before dashing off, cheeks chocked, to splash some more. Lily had made us a picnic lunch—cucumber sandwiches, apples, and cheese, even little jam tarts. A last supper of sorts, I suppose, for today was Lily's last day at Strandview Manor. I felt sorry to see her go, but my thoughts were overshadowed by the fact that my last day there was coming soon, and who knew when I could afford such a lovely spread again.

Though the house had not sold, there'd been several buyers interested. No doubt, my father would be back any day to wrap things up. To toss me out. I still had no idea where to go. Faith waded out a bit farther, the sunlight playing on her hair as the waves tugged on the hem of her skirt. The wind picked up, and with it the waves grew. "Not too far, now," I warned. I'd been looking at boarding houses this past week, but it was hard to find a suitable one close to both my work and my daughter. And it was impossible to consider that in the near future, I might have neither.

Unsettled, I turned aside to pour myself some tea from the flask, only to spill it all over my hand and lap. It burned, still kettle hot, and I gasped, tossing cup and flask aside, spilling tea all over our lunch. It soaked into the blanket, turning the few triangles of sandwiches into a soggy mess.

Bloody brilliant! I cursed myself for being so careless.

"Oi!" a man's voice shouted urgently, and I looked up to see Faith, waist deep, a wave bearing down upon her.

I'd only looked away for an instant. Just a few seconds.

But a moment is all tragedy needs. I knew that more than anyone.

Time slowed, playing every detail like frames in a film. The wave looming. Water crashing into my daughter, washing over her. Faith's dress like a white life vest against the dark. Her pink arm flailing. Her panicked face wide-eyed and going under.

Like Meg's.

Stones rolled like marbles beneath my scrambling and I stumbled as I ran the few feet between us. Those short seconds, that short distance, seemed to last forever.

The undertow pulled Faith's little body farther out, tumbling her head over heels. She hadn't come up yet. The man splashed into the water as I reached it, his hand already on my daughter, even as I grasped for her. He scooped her up and turning from me, ran back and laid her on the shore.

"Faith!" I screamed, hovering over them, sure I'd lost her. Her hair stuck across her face like blackened seaweed. Her eyes were closed. Skin, grey, and lips, blue-white—as still as the stones she lay upon.

I moved to pull her to me, but the man held out his arm, keeping me firmly behind as he bent over her to listen to her tiny chest. He sat up and kneaded it with the heel of his hand, like a round of dough. I wondered if it would ever rise again.

Dear God, not Faith. Not Faith, too.

"Wake up, love," I cried. "Come on, Faith. Wake up!"

After seconds of eternal silence, water spurted from her slack lips and Faith coughed and gasped. The man lifted her to his shoulder, patting her as she heaved and gagged. "That's it," he said. "A nice deep breath now."

I moved behind him, stroking her face in my hands as she gasped between retching. Breathing with her. "Breathe, love. Big breaths." She coughed once more and then started to cry, the sound of it as joyful to me as the day I first heard it.

He turned to give her to me, then, and I saw the face of the man who'd saved my daughter's life. A face I'd never forget. The man who gave my daughter back her breath and now took away mine.

For I was looking into the face of Jim Farrow.

⬿ *Chapter Forty-Three* ⬿

JIM TOOK MY ARM and helped me up the beach as I carried Faith. I felt as though I'd seen a ghost. But as he took up our blanket and wrapped it around me, his arms, his warmth, felt real enough. I slipped Faith's sodden smock over her head and sat on the ground, bundling her tight in the blanket, as if to protect her from a world of danger. But she fought her way free and reached for the jam tarts. She was shaken yet fine, thank God.

But not me. I wrapped her again and stood in my wet clothes, trembling from the shock of what I'd nearly lost. Of what I'd found.

"You're alive?" It seemed such a ridiculous question. For there he stood before me. The amazement at seeing him, the relief of it, was soon washed over by a wave of anger. "Why didn't you tell me? Why didn't you find me? For the love of God, Jim. All this time I thought you were dead!"

But why would he come to me? Hadn't he a wife and child of his own?

"I tried to, Ellie—"

My heart ached as he said my name. I thought I'd never hear it again.

"I went to your work, but the … the man at Strandview Manor said Ellen Ryan didn't work there anymore."

I lowered my eyes. *Oh, Jim. I never even told you my real name.*

"Is Faith … is she your daughter?" he asked.

I paused. I'd never told him about that story, either. About the farm, and Declan, and the Magdalene Asylum. "Yes," I said, ashamed, but not of her, only of the fact that I'd kept it secret from the man who meant the most to me.

He clenched his jaw, seeming angry himself. "And the father?"

"Her father is out of our lives." I looked at Faith. "All we have is each other."

He considered this for a moment. "I can't believe you never told me."

This from someone who'd clearly done the same?

"Don't judge me, Jim." I met his eyes. "You have your secrets too, don't you? All those nights at the rail, all the things you never said." Now it was his turn to look away. "I read it in your journal."

"You read my journal?" He ran his hand through his hair, flustered. "That was private. How did you even—"

"I got it from the reporter who interviewed William Sampson. It was in your coat—the one I brought back to *your family*."

I paused, hoping he'd deny that they were. But he didn't.

"Do you know how hard that was for me? To read about her, how she haunts your dreams, how you long for her? Even on that last night, Jim, when you kissed me. I read what you'd written moments before. How you'd decided to tell her everything and ask her to be yours." My voice rose as it spilled out of me, all that hurt and betrayal.

"Who?" He stood before me dumbfounded.

He should know. He'd *written* the bloody words!

"The one from your journal? Long dark hair? Red ribbon?" How dare he deny it.

A glimmer of recognition dawned in his eyes. "It's not what you think, Ellie."

I pressed on. "Do you know what it was like to have her open the door and stand there with your child?" The pain of it still ached. I'd buried it deep, thought it was past, and it surprised me how fresh it still felt.

"What in the hell are you talking about?"

"I'm talking about Elizabeth and Penny."

He blinked and frowned, puzzling it through. After all the ways we'd withheld our truths, I couldn't believe we were doing it still.

"The *mother* of your *child*?" How dare he deny it even now. "Your family, Jim."

"What ... Libby? Do you mean Penny and Libby?" He shook his head. "Christ, Ellie, they're my *sisters*."

I paused. That was not what I'd expected.

Could it be true? I was terrified to let myself think it. To trust again. "Well ... then ... who were you writing about that last night, about the ring and telling her everything and—"

"You!" he blurted. "Damn it, Ellie ... it was always you."

My heart flapped inside me, my truth bursting to be free. *Say it. Say it now. Tell him how you feel.* I took a breath.

"But I don't deserve you," he continued, and I closed my mouth. "Not after all I've done."

"What?" I wanted to tell him how much he meant to me. But I knew he needed to be honest first. This was it. His moment of truth. Would he say it? Would he trust me with that secret? "What did you do?"

"I—" He looked at me with such anguish in his eyes. "I—" He paused and slumped, defeated under the burden of his shame. "I can't, Ellie. I just can't talk about it. I'm sorry."

Without another word, Jim turned and walked away, just like he had in Quebec. No matter how much he said I meant to him, he would not tell me his story. And, unlike Steele, I had nothing to give that might persuade him. Except my love.

I guess it just wasn't enough. I wasn't enough.

I stood on the shore, Faith at my feet, and watched Jim Farrow leave me. Again. The pain of it as fresh as the day in Quebec. As the night on the *Empress*.

Maybe he is right, I thought, watching him walk out of my life, a lone figure walking the rocky shore. *Maybe it's better this way. Because if this is love, I want no part of it.*

It just hurts too much.

BY THE TIME I'D DROPPED OFF FAITH at the Buckleys' and walked the many blocks back to Strandview Manor, I was spent. Overwhelmed, really, by the day I'd had. Maybe that's why the for-sale sign in the garden upset me so.

I turned my back to it as I entered the gate, choosing instead to focus on the roses. I cupped one in my hand, marvelled at the layers of pink-tipped petals circling the still-blooming bud. Closing my eyes, I leaned in and inhaled deeply, holding its sweetness inside me. But I couldn't keep it. Any more than I could keep the flowers from fading. Sighing, I let go of the breath and blossom, thinking of Mrs. Winters's trellis.

What good is a trellis if the whole garden is being sold out from beneath you?

Father's ultimatum. Charlotte's hatred. Mrs. Buckley's negligence. Jim's secrets. Steele's article. All of it threatened the life I was working so hard to build.

Bates met me by the rose bush. We stood in silence for a few moments, just taking it in—hydrangea, lupins, pansies, and roses of every colour. A garden that would soon be someone else's.

I sighed. "Is it supposed to be this hard, Bates? Life?"

"Oh, it's work, right enough," he said. And didn't he know it. The man had worked tirelessly for decades. "But it's always full of surprises, too, isn't it?"

I thought of the many surprises I'd had just in these last few hours.

"Did you have a good picnic with your daughter?" His old blue eyes crinkled in the corners as he smiled. "I bet she loved the jam tarts."

I laughed at the memory of chasing after her as she bolted free, naked and filthy with jam and sand. Her joy in that moment. Despite the terrible experience she'd had only ten minutes before, she'd already let it go. Not that she hadn't learned from it. Faith was very cautious as I brought her to the water's edge to wash her down. But the trauma had not kept her from splashing again—or from making the most of a jam tart. Her resilience amazed me. It inspired me.

"You should've seen her," I said. "Jam from her head to her toes."

He laughed.

"Thank you, Bates," I said, thinking of all we'd weathered together. "For … well, for everything."

He laid his thick-knuckled hand on mine and squeezed.

"Oh, I nearly forgot." He pulled an envelope from his pocket and handed it to me. "Mr. Cronin dropped this off while you were out."

I figured it was routine paperwork from the will reading, but when I opened it I found a cheque. A large one. I looked up at Bates in shock. "What—what is this?"

"I believe your aunt called them royalties." He glanced at the number and smiled. "But I'd say it's a nice surprise."

❧ *Chapter Forty-Four* ❧

"I CAN DO IT, LILY," I chided as she cleared away my plates. "Good Lord, I've cleared away enough dishes to know I'm no better than anyone else." I'd taken to eating with them in the kitchen. It seemed silly to be sitting all alone at the dining table, and besides, I enjoyed their banter and bustle.

"Oh, it's no bother, miss."

"Ellie," I corrected. She smiled as she scraped the egg and toast crust into the bin. Bates entered, his face grim as he held out the paper. "You'd best read it for yourself."

My stomach sank as I took it from him. It was bound to happen, my article. It was only a matter of time. I'd exposed my secrets, my sins, my soul to Steele. And he, in turn, would expose them to the world. A headline that would change everything. And indeed it did, but it wasn't about me. And it wasn't just my world that had changed.

AUGUST 4, 1914—BRITAIN DECLARES WAR

Lily and Bates sat as I read the details.

"What does it mean?" Lily asked, her young face fearful.

"It means we will do what we must. As always." Bates nodded, fortified no doubt by the wisdom of his years. "We stand up for what is right, no matter what the cost."

LATER THAT AFTERNOON, I sat at the piano, Faith on my knees, ready for a war of my own. Ready to make my stand. Faith banged the piano keys with her chubby hands. After a few minutes of simply thrilling in the din she created, she began picking notes, making sense of it. I walked my fingers up and down the scale and she pushed my hands away, eager to try for herself.

Father entered through the front door, calling for Bates to get him a drink. He'd arrived back from London in a foul mood earlier today before setting out again to finalize his business here in Liverpool. He stopped dead in his tracks when he saw Faith on my lap. And so it began.

"Who is that?" He pointed at her, as if I'd let in the mangy mongrel from the back alley. As if he didn't know exactly who she was.

I kept my calm, though it had disappointed me that he hadn't softened at the sight of her. I'd hoped he might. She was his granddaughter, after all. His only one.

I stood and put Faith on the ground and handed her her stuffed bunny. I'd dressed her in a new pink frock, white bow at the back and a matching one in her dark hair. Yet he looked at her as though she were nothing more than a dirty street urchin. I realized then he'd never see her, never see either of us for who we truly were. It didn't hurt anymore, but I did feel sad, in a way. For him. For what he'd never know.

Bates appeared and handed the drink to my father, now sitting in the chair. He swigged it back and thrust out the glass for another. "Hurry up, man." He scowled. "For a man who requires a reference, you move very slow."

"Oh, about that, sir," Bates replied, refilling the glass. "I won't be needing a letter after all." He said nothing more as he placed the decanter on the sideboard and left the room.

"About time that old codger threw in the hat," my father muttered. "Never liked him anyway."

He turned his attention to me, purposely avoiding where Faith played at my feet. I waited him out.

Finally he spoke. "Ellen, you have blatantly disregarded my wishes."

I didn't bite.

He pointed his finger at her, even though his gaze did not follow. "I told you that child was not welcome in my house."

With Faith in the room, her gentle smile, her joyful heart, his hatred of her only seemed all the more ridiculous. She stood and toddled over to him, gripping the knee of his trousers in her fist as she looked up at him. No doubt his moustache fascinated her, but perhaps she knew on some instinctive level what he refused to accept. That they were family.

He clenched his jaw, not giving her a glance. After a moment or two, I leaned over and held out my hand to her and she toddled back.

"Your grandmother would have loved you," I said, lifting her to my lap. "You have Gran's eyes, so you do."

He cleared his throat and stood, silent as he looked out the window, hands clasped behind his back. Finally, he spoke.

"If you defy me, Ellen, if you insist on keeping this child ..." He turned to face me, angry again. "I have no choice but to turn you out of my home."

"There's always a choice, Father." I stroked Faith's soft hair. Inhaled her sweetness and kissed her head. "I've made mine."

"Foolish girl!" He spat the accusations. "Letting your heart rule your head—never thinking about the future! Living only for the moment!"

I stood to face him, lifting Faith and settling her across my hip. "This moment *is* what it's all about. If I've learned anything from all I've lost, from grief, from nearly dying on that ship, it's that I want to live. To love. Don't you see? It's not about how much money you can squirrel away."

"Blast, girl, it *is* about the money!" he thundered, turning from me. "When are you going to open your eyes and see—"

"When are you?" I sidestepped back into his field of vision and he finally looked at Faith's face next to mine. Looked in her eyes—Mam's eyes.

But he stayed blind.

Resolute, he looked back at me and saw only the daughter who bucked even as he tried to rein me in. "You know my wishes. Is that what you want then? To be thrown on the street?"

"I have plans," I said. "I'd just hoped you would have been a part of them."

"Plans?" he scoffed. "As a maid for those Morgans? You think I don't know what you've been up to? I've sent a letter to the colonel. Told him you will not be back. No daughter of mine is working as a servant. I won't have it."

"You needn't have bothered," I said, enraged that he had. How dare he? "I already quit yesterday."

"Yes, well …" He seemed put off that I'd stolen his thunder. "So what now, Ellen? Will you work as a lowly stewardess again? Maybe you can sneak the child on as a stowaway?"

So he did know about the *Empress* after all. It wasn't the judgment in his eyes that hurt me. I didn't care if he saw me as a lady or a labourer. What hurt was that he knew what I'd gone through in the sinking, the horrors of it had been in all the papers, yet not once had he reached out to me. For the first time, I wondered if he even knew how. For he'd been just as distant, just as cold, when I'd lost my mother. Something shifted inside me as I looked at him now—an overwhelming feeling, not the shame or regret he usually stirred. This time it was pity. I felt sorry for him, for his blindness, his small-mindedness. For all that he'd missed and was still missing. He didn't get it. He really didn't. He thought he was stoic. Strong. Even now. When I needed him the most, he was never there. And I realized in that moment, I no longer needed him at all.

"Your time is up," he continued. "I demand that you stop all this foolishness and come home. Quit your playing as maid and mother. It's over now." He paused, giving weight to his pronouncement. "Strandview Manor has been sold."

"Yes," I said, voice calm. "I know."

Perhaps he'd expected me to cave or beg. To cry, at least, as the old Ellen would have done. My self-control only infuriated him all the more.

"Don't be ridiculous! I just came from Cronin's office. It

just happened this morning." He scoffed at me. "How could you possibly know?"

"Because, Father, I am the one who bought it."

I'D TAKEN THE CHEQUE to Cronin's office the day Bates had given it to me. Surely there'd been some mistake.

"No," Cronin assured me. "No mistake. You inherited your aunt's literary legacy."

"Her books in her study?" I asked.

"Well, yes, I suppose, but also the dividends and royalties from her own writing." He'd pointed to a shelf behind his desk where, for the first time, I noticed he kept one of every Garrett Dean adventure. "Signed copies. Those alone would be worth a mint to a collector. Not that I'd ever part with them. Nearly fifty books, published in several countries and languages. Most of them bestsellers. Yes, quite the body of work." He seemed proud. "I represented her on every one of those contracts."

"What are you saying, Mr. Cronin?"

He pushed his glasses back on his nose. "I'm saying, Miss Hardy, that not only was your aunt a very successful author, she was a rich woman. And now, so are you."

This didn't make sense. "I thought my father inherited her estate."

"Her estate, yes. But I believe you've inherited something far more valuable and enduring. Her books are classics. They will never go out of print. They will never stop earning royalties. To put it bluntly, every copy that sells earns you money." He nodded at the cheque in my hand. "You can expect to receive one of those every six months. And that's not even considering the recent inquiries on the rights to scripts. Her death has only increased public interest. Just imagine that. A film based on her book—a Dean adventure headlining at the theatre." He shook his head and smiled. "Oh, she would have loved that!"

"I never dreamed—" I sank slowly into the chair. So *this* was her literary legacy. A hope and promise for my future. And for my child ... and her life to come.

"Actually ..." Mr. Cronin paused before continuing. "I'm glad that you're here. I've had an offer on the house. A little less than the asking price. I didn't want to be presumptuous, but I know you're living there. Have you ... have you considered putting in a bid yourself?"

"You mean buy Strandview Manor?" Could this really happen? Was he serious? "Can I? I mean—do I have enough—" I held out the cheque in my hand, like a child with a fistful of pennies in a sweet shop.

He raised his eyebrows over his round glasses, amused by my innocence, for I knew neither the asking price nor the real value of what was now mine.

"Miss Hardy," he explained, a grandfatherly smile on his face, "with the royalties and the investments, not to mention the rights you now own, you, my dear, have enough to buy Strandview Manor ten times over."

⊗ *Chapter Forty-Five* ⊗

"NO KIDDING?" Steele shook his head as I told him of the recent events. "And that's when you told him you'd bought the house?"

We sat on our bench at the park. It would always be that now, our bench. Even if he never sat here again.

"He'd no idea the literary legacy was worth so much. He saw it as my aunt's hobby—and an unladylike one at that. You should have seen his face, Steele. I've never seen my father at a loss for words." What was there to say? I'd found a way to keep Strandview Manor and my daughter. All my father could take from me was himself, and sadly, he did just that.

"He told me I would never be welcome in his house," I said, still stung by his words. "And I said he would always be welcome in ours."

"You never know," Steele said. "Dear old dad might surprise you one day."

I doubted it. But at least I had no regrets. I'd said all I wanted. It was up to my father now.

The one person I still had regrets about was Jim. I hadn't seen or heard from him since the day on the shore nearly a week ago. I couldn't stop thinking of him. Of what he'd said. Of all I hadn't.

The two boys from our kite adventures ran up the path to join us. "Did you bring it?" they asked Steele, their freckled faces bright beneath their cowlicks.

Steele took a folded newspaper from the satchel at his feet and peeled off one sheet.

"That's not a boat!" the younger one whined. "It's only a bit of paper."

"Hush up, Tommy." The taller lad elbowed Tommy. "Will you make us a boat, then, Wyatt?"

"Tell you what, boys. I'll do you one better." Steele spread the newsprint on the gravel at our feet. "I'll *show* you how to make one."

Tommy groaned. Learning how was not part of his plan—he wanted the boat was all.

"That way when I'm gone," Steele continued, eyeing them both, "you boys can make your own boats. As many as you want."

He creased and folded the paper, slowly explaining step by step. Then as if by magic, he flipped the pleats and popped them open into a—

"Boat! It's a boat!" Tommy snatched it and took off for the pond.

"Did you get it, Harry?" Steele asked the older boy who still stood before us. "Will you remember how?"

"I'm not sure." Harry scratched his head. "I think so."

"Show me." Steele handed the lad the rest of the

newspaper. Sure enough, fold by fold, Harry made his own boat. He held it up proudly, his face smudged with newsprint but aglow with pride.

"That, my boy, is one tight ship." Steele patted him on the shoulder. "Well, go on then. Give it a go."

Harry ran to join Tommy, who stood at the water gingerly launching his vessel. The paper crafts lingered at the edge but the boys prodded them with sticks, urging them over deeper waters. Sure enough, the boats caught the light breeze and rode the gentle ripples to the middle of the pond as the lads cheered them on.

"Writer. Kite flier. Shipbuilder. A man of many talents," I teased.

"I'm just glad someone has finally found a use for those damn articles. Speaking of which—" He leaned over and rummaged through his satchel once more. "Here." He gave me a file.

"The article?" My heart raced as I took it. I didn't want to read it. Didn't want to see how he'd spun my story, what angle he'd taken, what hook, what sensationalized secrets he'd set out in black and white. I swallowed as I opened the file.

I had to look. I had to know.

But inside it wasn't an article; instead, I found a dozen pictures. I lifted up the large prints and stared at the first one: Faith and I reaching to each other in Barnardo's garden, our faces full of joy. Our first meeting. He'd captured that moment and all the feelings that went with it. It amazed me how much a photo could say.

"A thousand words," Steele said, beside me.

I moved on to the next picture. Faith and I sitting on the

chair, several of the same pose—surely one of these would be the shot he'd run with the article. Then I came to the one of Faith and me caught right after our muck about. I held it up and laughed at the state of us. Our knees and hands muddied, our skirts stained, and the both of us with that same elfish grin, filthy and loving it.

"She looks just like you there," Steele said.

I'd never seen us together before, never noticed how similar we truly were.

The last two photographs were taken here at the park, on the day I flew the kite. In the first one, I'd been caught running and turning in the foreground, hat blown free as I clutched the bobbin overhead, skirts billowing behind. In the distance, I saw Steele frozen mid-leap and mid-yell as he launched the kite in the air.

"But who—"

"I gave Harry the camera," Steele explained. "He's not half-bad."

I skimmed the picture again, chuckling at the fun in it before slipping it to the back. "See?" I eyed Steele. "I told you I could fly a kite."

My breath caught at the next picture, at the memory of that moment. This one was a close-up of me and Steele together. He stood behind, his arm around me, tugging on the kite string. My hair fell in loose wisps across my face, caught up in the wind. Caught up in the moment. Our gaze was upwards at the kite in the sky, our faces full of wonder and excitement. I hadn't even seen Harry there with the camera.

"That's a great shot," Steele said.

It seemed so intimate, and yet, it wasn't. Not really. But it had captured Steele's childlike exuberance. And the moment I'd found mine again. The girl I was. The girl I now know I still am.

Under the last picture lay notebooks. Three black leather flip books, each filled with page after page of his sloping scrawl. Steele's notes. In the margins, he'd scribbled one-word questions—*Collision? Meg? Barnardo's?* Some were circled or underlined twice, but each one like a signpost along the journey we'd just taken. Clues he'd collected to help me find my way through that difficult telling.

Why was he giving it to me now? I looked up at him, unsure what this meant.

"It's a damn interesting story, especially when you add heiress to the end." He leaned forward, elbows on his knees, as he looked at the boys. "But I won't be writing it."

"But ..." I looked at the notebooks and back at him. "I don't—I don't understand," I stammered. "Don't you need an article?"

"I have one—a great feature on Dr. Barnardo and his orphanages. I even got some great shots of Winters and the home. It's running in the *Times* and I sold it to the *London Illustrated News*, too. Winters will love that."

"But what about the editor's job?" He'd told me my story would get him that coveted position.

"Chained to a desk while everyone else gets the scoop?" He waved away the idea. "That's not for me. No, I already told them I'm not interested."

Confused, I looked back at the notebooks, thumbing slowly through the pages.

"It's all there," he said. "Every word of it. And the

research, too." He paused. "Don't get me wrong, the world does need your story—God, and what a story it is. Of struggle and loss. Of survival and perseverance. Of finding Faith and hope and love. Great title, by the way." He looked at me and smiled his lopsided grin. "But I realized the story isn't mine to tell, Ellen. It's yours."

I sat there, at a loss for words. I would never have known my story if it wasn't for him. Though I'd hated him at first for making me speak all I'd thought unspeakable, Steele had helped me find my voice. He'd helped me find my daughter. He'd helped me find myself. Like a midwife, he'd been there coaching me through the pain and labour of birthing my truth, and in the end, he'd handed it back to me.

"Oh, and I got you a little something." He handed me a package wrapped in brown paper. I opened it to find a book of piano music.

I read the cover and smiled. "*Ragtime Favourites by Scott Joplin.*"

"And for the record, a piano is not furniture," he said. "You'd better know how to play at least one of those by the next time I'm in Liverpool."

I laughed and promised I would. "When will you be back this way?"

He shrugged. "That depends on the war."

The world was changing. None of us knew what lay ahead. But it didn't faze Steele.

"My editor has asked me to be the paper's war correspondent." His eyes sparkled with excitement. "I'm doing it, Ellen. It's not Africa—but it's my own adventure. I leave for the front tomorrow."

"But isn't it dangerous?" We both knew it was. I suppose every soldier did, too. But they wouldn't let fear stop them. And neither would Steele.

"If I survived your driving lesson," he teased, "well, then I guess I can handle just about anything."

He stood and picked up his bag, and I remembered the large envelope I'd brought.

"Wait, I got you a little something, too." I gave it to him.

Steel slipped out the thirty typed pages, his eyes widening as he read the title. "*The Hero's Journey: A Garrett Dean Adventure by G.B. Hardy.*" He met my eyes. "Is this ..."

"Aunt Geraldine's latest manuscript." I smiled at the reverence he had for it. If anyone would cherish this, it was him.

"I can't take this," he said, holding it out to me.

"I'm not asking you to take it." I stood and gently pushed it back, leaving my hand on his. "I'm asking you to *write* it. You know the characters and the voice. You love adventures. Hell, Steele, you even look like Dean."

Now it was his turn to be speechless.

"I've already talked to Cronin; my aunt's legacy is mine to manage. And I want the best. I want you. Who knows, maybe in this adventure he's a war correspondent." Already, I could see the seed of an idea sprouting in his mind. "Take as long as you like, but you'd better have at least one chapter by the next time you're in Liverpool."

"I don't know what to say," he said, breathless.

"Say yes."

He grinned like Harry with his paper boat. "You have no

idea what this means to me—to be given a chance to tell this story."

I stood on tiptoe and kissed his cheek. "Yes, Steele, I do. I know exactly how it feels."

∽ *Chapter Forty-Six* ∽

I WALKED THE SHORELINE, shoes in one hand, skirts held up with the other. It probably wasn't fitting for the lady of Strandview Manor, but it was exactly what Ellie Hardy would do. And that was how I'd decided to live from now on. To be true to myself, now that I knew her. Stopping, I picked up a handful of smooth stones and, tucking the ends of my skirt in my waistband, waded into the water. Leaning to one side, I pitched the pebble across the sparkling surface, counting the skips. *Six … seven … eight.* Circles rippled out from each place where the rock touched, but never stayed. That was the trick to skipping stones, to stories, to life, really—to keep moving forward.

"So that's where she gets it." Jim's voice came from just behind and I turned to see him standing on the shore. Just the sight of him, the sound of him, the nearness of him made my heart ache. After the way things had been left, I wasn't even sure I'd ever see him again. And yet, here he was.

But he didn't smile or meet my eyes. Instead, Jim took off

his shoes and rolled up his pant legs and, after picking up a few stones, waded in beside me.

I had so much to say. To ask. So much I wanted to know. But my time with Steele had taught me how to listen. How to let someone speak his story. And so, hard as it was, I let the silence hang between us and skipped another pebble.

Jim grunted as he forcefully threw one stone and then another. Each sank on the first splash. "I can't do this," he grumbled.

"Get low to the water. It's all in the wrist—"

"No, not that." He dropped the stones and plodded back to sit on the shore.

Unsure what to do, I followed and sat by him in silence for a moment, letting him find his words.

"You can tell me, Jim. Anything," I said, as though he needed permission to unload that heavy secret on my shoulders. Whatever it was, I could take it. I could carry it with him. I could lighten his burden, as Steele had done for me.

Jim breathed deeply. "I don't know what to say. It's too late, anyway. What's done is done. Why dwell on it?" His voice was low, barely a whisper. "Talking about it wouldn't change what happened."

He may never have spoken it, but clearly, he did dwell on it, whatever it was, for he'd been brooding over or burdened under whatever it was he carried in secret silence. I'd felt the same way when Steele first approached me. But he'd gotten it out of me, and after the painful telling I'd felt purged, relieved. I felt forgiven.

"Nothing will change what happened," I conceded. "But you can change what happens next."

His eyes searched the horizon, floundering in his dark thoughts, and after a while I threw him a line. Like Steele would. "Is it about your father?"

"Yes." He hugged his knees and burrowed his feet deeper into the sand. "I never told you ... he worked on the *Titanic*." Jim stopped and looked at me for a moment, unsure if he wanted to go on. "And so did I."

Titanic? It made sense, then. Jim's unwillingness to speak of it. His obsession with the *Empress*'s life-saving standards. "Oh, Jim, that must have been horrible."

He stared off into the horizon and I knew he was there now. Reliving that night.

"That girl from my journal—it's not what you think, Ellie. She was only a child. Four, maybe five." He turned his attention back to the stones in his hands. "A passenger on the *Titanic*. One of hundreds that died"—he paused, his next words barely a whisper—"because of me."

"What do you mean?" I knew that sense of shame for not saving others, of guilt for surviving when they had not, but surely he had to be exaggerating.

He shrugged, jaw clenched.

"Were you a stoker?" I asked, coaxing him onward.

He shook his head. "Bellboy." A smile haunted his lips. "God, Da was proud to see me in that uniform. Said I'd be chief steward in no time."

His smile faded. "Even when Captain Smith ordered the men to launch the lifeboats, I still didn't think we were in any danger. Not really. She was *unsinkable*, after all." He shook his head. "But I overheard Murdoch say the engine room was flooded and most of the bow, pulling her down by the head.

Compartment by compartment. I knew then she'd founder, for once the sea got a taste of her, it wouldn't stop until it had swallowed her whole."

I nodded, remembering that sense of shock, disbelief, and terror when the *Empress* had been hit.

"I found Da," he continued, "at his post—lower level by the third-class stairwell. Him on one side of the gate and a mob of steerage passengers on the other. Some of them had life vests. Most did not. But what did it matter with that black metal gate shut across the top of the stairs? They were crushed against it by the others pushing up from below. I'll never forget their pleas for help. Terror sounds the same in any language."

He paused and I knew he was hearing them still. I could almost see them surging against the rail, arms and hands stuck through the black bars, grasping for his father to save them.

"I ran up to Da and pulled on the steel grill." Jim mimed the action with his fists. "Maybe together we could do it, but it would not budge. When Da shoved me aside, I saw the key hanging round his neck. I knew the truth even before he told me he'd locked them in."

Jim dropped his hands. "'Captain's orders,' Da said. Like that explained it. And I looked at them, all those people, mothers, children. I looked at the terror in their faces. There was a little girl of four or five, down in the bottom corner in a white nightdress, a red ribbon knotted at the end of her hair. God, I'll never forget her—the way she reached out to me." He paused and rubbed his eyes, but I knew it wouldn't get rid of that sight. "I begged Da to see sense and let them out. But he wouldn't listen, so I lunged for the key. I don't remember exactly how it happened, we struggled, he must have hit his head. Da fell, splashed into the water flooding the alleyway hall, and just floated there face down, arms sprawled, blood blooming in the water around his head."

Jim stopped, his breath laboured.

"It was an accident, Jim," I said softly. I rested my hand on his arm. But he wasn't with me. He was still there, still in the hold of the sinking *Titanic*.

"He was alive," he continued. "But neither of us would be for long if we didn't get out of there. I hauled Da to the stairwell and up a few steps as the water rose behind. The passengers cried out to me. But what could I do? I couldn't save them all, so I took the key chain from around Da's neck, threw it at their grasping hands, and hauled him out. I didn't wait to see if they caught it. I didn't care if they lived or died. All that mattered in that moment was saving my da. And in the end, I couldn't even do that."

Jim hung his head, gasping, labouring under the weight of his guilt. He'd shouldered it along with his father's lifeless body. Carried it every step since. Borne it two long years.

No wonder he seemed so burdened.

ᢒ *Chapter Forty-Seven* ᢒ

"THEY GOT OUT," I SAID, suddenly recalling where I'd heard this story before. "The third-class passengers—they opened the gate, Jim!"

"You can't know that." He wouldn't be so easily comforted.

"No, it's true. I read it in an article about the *Titanic*." It was one of the stories Steele had given me when we first met. "No one could have told the reporters about the gate being locked ... if they hadn't *lived* to tell."

I paused to let that truth settle. "You saved them, Jim. Maybe not your father. But some of them, at least."

He sat with that knowledge for a few moments. "It should have been me, Ellie," he finally said, lips trembling. "I should have died."

I knew his pain. Hadn't I felt the very same about Meg? But I saw things a little differently now.

"I know the guilt of surviving," I said. "I wanted to die, too. How could I live with myself, how could I live a happy life knowing Meg never would?" I paused and thought of all I'd learned these past ten weeks since the sinking. "But a life of regret and shame is no life at all. They wouldn't want that for us. Not Meg. Not your da."

He clenched his jaw, afraid to speak. But he nodded and I knew he understood.

"It was an accident, Jim. The iceberg. The *Storstad*. Each one a stupid mistake that ended in horrendous tragedy. But the captains, the crew, your father, you, me … we each did what we thought best in that moment."

I thought of my aunt, of my father, of everyone who'd ever hurt me, and realized I needed to accept that truth for those situations as well.

"We need to forgive them," I said. "We need to forgive ourselves."

"But it's just so"—his voice hitched—"so unfair."

"You're right." I paused. "A tragedy is exactly that— tragic. But dwelling on its senselessness, wallowing in our grief and regrets will only sink us to deep, dark places. If we let it."

He took a deep breath and exhaled; I could almost see the weight easing from his shoulders. But it wasn't just about letting go. We had to look forward. To skip on to the ways we'd make ripples in the next parts of our lives.

"Jim, we survived—asking why will only drive us mad. We need to ask *what for*? What are we living for now, here, today?"

He picked up a stone and discarded it. Then another and another. Something still weighed upon his mind.

"Knowing about what happened, what you did on the

Titanic, doesn't change how I feel about you," I said, treading into new waters.

He chucked the last pebble and stopped. "What does it matter anyway? It's too late for us. You're with him now and—"

"With who?"

He looked at me sideways. "The man from the park. The one at your house?"

"Who? Steele?" I said, surprised.

"The day my ship docked, I came looking for you at Strandview Manor. You were the only thing that kept me going in the hospital in Quebec. They said I kept calling your name, even when I didn't know my own." He paused. "And this Steele fellow answers the door and tells me you don't work there anymore. And I wondered how I'd ever find you. How I'd live without you."

"That was you?" I remembered that day. "We thought you were a reporter. That's what he is, Jim. He's writes for the *Times*. He was interviewing me for a story on the *Empress*."

"He's not Faith's father?"

I shook my head. But it did nothing to ease his mind.

"I saw you with him a few times, Ellie. You didn't seem to miss me all that much, then."

"Of course I missed you." If only he knew. "Jim, there is nothing between me and Steele," I said, as if convincing myself as much as him.

"Really?" He looked at me accusingly. "So you kiss all the reporters?"

I wanted to defend myself, to push back at his hostility with some of my own. What did he know? Where was he, then, when I needed him? Had he been spying on me? Instead, I reached for his hand, taking that chance, risking that pain of having him get up and walk away from me once more. Knowing it might kill me if he did.

But Jim was worth it. We were worth it. And I had to speak my truth. I owed him that. I owed it to myself so that, whatever else happened, at least I'd know I'd left nothing unsaid.

"It's you I want, Jim," I said, my fingers taking his. "You're all I've ever wanted."

His eyes softened.

"Losing you," I continued, "thinking you were gone forever, only made me realize how much ... how much I love you." I'd found my voice and I would no longer be silent. "I thought I'd lost you. I thought I'd lost Faith—they told me she'd died when she was born. And yet, here we are." I took a deep breath, my heart pounding in my chest, and kneeled beside him. "Lots of people have tragedies, Jim. We have all faced incredible loss. But we've been given a second chance. Let's focus on that. Let's not waste it." I gripped his hand. "I want you in my life, Jim. In Faith's."

He knew how I felt. What I wanted. The choice was his now.

Jim looked at me, searched my eyes, and found truth. As I did in his. No secrets. No shame. Just acceptance. And love.

"God, Ellie, you don't know how long I've waited to hear you say that." Squeezing my hand, he leaned in and slowly brought his lips to mine. His mouth warm and reassuring. Familiar. Like we'd done it a thousand times before, even though this was only our second time. We breathed our souls into each other in that moment, knowing this was the first kiss of forever.

"I love you, Ellie," he whispered. "I love you."

I smiled and circled my arms around him, rested my head against his chest. Jim kissed my forehead and I felt hopeful, safe, comforted by his warmth, his breath, the beating of his heart. No matter what the future brought, we had each other. We had our love to buoy us up through any storm. Nothing else mattered.

It must have been so hard for him to confess his secret, to risk losing me. And to voice his fears about Steele. I sat up and looked into his eyes once more.

"Just so you know, Steele is leaving," I said. We'd be in touch about the novel, as friends, but nothing more. I wanted to reassure Jim of that. The kiss on Steele's cheek meant nothing. "When you saw us, that was goodbye," I said. "He's going to war."

A sad smile tugged on Jim's lips and on my heart. And I knew what he was going to say even before he spoke the words. "So am I," he said. "I enlisted this week."

❧ A NEW DAY ❧

September 1914
Strandview Manor, Liverpool

✺ *Chapter Forty-Eight* ✺

SETTING MY TROWEL ASIDE, I dug into the rich, black earth with both hands. Bates was right, there was something so peaceful about gardening. A connectedness. A rootedness. A sense of time—of season. Jim had left for his training with the King's Liverpool Regiment last month and I had no way of knowing when he'd be back, for how long, or where his duties might take him next. I couldn't change the past or jump ahead to the future any more than I could change the seasons. My life no longer revolved around the number of days since a past loss or in anxious countdown to a future worry. I'd finally learned that life was now. This moment. To feel the sun on my shoulders and the cool, moist earth on my fingers. And to sow hope for tomorrow.

I lifted the plant from its pot beside me and shook the dirt off its hairy roots. Among the green leaves bobbed dozens of tiny flowers, each one a brilliant blue, its five petals buttoned to its stem by a bright yellow centre. I gently set the plant in the hole I'd dug between the rose bushes.

"That's the perfect place for it," Bates said to me, as he and Faith came down the front steps. She ran over to me and, picking up the trowel, patted the earth I'd mounded back in the hole.

It had been Bates's suggestion that I add a plant of my own to the garden. Something meaningful to me. At first I'd picked this one simply because I liked its vivid dots of blue and yellow. Learning it was called forget-me-not made it all the more fitting, not just because I wanted to remember my mother, Aunt Geraldine, and Meg—they had flowers of their own here—but because now that I knew her, I never wanted to forget who I was.

"Ducks! Ducks!" Faith said, running back to Bates. He handed her the small paper bag full of the crusts they'd saved from their morning toast.

"Are you sure you don't want to come with us today?" he asked, as they opened the gate.

"No, no." I waved my dirty hand at them. "Go off with yourselves. I'll come next time."

I washed my hands at the kitchen sink, smiling as my ring rinsed clean and caught the sunlight. I hadn't taken it off since he'd put it on my finger the day he left, over a month ago. A band of gold with two hands clasped around a crowned heart. A claddagh, a traditional Irish ring. But more than that, a promise of friendship. Loyalty. Of love.

"Will you be my girl, Ellie?" he'd asked, almost shy as he slipped it on my right hand, heart facing in—a sign that mine was taken.

"Always."

He'd kissed me then and we'd said our long goodbyes.

But not our last. Though it was hard to let him go, to watch him leave, I knew, somehow, that this was only our beginning.

I climbed the stairs to Aunt Geraldine's study. To my study, now, but I'd always feel closest to her there. I'd moved the desk near the window, her typewriter still sitting upon it, though I'd set it aside to pen long letters to Jim. We wrote every few days. Even Steele had dashed off a postcard now and then, scribbling me bits of his adventures, of his story, asking if I'd started mine.

The rows of shelves were empty still but for the ivy plant, my aunt's novels, a portrait of my mother, and the framed picture of Faith and me meeting in the garden for the first time. But the vacant shelves no longer saddened me. I knew, in time, I'd fill each one with my favourite things, with mementoes from every adventure I'd yet to have. It excited me to see them. To wonder. To dream.

I sat at the desk and stared out the window, thinking of that fairy queen I used to imagine as a child. Realizing, for the first time, that she was me. Beautiful. Strong. Powerful.

Absentmindedly, I pressed a worn-out button on the typewriter and the key struck the paper. The *clack* broke the silence, leaving a black *E* on the white page. I liked the look of it. The sound of it. The power of creating something where there'd been nothing. That sense of making my mark.

I hit four more keys.

… L … L … I … E.

Stopping, I stared at the portrait of my mother. I thought of her often, even more since I'd become a mother myself, and yet, I never really knew Mam's story. I gazed at the picture of me and Faith on the shelf next to it.

Would Faith know my story?

Sliding the machine in front of me, I pressed the metal arm, cranking the sheet up one line, and started to type.

```
We write our lives by the choices we
make. Like it or not, that becomes our
story. Parts of it are sad. Parts are ugly.
Some parts are downright embarrassing. But
stories need to be shared. They need to be
passed on and remembered--even the ones that
terrify or shame us. Especially those parts,
I guess. Because if we don't learn from
it, we live it over and over. Stuck in one
chapter of ourselves.
     And in my heart, I've always known there
is so much more to my story than that.
     For a long time, I lived a story that was
not my own. I let someone else be the author
of my life. I wore what I should. Acted as
I should. Spoke how I should. I let others
tell me who I was.
     I even let a handsome young man spin
me a new story--a romance. He told me I
was beautiful and desirable. I knew who
he wanted me to be and I played the part
for a while. It got to the point where I
would have been anyone he wanted if only
he'd stayed. But he didn't want a sixteen-
year-old girl. Especially a pregnant one.
     No, nobody wanted that girl.
```

And though I have been a daughter and a niece, a victim and a survivor; though I have loved and lost and found it once again; though I've been mistress, maid, and unmarried mother--I've come to realize that, though it's all true … it's not all I am.

I am a fairy queen. I am a dragon slayer. I am the hero of my own adventures.

Yes, I am every one of those things. And so much more.

I am Ellen Geraldine Hardy--and this is my story. So far.

❧ AUTHOR'S NOTE ❧

The *Empress of Ireland*
The sinking of the *Empress of Ireland* was Canada's worst
maritime disaster, and is one few people today know much
about. For whatever reason, it seemed to be lost in both the
St. Lawrence and in history. Maybe it happened too soon
after the sinking of the *Titanic*, a similar tragedy only two
years before. Maybe it was forgotten because her passengers
were not rich and famous New York socialites. Most likely,
it got lost among the headlines, overshadowed as the First
World War broke out only ten weeks later. In any case, the
story of its collision, of its foundering, and of the 1012 souls
lost with the *Empress of Ireland* sank from memory.

Now, a hundred years later, we try to piece together that
part of our story. We must remember, to honour the people
who lost their lives in the tragedy and all those who lived on
in silent grief.

Though Ellen Hardy and Jim Farrow are fictional
characters, I hope their journeys ring true. Their experiences

are based on research and accounts of surviving crew and passengers, in particular *Fourteen Minutes* by James Croall and *Forgotten Empress* by David Zeni. These two books were vital in preserving the history of the *Empress of Ireland* and for that we all owe both authors our gratitude. *Titanic Survivor: The Newly Discovered Memoirs of Violet Jessop* by John Maxtone-Graham provided great insight into life as a stewardess and a survivor. After researching hundreds of *Titanic* survivor accounts, I wondered how someone gets past such a horrific tragedy. Most people, it seemed, simply did not speak of it. Many lived half-lives burdened by the guilt of having survived when their loved ones did not. Yet Ms. Jessop lived all her days as much more than "*Titanic* survivor"—she never limited her extraordinary life by her losses or by others' labels.

No one wants to talk about what is painful. No one seeks out grief. We'd rather ignore regrets and stay blind to hard truths. But as Ellie journeyed through the stages of denial, anger, guilt, depression, and, eventually, acceptance—so did I. I thought I was writing a story of loss, of tragic events that some people might rather forget. But it is really a story of finding Faith, hope, and love. Because if Ellie taught me anything, it's that life is meant to be more than just survived.

I can be the victim of someone else's story—but I choose to be the hero of my own.

Magdalene Asylums

Magdalene Asylums existed from the eighteenth to the late twentieth century. Supervised by nuns, the asylums, originally an option for employment for marginalized young women, increasingly became more of a prison of enforced penance.

These asylums in Britain and Ireland were for prostitutes, unmarried mothers, mentally challenged women, and abused girls. Families also sent daughters who were too flirtatious or attractive. Until a family member vouched for them, the young girls would remain in the asylum. Today, advocacy groups such as Justice for Magdalenes exist to promote justice, to support survivors, and to give them a voice. The last asylum in Ireland closed on September 25, 1996. On February 19, 2013, Irish prime minister Enda Kenny issued a formal apology.

Barnardo's Homes

Although poverty, at the time, was seen as a shameful result of laziness or vice, Dr. Thomas Barnardo insisted that "every child deserved the best possible start in life, whatever their background." By the time he died in 1905, his charity had founded ninety-six homes caring for more than 8500 children. He'd also introduced a support for unmarried mothers, securing work in domestic service so they could pay for a portion of their child's fostering. This was at a time when most charities denied help to unmarried mothers. At the beginning of the twentieth century, Barnardo's Homes sent about a thousand children a year to Canada. Children were to receive education and training, and foster families, in turn, were paid five shillings a week per child. Many Home Children sailed on the *Empress of Ireland* and its sister ship, the *Empress of Britain*. Today, Barnardo's continues to work for "the abused, the vulnerable, the forgotten and the neglected" and is the U.K.'s biggest children's charity.

∞ FASCINATING FACTS ∞

Though a member of the *Empress* crew for two years, Emmy, the ship's cat, deserted ship right before its final sailing from Quebec.

Of the 1477 people who sailed from Quebec aboard the *Empress*, 1012 died—840 passengers and 172 crew.

More passengers died on the *Empress of Ireland* (840) than either the *Titanic* (832) or the *Lusitania* (791).

The ship filled with 60,000 gallons of water per second.

Within one minute of impact, the tilt of the ship was enough to jam the watertight doors.

Most passengers had only a few minutes, and some, mere seconds, to escape their cabins. Passengers on the lower right side of the *Empress* most likely drowned where they slept.

The *Empress* sank nine hours and forty-three minutes after leaving Quebec—and just fourteen minutes after being struck by the *Storstad*.

Chief Engineer William Sampson, an Irish veteran on his ninety-sixth voyage of the *Empress*, gave his account of the sinking from the engine room. He escaped with the help of his younger crew members and was eventually rescued by a lifeboat.

Dr. James Grant was on his second voyage as ship surgeon. Thrown from his bed as the ship rolled, he crawled through the passageway and escaped through a porthole. His heroic efforts on the *Storstad* saved the lives of many.

Of Matron Jones and nine stewardesses, only one survived: Helena Hollis. She'd tried to keep her fellow stewardess Ethel Dinwoodie afloat, but Ethel, weighed down by two coats, sank from her grasp.

William Clarke worked in the *Empress* stokehold and escaped to a lifeboat. He was also a *Titanic* survivor. There is also a legend of a man, Frank "Lucky" Tower, who survived three sinkings: the *Empress*, the *Titanic*, and the *Lusitania*.

Though both the *Empress* and the *Storstad* captains claimed they maintained their heading and accused the other of changing course in the fog, an inquiry of sixty-one witnesses ˜ nine thousand questions concluded that the *Storstad*

ation Army members, just over two dozen
/ died heroically helping others. Not one

surviving Salvationist wore a lifebelt. The convention in London went on without them but kept 148 chairs empty and marked with white sashes, one for each member who had died.

Salvation Army bandsman Thomas Greenaway had resolved to go down with the ship when he thought his wife drowned. They'd been married only a week before. Thankfully, he was rescued, as was his young wife. The couple wept for joy when they found each other in Rimouski.

Gracie Hanagan had just turned seven when she boarded the *Empress of Ireland*. One of the four children who survived, out of the 138 aboard, Gracie was the youngest and the last living survivor. She attended annual memorials held by the Salvation Army of Toronto until her death in May 1995. In her account of the sinking, she mentioned being terrified of sleeping by the portholes where the water would come in. Though she lived to be one day shy of eighty-nine, Gracie never overcame her fear of running water, even in bathtubs.

∞ ACKNOWLEDGMENTS ∞

Thank you to:

Lynne Missen and the Penguin Canada team for giving me the opportunity to explore and share the story of the *Empress of Ireland*.

Marie Campbell for your steadfast encouragement and support.

A special thanks to experts:

David Zeni and James Croall for your meticulous research and detailed accounts.

Dr. John Willis, curator; Jonathan Wise, archivist; and reference librarians Anneh Fletcher and Brigitte Lafond of the Canadian Museum of Civilization. Thank you for being such faithful stewards of our history.

A heartfelt thanks to my friends and family:

Elizabeth Tevlin, critiquer extraordinaire, for always being there and for all the ways you helped bring Jim to life and love.

Kerri Chartrand, Alan Cranny, Peggy Cranny, Fiona Jackson, and Tony Pignat for reading draft after draft.

My kids, Liam and Marion, for always putting on the kettle and especially for reminding me of what matters most.

And especially to Granny, for your inspiration of faith and fortitude. I miss you.

Thanks to each of you for not only sharing in the stories I write but especially for being such a big part of the story I live.